I0747030

BURN THE SKIES

K.A. WIGGINS

SNOWMELT & STUMPS

FOR THE ONES STILL LEARNING TO LET IT GO

Copyright © 2021 by K.A. Wiggins

A Snowmelt & Stumps book

This book has been published in Canada and adheres to Canadian grammar and spelling rules.

All rights reserved. This book or any portion thereof may not be reproduced or used in any manner whatsoever without the express written permission of the publisher except for the use of brief quotations in a book review. Under no circumstances may any part of this book be photocopied for resale.

This is a work of fiction. Any similarity between the characters and situations within its pages and places or persons, living or dead, is unintentional and co-incidental.

Requests for information should be addressed to kaiewrites@gmail.com.

ISBN 978-1-7775174-2-7 (paperback)
ISBN 978-1-7775174-0-3 (ebook)
ISBN 978-1-7775174-1-0 (Kindle ebook)

First Edition: July 2021

Printed in Canada.

Cover design: Christian Bentulan, CoversbyChristian.com, modified
Heading Font: Cinzel Decorative by Natanael Gama
Body Font: New Athena Unicode by American Philological Association

PARADISE

THE EDGES OF this world's map are not bordered with monsters but with ghosts. Or maybe they're just nightmares.

Don't get me wrong—in many ways my life, such as it is, has never been better. I was always a little jealous of Cadence's altered existence. Nothing could hurt her. Nothing could reach her. No one looking at her and judging or wanting or demanding or expecting or . . .

Anyway, what I'm trying to say is: being disembodied has its perks.

No sweating. No acne. No barriers between me and whatever I want to do, wherever I want to be, whoever I want to be with.

Just so long as I don't mind being completely powerless to affect the waking world, or having to dodge those grasping, howling things that line the border between *here* and *there* whenever I want to cross, or the way almost no one can hear me. Or even knows I'm here.

Which is less of a problem than you might think when you have a near-limitless world all to yourself—one you can shape at will.

It starts with the familiar, the known. The formless mists clear to reveal an empty room. Look for a door and open it to let in the light. Step into a rainbow field of wildflowers and make your way to the welcoming trees beyond. Stand at the edge of a towering cliff overlooking a churning grey sea that comes alive with the salt-tinged scent of flowers and crushed herbs as it floods with sunlight. Ignore the edge—the edges don't mean anything anymore—and keep walking out over the now-sparkling waves until you're ready to dive. Part the waters without a splash, without even the need to hold your breath, and wander the playful kelp forests that soon give way to the buzz and bustle of coral reefs. They twist and spiral into a fantastical underground kingdom just for you, populated by colourful inhabitants that want nothing from you, expect nothing from you. They exist simply for your pleasure and can be undone in a single, guiltless glance should you wish for solitude once more. Let yourself bask in the coolness of the deeps, and when you're tired of floating and breathing through new-grown gills just for the alien thrill of it, shake off the feathery touch of newly candy-coloured waves and step onto the ever-changing land. It forms itself to your will, instantly and seamlessly responding to your slightest whim.

This is the dreamscape: more than just a passageway, a space between, it's another world where the rules don't apply. The most perfect paradise you can imagine. Just so long as you imagine perfection.

Which is why I think the ghosts must be nightmares. My nightmares.

The forest isn't so sure.

"It talks to you?" Ash plucks a series of berry-flavoured notes out of the air and sets them spinning in a jaunty tune. They cast cheerful kaleidoscopic beams in every direction.

I brush my fingertips over the knotted lump of wood in my lap and shiver when the grain shifts under my touch. "Not quite. It's more like Victoire. No words, just . . . feeling."

Not that he'd know; that attention-hungry creature never came out around him. I've only ever been myself in his presence, even at the beginning, before he understood I wasn't his Cady. And I'm still not entirely sure if Victoire really is something *other*—like Cadence—or just a name and a face for all the things about myself I can't accept. I flinch away from a particularly alarming beam of chartreuse. Ash dismisses his radiant music with a wave.

"If you don't like it, you know you can just change it, right? I won't be offended—I already know you lack the capacity to appreciate my musical genius." He smirks, teasing to cover how uncomfortable he is with my . . . restraint.

Apparently it's not normal to be so unwilling to shape the world to one's whims. At least not to him. But he didn't grow up in a city where desire was deadly and dreams were a sure path to death-by-Mara. His whims don't call up tortured ghosts from the space between.

The forest's gift trembles in my hands. Ash's dream-bright form wavers as a layer of mist slides between us. I stroke the smooth grain of the living wood, and it settles.

The knotted ball acts as both an anchor and a bridge, mooring my disembodied consciousness to this reality while spanning the vast spaces between the body Cadence stole, this dreamscape, and the ancient forest outside Nine Peaks where Ash's physical anchor waits with both hands pressed against mossy bark.

"Cole?" His lines are crisp once more, his touch warm as he reaches out in concern.

"It's nothing. What did the council say?"

"Oh, you know what they're like . . ." He leans over to pluck at the soft grass beneath us, drawing it up into a swaying line of extravagantly and improbably patterned flowers. They hum a low, gentle chorus scented, oddly, of spruce. "I'd rather see what you've been up to. I'm sure whatever you've chosen to dream is as beautiful as you are. Why don't you show me?"

I wrinkle my nose. The flattery, I'm almost certain, is an attempt to cover up his guilt for leaving me behind. Even though every disastrous choice I've made has been mine and mine alone.

Besides, he doesn't need to see my clumsy attempts at creation. Those are private.

I swat his distracting blossoms down into prickly, purple-barbed spears. How's that for beautiful? "Don't change the subject. What did the elders decide?"

He shifts his weight gingerly, wincing at the ungentle groundcover. "That reminds me—Grace wants to visit, did I tell you? She's been bugging me about it all week. You won't believe how much more fun you can have over here with a group. If we can get her and Banshee tapped in at the same time, you'll see some real fireworks—"

"Ash. The council. When can we expect their help?"

He plucks at his old, disreputable scarf, brighter and cleaner beneath his jacket than I know it to be. Ash likes to dream things unbroken. "It's not that they don't care, it's just . . ."

"They don't believe us." I wait for a response, but he's busy rearranging the scarf in lieu of the landscape, hesitant to dismiss my spiky contributions after insisting that I participate in the shaping. "We're running out of time. Just tell me already."

Ash meets my gaze and the weight of it is more than I can bear. He gestures. The sunny meadow becomes a cozy little cabin; wooden beams overhead, fire crackling at our feet. In the way of this place, there is no sense of movement, no conscious choice, between staring him down and finding myself curled against his side, his arm slung around my shoulders, holding me just a little too tight at an angle where he doesn't have to meet my eyes.

I dig an elbow into his ribs, trying and failing to spring to my feet. His dreaming is the stronger, though he has said that was never true of him and Cadence. And she's not here to test how things have changed.

He whispers into my hair, his voice low to cover the shaking, "Isn't this enough? Just be here with me."

But for all his strength—of will, of vision, of magic—I'm still holding the forest's gift. I could let it go, break the bridge linking us through the dreamscape. I will if he doesn't release me.

As if he can sense my resolve, his grip slackens. I pull away, the ceiling and walls crumbling as they shift up and out, light breaking in dust-thick golden beams through the bare shards of high stone arches.

"I'm on your side," he says into the cold, echoing ruins—and I even believe him. "Always have been. Always will be."

It would be nice if that were enough. Once upon a time, maybe it could have been.

"They're not going to help, are they?"

"You know we can't risk it." He flicks a murky-hued bench into and drops onto it; his shoulders bow in surrender to that unconscious "we." He's not talking about me.

I'm not the only one who struggles to throw off years of submitting to authority. But he still thinks of himself as part of Nine Peaks, even if he doesn't agree with the elders' orders. I have learned very well that I don't belong. Not there, nor in the city I've trapped myself in, nor even in this paradise of make-believe.

Ash continues, "I don't know that we could take the Mara anymore, not at our current strength, not with enforcers attacking at the same time. Crossing that barrier takes too much of a toll."

"Not on me. Ravel didn't seem too bothered by it, either. Isn't there a way to, I don't know, shield yourselves or something? Nine Peaks literally teaches people to put down monsters. What's the point of all that training if you guys won't actually fight when it matters?"

"Self defense is one thing. But you know we're not an army. Our training and missions are about restoring the Earth, not battling those that inhabit it."

I roll my shoulders, impatient. The crumbling stone hall disappears, along with Ash's bench. By the time he hits the ground, we're on a familiar simulacrum of Refuge's gravel-strewn rooftop, overlooking the drowned city. "We've been over this. Just tell me what the council is willing to do."

Ash, gravel biting into his elbows, glares. I tighten my grip on the anchor-knot, ready to ask the forest to fight him if he tries to run away. But he just blows out a frustrated breath and flops back.

"What was that?"

"You're not going to like it. You already know their answer. You really have to make me say it?" He pulls an exaggeratedly pouty face and reaches a lazy hand towards me as if I'll let myself be pulled down to the rooftop, which is suddenly and improbably covered in soft-looking grass. As if I'll be cajoled into indulging in a few moments of escape . . .

I stamp, the grass rippling away from a clattering hail of gravel. I can ignore his outrageous attempts at distraction all night if I have to.

He sits up, wincing. "Fine. The elders said what they always say. Too many lives wasted already on a lost cause. They're not sending an army—not that we have one to send. But the Council of Nine has made it clear no one will be permitted to volunteer this time, either. Everyone who helped before you left us, they—we—are all grounded. Grace included. They barely let me out to talk to you."

I nod. None of this is a surprise. It still hurts. "What else? What about Susan? Surely she had something to say about them abandoning Cadence and me out here?"

"Your *grandmother* was released from her seat on the council. The other elders declared her overwrought. They sent her away to mourn the loss of her granddaughters in seclusion."

"We're not dead." And I'm still not convinced she's *my* grandmother.

"That's the spirit." He laughs, sending the gravel rippling in joyful clattering waves. "Get it? 'Spirit?'"

"Really?"

He stops. "Sorry."

The sky wheels from hazy afternoon through a lurid sunset to icy starlight.

"There has to be more," I insist. "Something I can try, if they won't act. Something—"

"There is nothing else."

Too fast. He's nearly as clumsy a liar as I am.

I lean in to force a confession—and my vision doubles. Cadence just woke up.

"We'll pick this up later. I'm not letting it go, Ash."

He nods, eager to wriggle off the hook for one more day. "No problem. Happy haunting, C."

I loosen my grip on the anchor, snapping the bridge out from under him and hurling him back into his world before he can retreat under his own steam. It's petty—and amazingly satisfying.

Might as well flex what little power I have here while I can—because the next item on my agenda is about sixteen hours worth of harassing the heck out of a duplicitous body snatcher in an almost certainly futile attempt to save the world.

NAGGING

RELENTLESSLY PESTERING SOMEONE full-time turns out to be yet another one of the skills Cadence is just naturally better at. I'm running out of ideas. I've already sung through every one of Ash's marching songs I can remember, a dozen times each, fabricating words as needed. Staying on tune is not aligned with my goals, so that part's fine.

Cadence is scowling. It's unclear if that's a result of my pitchy efforts or just her face. Our face. Whatever.

When even I can't stand my singing anymore, I revert to peppering her with questions about everything she sees, or does, or says. It kills a few more hours. I like to think her heavy pauses before responding to anyone who speaks to her are due to my efforts. But it's more likely that she's just trying a little too hard to seem intimidating.

Which gives me an idea.

"Why do you look constipated?" I chirp in her ear, swinging around to the other side to stage-whisper, "Do you need to go to the bathroom? Go ahead—say, 'May I please be excused to use the toilet, Your Worship.' You know there's no bathroom break in the schedule, right? The mayor is like nine thousand years old. She probably wears diapers. Wait . . . Are *you* wearing a diaper?"

Cadence glowers at the fawning supplicant "You heard me. It wasn't a suggestion."

The witless Division Head grovels. "Of course not, Your Worsh—Hon—Majes—Lady?" He darts a glance at the mayor's inhumanly lovely face, trying to guess the correct honorific from the slightest variations in the curve of her full lips. When he gets a delicate moue of disapproval, he whimpers.

"There is no need to address us," Her Worship Maryam Ajera, Mayor of the Towers of Refuge, Chief of the Council of Guardians, First Mother to the Citizens, Breath of Tower Regulation, kidnapper, murderer of our parents, purloiner of memories, and agency, and freedom, and all that's good in life—says in a dangerously throaty purr. "This is my Right Hand. Her words are as my own and will be obeyed as such."

The man bows his dual-banded hood to the golden floor of the opulent receiving room and cowers.

"See? He's not even looking. You could totally sneak off for a little private time. It's not good to hold it in, you know?" It would be impossible to tease her like this straight-faced—if I had a face.

Cadence emits a faint, low noise, almost a growl. The man prostrate at the feet of the two ornate, throne-like chairs whimpers. "You waste our time," she says after too long a pause, her voice thin and pitchy next to the mayor's. "Patrols won't arrange themselves. Or do I need to handle this matter personally?"

"No, your . . . your Handliness. Enforcers will be posted. Immediately. Without fail."

"If he pees himself, do you clean that up?" I'm genuinely curious—and also committed to this new bathroom-themed torment strategy. I can see a vein throbbing in Cadence's flushed forehead. "Or is there a housekeeper lurking somewhere? How does it work? I mean, someone's got to do the chores, right?"

Cadence scoffs. The division head darts a panicked look from her to the mayor and back again. At a sign from Maryam, he scuttles off to execute his orders.

"Embarrassing," Cadence huffs. "Is there no one better to put in charge of Refuge Force? It's not exactly a low stakes job."

Maryam hums amused agreement. "You clearly haven't had the misfortune to learn, child, that putting clever and powerful men in charge of your armed forces can backfire.

Much better to have a predictably venal and spineless puppet to use or dispose of as needed."

"And what does that make you?" I snicker, finally coaxing a futile swat from Cadence. "Gotcha."

"The other one is here, I take it?" Maryam flutters elegant, bejewelled fingers vaguely in our direction. "Hello, darling. I do wish we'd had more time together. I understand my boy was quite smitten with you."

Cadence pouts. "I hate it when you do that."

"Yes, dear. I'm aware." Maryam reaches over and digs manicured nails into Cadence's sleeve until blood mars the fabric.

The girl wearing my body hardens her jaw and glares back, refusing to flinch.

A warm glow of pride flickers despite my best intentions—she's stubborn, but oh is she strong.

"I heard that, stupid," Cadence thinks smugly.

I blow a raspberry in her ear and follow it up with a series of inventive mouth noises despite not actually having a mouth. It works better when you don't think too hard about it. And it's one of the irritating activities that repetition makes worse for her and easier for me.

Maryam peers at Cadence. I freeze mid *pop.*

It's as if she's staring past Cadence to me. Which is impossible.

I pop my lips at her once in defiance. Her eyes narrow.

I shudder and hurriedly direct my noises back at Cadence—just in case.

"I'm going to change," Cadence announces.

"No need." Maryam licks one wet red nail and smiles.

"I don't like you very much." Cadence's fists tremble at her sides, ever so slightly.

"Hurry back. We still have so much to do."

Cadence turns on her heel, muttering, "I chose to work with you, stupid-head."

"What was that, dear?" Lazy. Amused.

I almost feel sorry for Cadence. Almost. "'Stupid-head?' What are you, four?"

There's no need for the dig. I've clearly already pushed her over the edge. But it's hard to turn off the harassment once I get going.

"Like you could do better." She stomps so hard her heel snags on the carpet. She barely manages to get her hands up in time to keep from face planting.

"Now who's the clumsy one?"

"Whatever. At least you had time to get used to it. The last time I walked in my own skin my feet were half this size." She waggles one foot to emphasize her point and has to scramble for balance again. "Uh. . . that sounded creepier than I meant."

I snicker, but the truth is her complaint lands a little too close for comfort. She's not the only one who lost years to this place. To Maryam.

"The difference is I'm a real person," Cadence sneers, eavesdropping again. "I don't know what you're whining about. This was never your body to begin with. My parents were the ones who died. My life was the one ruined. You're just in the way."

I sigh heavily as if exasperated. I can't let on how terrifying her words really are. Because if she is wrong, if I'm not some kind of mistake, some half-formed remnant or ghost, that means she is.

And while she might be the one with memories of our past, I'm not the one stuck in it. She can't seem to move on—

"Save it," she snaps, throwing open the door to her dressing room. "You know you can't hide anything from me, right? I'm not stuck in the past. I'm just trying to fix it."

"By working with a murderer?"

"By doing whatever it takes." She strips off her bloodstained top and tosses it in the corner.

I look away, absurdly. Not like it's anything I haven't seen before, though the clusters of small, dark bruises and the long, pale scratches are new. "I spoke to Ash while you were sleeping.

He reached Nine Peaks. Everyone made it. They're doing well. Susan—Gran said to say hi."

"Liar." Her voice is muffled behind a fresh tangle of glittery fabric.

"Um, I don't think it's meant to go on like that . . ."

She struggles for a full ten count before hurling the offending item to the floor. "Whatever. Didn't want to wear it anyway."

I grant her a few moments to pick through the complicated, ornate garments in peace.

"Did Ash ask about me?" she says, nose buried in the closet.

"Of course."

She knots her fists in fabric and rips everything within reach from the hangers, casting it down at her feet. "You're a worse liar than he is."

"He didn't have to ask, okay? Of course I told him. You're all we talk about. You, you, and only you. Happy?"

"He's my friend, not yours." She stamps a foot, fists clenched, face flushed.

I take a deep breath, absurdly reminded of a small child throwing a tantrum. "He's worried about you. We both are."

"Stop it. Leave me alone. *I don't want you.*"

The tantrum is escalating—which would be great if I were trying to distract her right now instead of convince her to switch sides.

"I hate you. Just die already." She flails, teary-eyed and red-faced, entirely ridiculous.

Somebody needs a nap. The fact that she's wearing my face makes it all the more uncomfortable.

"Not yours! Mine!"

You'd think switching places would finally get her out of my head. No such luck, apparently. "Cadence—"

"*Mine!*"

"Yours," I soothe. "You're right. You are the original. You are the one with all the power. You're the one Ash cares about, and Susan—Gran. Everyone."

The insane thing is she's the one I care about too. More than I should, after her betrayal. I think it's force of habit keeping me from strangling her, as much as anything, but I just can't shake it.

"Mine?" She peers suspiciously into the middle distance—not that she can see me any more than I was able to see her when our places were reversed.

"Which is why I need to talk to you." Like adults, preferably. This kiddie behaviour is giving me the creeps. "You're in charge. What you choose to do matters. So—so the Council of—I mean Susan—Gran, and Ash, they wanted me to pass a message to you."

Cadence sniffs, rubbing a careless arm across the damp mess she made of her face. "Ash has a message for me?"

"And your gran. They miss you. They don't like that you're so far away. They want to see you."

She nods. "'Course. But I'm busy—tell them to wait a bit."

"That's just it—they can't wait. They need your help. There's, um, monsters attacking Nine Peaks."

She snorts, her childish tones flattening suddenly to adolescent derision. "What do you think I am, three? Ash did not tell you he needs me to save him from monsters."

Oops.

"What's that about monsters, dear?" Maryam lounges in the doorway, elegant and deadly.

Cadence plants hands on hips and glares. "I'll be out in a minute."

"Oh, don't go cutting me out of the girl talk," the mayor pouts, her head tilted just so. "Especially when it's about boys. Especially *mine*."

"Mine," Cadence snaps back automatically—and then flushes.

"Hmm?" Maryam's eyes glitter wickedly, but she wafts away in a cloud of cloying gilt chiffon without further comment.

I have to stop wasting time. Maryam isn't likely to leave us alone together for long. "Fine, you're not a kid.

So here's the truth: you screwed up. You made a stupid mistake way back when you *were* little and it cost you everything. Now you're trying to fix it, and only making things worse. You can't work with a monster to stop the monsters. You can't bring mom and dad back from the dead. And bringing down that barrier is only going to put more lives at risk. You don't have to give me back my— your—body. Keep it. Keep Ash, too. It's your life—take it. Just run away before it's too late."

"If it's my life—which it is—I don't have to take it from you. I already have it, stupid. Besides, since when have you ever known what to do? If it weren't for me, you'd still be mindlessly plodding along like the brainless drone you are."

I choke on a dozen different comebacks at once, giving Cadence time to wrestle her way into halfway decent attire and stalk out into the corridor. Thankfully, Maryam isn't lurking around waiting for her.

"She doesn't lurk," Cadence huffs.

Does so—but . . . "Look. I don't want to fight. But if you destroy that barrier, sure the Mara won't be trapped here anymore. Instead, they'll be able to go wherever they want. Eat whoever they want. If you keep working with Maryam, it's only a matter of time before they kill everyone you care about. Susan. Grace. Lily. Ash. Come on, Cadence. You don't really want Ash to die."

She huffs. "You can't trick me. The Mara are only dangerous because they're trapped. I'm saving the city like mom and dad wanted, not destroying the world."

This is where the conversation always breaks down. Every time. "Cady—"

But she takes off, dashing back to the audience room to plot destruction with her volatile new bestie. And there's nothing for me to do but tag along and be as disruptive and distracting as I can manage until she's too worn out to be any use to Maryam.

But if Ash doesn't have a better strategy for me tonight, I'm afraid I'll be the one to go mad long before Cadence breaks.

MURDER

"**I** DON'T LIKE it." I turn my back on Ash and his marching band of uniformed woodland creatures. The chipmunks are particularly shrill. "And that is not helping."

He dismisses the adorably fuzzy little musicians with a gesture, but the music still trips along in the background, as if a sufficiently jaunty tune can make this better. "Sorry. I just—I don't know. I wanted it to sound less scary than it, uh, does. It's not that bad—"

"Really? 'Cause it sounds like an assassination to me."

"That's hardly fair. I just said there could be some risk."

"Of *dying*. 'Risk of death' means murder."

"No, it means there's some risk involved. This isn't exactly well-charted territory. Things could turn out. Or, um, not."

"I'm not killing a kid, Ash."

"Technically, she's our age. Practically an adult. Probably. Anyway, it wouldn't be like that—"

"I'm not murdering Cadence. Period. Not even to save the world."

"And I wouldn't ask you to. I don't want to see her hurt either. But we don't exactly have a lot of options here."

Lightning crackles. A tree bursts into flame. I watch it burn—until the anchor knot squirms under my touch, emitting an ominous rumbling. The forest doesn't appreciate this show of temper. I nod a downpour into existence and watch it flatten fire and foliage alike.

Ash took his sweet time getting here tonight, too. I had been tossing around the idea of showing him what I'd been working on, but now . . . It's not like it really matters. I mean, I'd even gone to the trouble of reproducing a patch of wasteland so I could test different ways of restoring it while I waited, never mind those improvements on Nine Peaks' layout that the forest had nudged me toward, but now . . .

I blink, and the half-finished structures in the distance are gone as if they'd never been.

Ash shoves dripping hair out of his eyes and swirls up a clear dome to deflect the rain. "See why I didn't want to bring it up?"

I cut a dark look in his direction. The rushing water has finally drowned out that gratingly cheery tune of his. "Explain properly this time."

"They're not even saying it's what you should do. It's just one option."

"The only option they're willing to share, at least."

"That's—"

Lightning strikes in quick succession, a ring of flames springing up in defiance of the downpour. "Seriously? What else are you hiding? How much worse could it get than murder?"

He makes a fist, suffocating the wildfire out of existence. "*It's not murder.* No one is saying you have to do anything you don't want to do. I mean, the council would really prefer you just hang out here and stop stirring up—"

"Not an option. Did you explain properly? Putting aside the elders' willingness to sacrifice a whole city of innocents, if Cadence and Maryam bring down the barrier and set the Mara free, *no one* will be safe. You did mention that part, right?"

"They don't see it that way. Grandfather said there's no reason to believe your Mara are especially dangerous. If anything, the majority opinion is Cadence might be onto something. The Coles were sent to remove the barrier in the first place. She might even manage to save a few lives if left to her own devices.

I'm not"—he holds his hands up to forestall my protest—"saying I agree. Just relaying the message. It was your gran who brought up the idea of taking back control from Cady and switching places again."

"That was Susan's idea?" I pace, shrugging the rain away.

Ash doodles a few sunset streaks across the watery-pale sky. I glare. He stops guiltily.

"You're saying Cadence's own grandmother suggested I risk her life?"

He shrugs. "*Your* gran didn't put it like that. I would have brought her to explain, except the council has really cracked down on gate access since we all snuck down to the coast, and she's supposed to be holed up getting over grief-induced insanity or something. Technically, I wasn't even allowed to be talking to her."

"Uh huh."

"She didn't seem insane, though. Sad, sure, but no more crazy than usual."

"Murder seems pretty crazy. Not to mention, if it was that easy to switch places with Cadence, don't you think I would've done it by now?"

"So you have tried? Can you use your powers at all like this? You know, on the other side? Maybe—"

"It doesn't matter"—the forest's gift squirms at the evasion—"I'm not doing anything that could put Cadence at risk."

Ash chews his lip, peering at me. I turn to examine the misty clouds chasing each other in the distance.

"Cole, you know I—I care about both of you, right? I don't want Cady hurt any more than you do. But if she brings down that barrier and it is as bad as you say . . . maybe it's worth the risk, you know?" He digs a toe into the dirt, continues, "After what she did to you?"

I heat with sudden anger at the reminder of Cadence's betrayal, at the way she used my desperation against me to steal back her body, but the flush cools before I can even muster a response. The sensation is almost alien, distant and unfamiliar, as if the fury is being stolen from me before it can fully ignite.

I look past the clouds, beyond the vast sea of unreality to the very edges of the dreamscape. To the place where my ghosts wait for me, drowning in their darkness. The tortured victims of the Mara: the ones I failed to save and the ones I never had a chance of saving. If it were within my power, is there anything I wouldn't do to keep their ranks from swelling?

Every night I look into that void and count the names of those I desperately hope not to see tortured within. Ange never made it out of the city—it can't be long now until she joins her partner Cass's ruined shade in the darkness in-between. And when the barrier hemming in the Mara falls, how long until she's reunited with her sister Amy in death? Her young niece, Lily? The thought of stubborn, fearless, pixie-faced Lily sucked dry by the Mara makes me almost physically ill.

This is the nightmare that lurks at the edge of the dreamscape, and I would do anything to keep it from becoming real. Anything—except trade one child's life for another's. And in my nightmares, Cadence doesn't wear the gawky, spotty, nearly grown body I left behind, but a form not much bigger than Lily's . . .

"Everything could go back to normal," Ash lies. "You don't know for a fact that anything bad would happen. You might just switch places again."

Or I might wipe one or both of us from the face of all worlds at once. I know I should be angry at her, furious at her betrayal, but . . . "I took the chance to grow from her once, without meaning to. I won't take it away again, even if I could. Besides, I think I'm making progress getting through to her. It's not like she's evil, just stubborn and stuck in the past."

"None of this is your fault, C."

I blink. Then I swirl up a couple of straight-backed chairs with a scratched-up table. The legs sink into the damp earth when I sit, so I waft the whole setup a couple inches into the air and glare until Ash hoists himself into the opposite chair. "What else are you hiding?"

He drums his fingers against the top, studying me. "What do you know about the dome?"

I narrow my eyes at the change of topic. "It keeps the monsters in. Keeps everything else in too. Something about it is toxic to dreamwalkers. Not deadly, but damaging. And it burned when I touched it, crossing with Ravel. I didn't have access to any magic at that time, so the barrier may or may not burn regular humans, too. That's about it."

He reaches across the table, palms up, hands open. "I hate that you keep getting hurt by all this."

I shrug and pointedly cross my arms. It's not like I love getting hurt either. Where's he going with this?

"I want you to listen, okay? Just listen and don't interrupt." His eyes are wide and dark, his gaze too steady, too intent for me to meet for more then a moment at a time. "You do not have to go back there. You don't have to do anything that hurts ever again. You can just stay here. With me. If you want to. Because I want you to. Stay here. With—with me. Wow," he lets out a shaky breath, grimaces. "I sound kinda lame, huh? But for real, Cole. Or C. Or whatever. I'll call you what you want, be happy with whatever you want to be, and do, and have me be. Just . . . just *stay*."

He isn't supposed to lay it all out there like that. Dancing around it is one thing—that, I can bear. But this—this is unfair. Cruel, even.

In another world, if I were another me, maybe I'd feel differently. That other me might want to reach back—and even know *how*. Maybe she would be able to find the right words to give back to him. Maybe she'd be able to make a different choice.

I could say something like, "You have dreamed of me for years—"

"Decades," he'd interrupt, staring at me with those wide brown eyes brimming with adoration.

And I would gaze back, maybe a little teary with the emotion of it, maybe bashfully glancing away, saying something like: "While I have only just begun to dream again."

Or maybe something more like, "While my dreams have only just come back to life." Something eloquent. Restrained. But I would leave the door open to more. Maybe he'd kiss me. Maybe I'd want him to. Maybe it would be enough to help me forget all worlds but the one we'd make together . . .

But the me that I have become, that I *choose*, only has the capacity to care about one thing right now. And it's not him.

"Don't." I let him see the fantasy dying in my eyes, my tone flat with finality.

He flinches. Closes his eyes. His hands tremble as if he's only just stopping himself from covering his ears.

"If you care about me at all, Ash,"—he starts to respond, but I cut him off before he can embarrass either of us further—"*If* you want to help me, you'll help me save them. Now: the dome. Impenetrable to monsters and to most humans. Burns on contact, probably. Toxic to dreamwalkers. Cadence's target, and apparently Maryam's. Am I missing anything?"

He shakes his head, draws his hands back and braces them against his knees, knuckles whitening. " No, that sounds about right. I'm not sure anyone knows much more than that. But the elders—let me back up. You knew I ran away from Spectre to come find you, right?"

"Not that you told me, but yeah, if that's what you call your little team or whatever, then that's the story I heard."

"Did anyone ever mention what we were doing on that mission?"

"Does anyone ever explain anything to me?"

He shrugs. "It's hard to remember what you know, sometimes."

I drop his chair into the mud so he has to peer over the table.

Ash rolls his eyes. "Abuse of power. I'll take that as a 'no.' And also a 'hurry-up.'" He tries for a grin but doesn't quite pull it off. "Here's what you need to know: most large bodies of water are infested with creatures who are none too fond of anything that looks human, so we obviously try to keep our distance."

He holds up a hand to quell my protest. "Stay with me, that is not the important part. The thing is, my squad came across the rumour of a boat—a ship, really—crossing between our shores and an island off the coast. And the source of that rumour claimed to have encountered a dreamwalker crew. Her descriptions were dead ringers for some of our missing-presumed-killed parents. You know you weren't the only one to lose most of your family when you were young, yeah? Nearly all of us have lost at least one parent, if not both, in missions gone wrong."

I blink. That is news, actually, but . . . "Where you going with this?"

He leans forward, tapping the table in emphasis. "Look at it this way: how does the council know what to expect from a barrier dome when yours is the only one anyone's ever heard of—and the only mission to crack it failed?"

"I don't know, how do they know anything? Mystical dreamwalker libraries?"

". . . Okay, sure, maybe. But there were never many big cities around here in the first place, and I'm telling you, yours is the only one I've ever heard of that ever had a barrier like that put up around it. It's also one of the only ones still inhabited. But that island I mentioned? On the old maps it's huge. Once it held the biggest city in the region, next to yours. If my parents are still alive, there's nowhere they could have survived in hiding all this time . . . except, possibly, across a sea-monster infested ocean."

"And?"

"And what? That's like—like—it's the biggest news in pretty much forever. It could change everything. Just imagine: a whole generation of fully-grown dreamwalkers out there somewhere. What have they learned since they left us? What skills have they honed? I mean, there's your army!"

I flick the landscape past until we're standing on the edge of the cliffs staring out to sea. Not the sea he's talking about, but my pulse still ticks up as if a ship will appear on the horizon.

Forces unconstrained by Nine Peaks' elders. Adult dreamwalkers who could fight and choose their fate—instead of a bunch of teens on the edge of childhood with half-manifested powers and more enthusiasm than sense. Surely they could save my city, defeat the monsters, even rescue Cadence from her misguided quest . . . But—"Why didn't you bring this up sooner?"

Ash kicks a pebble off the edge of the cliff and watches it fall, mumbling.

"What was that?"

He dangles his legs over the edge and flicks another pebble. "Spectre didn't actually find anything. No traces of boats run up on the shore. No pier for a ship to dock at. No more survivors to corroborate the story. Just one traumatized little kid with a wild story. That was when I left my squad behind to look for you, and all they found while I was gone were swamp monsters and gnawed bones."

He hangs his head, intent on rolling a stone between finger and thumb. I snatch it away and hurl it into the shimmering ocean. "So? Those guys suck. I mean, have you met them? I did—hardly confidence inspiring."

His eyes spark at the insult to his friends, but I keep going without pausing for his protests. "You'll do better this time. You'll find the way across, I know it. How far are you from the coast? You know what—doesn't matter. Just get going. I'll do my best to stall Cadence until you find the ship. Bring me that army, Ash."

"It's not that easy—"

"And killing Cadence is? Look, it's not like—ugh." My vision doubles. She's waking up. Back to harassment duty. "Look, I don't care what it takes. I'll stall her as long as I can, but I'm counting on you to find that ship. You promised not to bring Nine Peaks' forces back to the city, but you never said anything about other dreamwalkers, right? You owe me this."

I leave him on the cliffs overlooking the dreaming sea, still protesting, and hurl myself through the ranks of nightmares at the edge of the dreamscape with barely a sideways glance.

UNWEAVING

THE UNEARTHLY MAYOR of Refuge rarely descends from her golden perch at the top of the tower—or so I've always imagined. As it turns out, she just has her ways of moving unseen. They're called "guards" and "elevator keys."

"Can I have one of those?" Cadence points to the unassuming little slip of metal.

"When you've earned it." Maryam holds the key card against a panel until it beeps, then presses the button for the lowest level with the very tip of her pointed nail. When the disc fails to light up, she frowns and stabs harder, cracking the age-fogged plastic.

"When will that be?" Cadence whines.

Maryam whirls in a tinkling of gold chains and grabs the toddler-masquerading-as-a-teen by the chin. "When you've learned to block out that traitorous ghost. No offense, darling."

I don't know how she knows I'm here. Unless she just assumes I'm always lurking—accurate, if so. Maybe it's all just a ploy to get under Cadence's skin, but it works. Cadence subsides into sullen scuffling and heavy, pointed sighs, while I do my bit with an assortment of lip pops and inane questions like: "Why did she send her guards on ahead? I mean, the B.O. was *bad* but it's not like she can smell it over that perfume, right?" and "I do kind of like her fashion sense. You should try harder, you know. You're not a kid anymore."

But when the elevator doors slide open, my brain goes numb.

Once, I thought the lower levels of the Towers of Refuge abandoned. When the ocean rose, they were supposed to have flooded, but obviously, by the time Ravel turned them into his sprawling playground of hedonism, they had been reclaimed. Probably with the help of Ange's Underfolk, now that I think of it. Their engineers had all sorts of clever pumps and turbines and such that could have made it possible. But the last time I saw these halls, they'd been a disaster zone.

Now they're gleaming.

The bloodstains have been scrubbed away, the gouges in the floors and walls filled and smoothed, the fallen-in ceilings replaced. Everything is painted in blinding white with the strongest lights I've ever seen bouncing pain-bright rays off the sharply bland surfaces. Sanitized.

"Oh, Ravel is gonna *hate* this," Cadence crows, earning from Maryam what would have been a smirk on any lesser visage.

But, "It was getting a little dingy," is all she deigns to say.

Her enforcers stalk ahead of us; the distant tromping of their boots and the flickering hems of their uniforms always just at the edge of human senses as they clear each new hall ahead of us. Which begs the question: who is it that still inhabits these sanitized spaces? Not Ravel—presumably under house arrest in far away Nine Peaks with a flock of traumatized refugees to look after. And surely Ange and whatever is left of her flock must have been imprisoned or sacrificed to the Mara by now.

So, why bother with guards? Are they here as a snack? An offering to the hungry monsters? Cadence seems unconcerned when I bring it up.

Maryam laughs when I finally nag Cadence into asking. "Well, *I* wouldn't want to eat them, dear, but I suppose it's possible."

This makes Cadence uncomfortable enough it feels safe to give her a break from the constant irritation I've been so diligently supplying. After all, it's not as if she's being particularly useful to Maryam right at this moment. And I'm a big enough person not to indulge in undue harassment just in petty revenge for all she put me through.

Probably.

More to the point, I want to have a look around. I can see through walls. And floors and ceilings—yet another advantage of turning ghost. But it does take some focus.

There's no one behind us, which isn't all that surprising. Above—nothing for the first couple floors. Not that there would be. Below—no one nearby, at least. The lack of inhabitants gets more concerning the further we go. Ravel hadn't managed to free that many in those desperate final hours of our ill fated rescue—probably more of Ange's folk than his own since so few of Freedom's dancers were permanently in residence. Most snuck down night after night from Refuge to seize a few hours of escape and would have fled back to its "safety" at the first sign of enforcers. But there should still be someone around.

And then there is—in the distance. A flickering of life at the edges of these tunnels. Someone survived. More than one someone.

"Probably just enforcers on patrol," Cadence says carelessly.

"What was that, dear?"

"Nothing."

"Is your ghost curious about the remnant? She is, isn't she? She thought I'd have used them all up at once."

Cadence trips, catches herself against a too-white wall, and flinches when Maryam slips an elegant arm through hers.

"Don't you think me silly, dear," the ancient hisses into her ear. "I didn't last this long being wasteful."

Cadence swallows hard—and yanks her arm free. "Stop screwing around and just tell me what we're down here for already. Do you want my help or not?"

Maryam cocks a full hip and tilts her head. "So sure of ourselves, aren't we? What if it was never your help I wanted?"

Cadence is too belligerent to back down, but if I had blood, it would have been rioting to escape by now. I don't know how sacrificing us would be of any particular use to Maryam—but I'm not at all eager to find out either.

"Oh, you're just so much fun!" The sharp pinch leaves fading white dents on Cadence's cheek. "I'm not going to eat you, child. I don't play with my food. Often. And you, my dear, are much, much too valuable to waste."

Cadence pretends to sulk, but I never realized how susceptible she was to flattery.

"Not far now," the mayor trills with an elegant sweep of her hand. "Watch your step—it does get a tad tight."

It is not the same tunnel Ravel used—at least, I don't think it is. But it comes to the same thing. Maryam has led Cadence to the edge of the barrier.

Time's up, and far sooner than I'd expected. I should have pushed Ash harder, should have been willing to risk—

"Well?" Cadence raps the barrier and recoils.

"Silly girl. It takes more than a tap to knock down that wall."

"It burned me!" She doesn't bother cloaking her outrage. "That actually hurts!"

"Now, now. So easily distracted."

Cadence growls, lunging to her feet. But instead of going after the mayor, she squares up to the barrier. "What is it?"

"This and that." But Maryam's tone has lost all its slyness. "Mostly this." She flicks one of the delicate golden chains that drip from her wrists.

The barrier is made of gold? It kind of makes sense. Dreamwalkers—and, supposedly, monsters—aren't too fond of the stuff. But the surface before us seems amorphous and indistinct, a sluggishly churning translucent mass with a near-pearlescent oil-slick gleam.

"I don't understand." Cadence steps back as if afraid it will leap out at her. "That's not gold."

"Well. Not all of it, more's the pity. Perhaps I should say: It was gold, or, it started with gold. But if that were all, I would have no use for you dear."

Cadence has gone back to staring at her blistered hand in disbelief. She must've assumed the noxious surface only burned me because I couldn't use a dreamwalker's magic at the time. After all, when she crossed with her parents, she passed through the barrier without lasting harm, we've both encountered small amounts of gold in Freedom and Refuge, and I'd been fine the times Ravel and Ash took me across—

"It's all your fault," she snarls.

"Perhaps." Maryam's lips curve, though I doubt she's the one Cadence meant. "But assigning blame moves us no closer to solving my little problem. Get on with it, child."

Cadence blinks, apparently lost in the conversational whiplash.

"Go ahead. Take it apart," Maryam prods.

"Does—does she think you know how to destroy that thing?" I stage whisper, amused at Cadence's blank expression. "How disappointing."

But this time, when she fixes her glare on the poisonous swirl of the barrier, something is different. There's more definition to the sickly churn, a loose pattern that wriggles its way through the fog, almost like—

"Ugh. You tattooed your son after this thing? That is some fashion choice," sneers Cadence.

"Try the other hand, dear," Maryam says coolly. She means the one I burned on the other side of the dome when Ravel let go of me for just an instant. The one etched in a swirling pattern of burn scars eerily like his tattoos.

Cadence darts her a venomous look but after a moment shrugs and reaches out a tentative fingertip. This time she doesn't flinch. Her hand sends ripples across the barrier and sinks to the second knuckle below the murky surface.

When she pulls back, something comes with her. Long, sticky strands trail from the barrier for several inches before snapping back with an audible *glop*.

"That's not—" she starts.

"You recognize it, then?" Maryam sounds too eager for comfort, and I think I know why.

Those strands, that swirling pattern . . . they're warped, but all too familiar. The reason Maryam wanted Cadence, or me, for that matter, wasn't about either of us in particular.

She just wanted a dreamweaver—any dreamweaver—to tear these twisted threads from the fabric of the barrier. I'm almost sure of it.

"They can't be . . ." Cadence hunches, hands braced against her knees, a sickly pallor washing over her.

"It seemed like a good idea at the time," Maryam drawls with an elegant shrug. She examines one shimmering nail. "And it worked, of course. Much, much better than expected."

Cadence empties the contents of her stomach onto the floor. The barrier pulses, slurping away the mess and swirling more energetically. I gag.

"It's not alive," Cadence says, pleading. "It can't be alive—"

"Of course not, dear," Maryam says, all flat white teeth, blood-red lips, and black, black pupils. "Not anymore. Not in any way that matters."

5

LIVING

HREADS OF DREAMS.

Threads of desire, of hope, and fear, and longing, and lust.

Threads tangling between my fingers and singing of life and death and that which lies beyond.

Every single one feels distinct, unique. But they all have one thing in common: every single thread was born in the heart of a human.

So how the hell does this clotted nightmare of a wall have threads of its own?

"Don't act so shocked, dear," Maryam strokes the inner surface of the dome, rings sparking and polish crackling in the heat of its arcane force. It roils beneath her touch—in panic or pleasure, I have no way to divine. "So I had to sacrifice a little blood in the process—just look how many lives I've saved over the years."

Cadence's thoughts are frantic, inarticulate. A welter of emotion, gibbering horror wrestling with disgust, a torrent of half-formed words, choked pleas . . . and, finally, from the depths of terror, one overwhelming imperative: *get me out of here.*

She offers it all to me. I don't know if she means to, but that's what it feels like—she's holding out the reins, the key, the right to take control, and I have only to take it and return to what I was. My body, my life, my mission. She the powerless, helpless ghost; I the original, the real, living girl. The one with the power to choose. To act. To change the course of the future.

I could take it all back, right now. But at what cost? Would we truly revert to the 'normal' I've always known? Would she still be around to taunt and harass and save and simply be with me, or would I be finally, devastatingly, alone in my head at last?

Deciding what I want, and on short notice no less, isn't a skill I've had the chance to develop. But I know I don't want to risk her. I can't.

I choose to believe she'll do the right thing. After this, how could she not? It's impossible for her to go on working with Maryam, now that she's seen into the ageless depths of her depravity firsthand. I doubt Cadence will be able to bring herself to so much as touch that barrier after this. And even if she could . . . No.

I can't let her go.

So I take that key—that right to take back control—and fold the open hands of her soul tightly back around it.

Not mine, but hers. Not taken, but given.

She sighs. Rocks back on her heels, subsiding into the body that is now no one's but hers. And reaches for the barrier.

I gasp. "Don't—"

She withdraws quickly, strands oozing from her fingertips, and closes her fist before they can snap back into place. Then she yanks, crying out with the effort.

The strands fray. And snap, the barrier where they were raised suddenly hard and brittle. Cracks splinter across a hands-breadth of the diseased surface, now gone dull and still.

Cadence yelps. She shakes the slimy, torn mass in her hand to the floor. It patters to the ground, desiccating in midair, followed moments later by her knees. Her eyelids flutter. Her skin turns grey and damp with cold sweat.

"Shh, shh. It's a wonderful start, dear. You've done well. So, so well." Maryam croons, cradling Cadence's head as she slumps into unconsciousness. "And you too, darling. You tell my boy it won't be long now. Not long at all."

She looks up, mad golden eyes swirling like the barrier, burning straight into my soul as if she can see beyond the fabric of reality itself.

I could stay, even without Cadence's consciousness linking me to the waking world. I should. I need to know more, need to make sure this foolish child is safe, need to stop her before she can do more damage.

Instead, I flee to the clean sunlight of my safe, unsullied world of dreams and leave the waking nightmare, at least for now, behind me.

I DIVE DEEP, desperate to feel clean again. But the sinuous plants dancing beneath the dreaming waves are too like those wriggling strands, revoltingly lifelike in that wretched, brutal moment before they turned to ash. I scale the cliffs to the forest and keep right on climbing, revelling in the rough solidity of cinnamon and ginger-scented branches until I reach too high in one towering oak and the frail slenderness of a handful of twigs turns my stomach.

So small. Alive, and yet not. Joined, and then . . . not.

I let my weight drag me to the ground as if gravity is a rule and not one option out of countless opportunities. The thud of impact pushes air into my lungs. I crawl from the cool shadows under the trees to the lush grass of a clearing, curl up in the sunlight and shudder until Ash finds me and makes me get up again.

He conjures food and drink and does his best to get me to take it. He flips through landscapes, making the world around us larger, then smaller, more brilliant, and then peaceful and muted, increasingly frantic about my silence.

It's not until I realize he thinks I've killed Cadence that I find my words again. Even so, it's nearly impossible to hold onto any semblance of coherence.

He slumps in relief when I start to explain—starting with "I didn't do it"—and gets increasingly rigid as I haltingly choke and stutter my way through the rest of it.

"I didn't think—how could she?" I finish on a sob, arms clamped tight around myself to keep from shattering. I should have stopped her. I never even imagined she could bring herself to do something like that . . .

Ash paces, face drawn, muttering under his breath. Every few circuits, he stops, scrubs his hands through his hair, and shakes his head before starting up again.

It's odd, but the more he freaks out, the better I can think.

"So?" I ask, finally.

"Hmm?"

"Did you find that ship yet?"

He stops. "Did I what?"

I clear my throat. "The ship. To the island. To get my army. Did you find it yet? How close are you?"

He stares, still frozen. "You really have no idea, do you? It's not like I can just pop over there in an afternoon."

"We're running out of time. How much longer do you need?"

". . . We might reach it tomorrow. But only because we're doubling up on bikes and taking it in shifts. And there's no guarantee we'll find anything once we get there."

"'We?'"

"The whole squad wanted to come. Not just Spectre—Steph's Nightwitches, too. Your Ravel even tried to sneak out after us. Nearly blew the whole thing up. I made Rei take him back."

"He is not my Ravel." But I'm not unhappy to hear he's safely tucked behind Nine Peaks' walls. He'll look out for the refugees there, if only because it gives him an established power base. Plus, Maryam seems bothered by his absence, judging by her repeated references to 'my boy.' "So who's actually with you? Besides Banshee."

I didn't mean to add that slant to her name, honest.

He snorts. "You too? She's good in a fight, that's all. Hatif's riding with me, Aleya with Banshee. Mogwai, as squad captain, couldn't get away without the elders catching on, but she and Dybbuk distracted Steph and Grace long enough for Banshee to sneak out so that's something.

Qareen would have ridden solo, but she had to run interference with Nightwitch squad or we would have had the whole flock tailing us."

"... You know I have no idea who, like, half of those people are, right? Doesn't matter—it only takes one messenger to rally an army, and it sounds like you're on your way. By tomorrow, right?"

"Maybe. Look, don't expect too much, okay? There is no guarantee there's anyone actually out there to help, even if we could reach them in time. Have you put any more thought into—"

I stomp, rippling the pleasant meadow surrounding us into mirror-smooth glass, and summoning an abomination from its still surface. "This. Just like this. She just reached out and broke it in a heartbeat."

He steps closer to the slight curve of the ugly mass jutting up from the ground with its still, cracked patch at shoulder height. He reaches out to trace his fingers over the dead section.

I flinch, but of course, nothing happens. It's not the real barrier, just a reconstruction. I plant both hands beside his; spreading my fingers to show how much damage she could do with a double handful, how easy it would be to tear the barrier apart.

"But you said she passed out afterward, right?" He raps the dead patch. "A single handful laid her out cold. The barrier is huge. Does she have to reach every part of it to destroy it or just punch one small hole through? How much damage can it take before coming down entirely? Did she collapse from shock, or did it take something, do something to her, retaliate, or drain her energy, or—And will she get stronger, or weaker as she continues?"

He's pacing again. And making me more anxious with every horrifying possibility that comes out of his mouth.

I snap the model of the barrier wall into nothingness and beckon back the reassuring flowers, nodding the sunlight's warmth around us to ward off the chill of that remembered death. "Don't know. Maryam seemed pleased, but whatever Cadence did to that wall didn't exactly blow a hole through it.

Assuming that's even what she was going for in the first place. Hurry. I need that army yesterday, Ash."

He raises a softly chiming cloud of citrus-scented petals on the breeze—probably to hide his face as he says, "You know I'll do whatever I can to help. But you need to prepare yourself to act alone if it comes to that. If you're right about the barrier, you'll have to be the one to stop Cadence before she frees the Mara."

"You mean 'to kill her.'" I swat the dancing petals back to earth.

"To take away her ability to do damage," he says reprovingly, as if he's not the one who raised the idea of murdering his childhood friend. "Again: there is no guarantee she would actually die if you switched places. Just some risk."

I don't bring up that desperate moment when she offered it all to me, practically begged me to save her. She hadn't wanted to touch the barrier, hadn't meant to destroy it. I know she hadn't.

So why did she?

"Cole?"

I look up from my hands. "I just—"

He sighs. "Look, I've got to get some sleep. I'll try, C. We'll all do whatever we can. This shouldn't all be on your shoulders, but—"

"You're right," I interrupt, all but backpedalling from the soft sympathy in his voice. "Get some sleep. And get me that army, Ash. I'm counting on you."

I snap the bridge shut, sending him back to whatever stretch of wilderness his squad is racing through at the moment and move the land beneath me until I'm back on the edge of the cliffs. It's easiest to breathe here, even if it is an illusion.

I blow the sun to the horizon and drink in the nascent sunset, breathing the air brine-sharp instead of floral and fluttering gulls into existence so their piercing cries almost drown out the howling ghosts beyond the edge of the skies.

Their numbers swell with each passing day, and that is not just my nightmare. The Mara grow ever more hungry. And I can't kill Cadence, even to stop her unleashing them to devour the world.

Which means I have to find another way of stopping her. Today.

6

UNCHANGED

"I DON'T KNOW what you're talking about, but that sounds disgusting." Cadence flicks through her wardrobe, considering each impractical garment with undue attentiveness.

"It was disgusting, which you know full well. You were there. Goopy strands of sacrificed people-puree? Sentient walls slurping up puke? Severed soul-threads turning into dust? The barrier freeze-drying? Or dying? Or shrivelling, or whatever."

"Gross." She wrinkles her nose. "But nope. Doesn't ring a bell."

I'm supposed to be the one pestering her, not the other way around. But more than that, I'm caught off-balance by her stone-cold refusal to acknowledge reality.

Could Maryam have wiped her memory? Or was she shocked into amnesia? Or is she so embarrassed she's just going to pretend it never happened?

"Who's embarrassed? I'm finally doing what I want." Cadence assembles an eye-bleeding combination of gold, green, and pink with black accents, twisting her hair and pinning it back with glittery clips.

The ornaments don't burn on contact, though they do make her thoughts a little fuzzy-sounding. "Funny, you didn't seem so in control yesterday when you were begging me to swap places with you."

"Creative." Cadence says dryly. "Finally ran out of ugly noises and moved on to storytelling, did you? Thing is, it's not so easy to pull one over on a girl when she already knows all about the real world."

Huh? "Just because you don't want to admit breaking down yesterday doesn't mean it didn't happen."

"Can't you go haunt someone else for a while?" She considers the result of her efforts in a tall mirror and stalks into the corridor.

"Ash asked after you," I lie.

She falters, huffs, and resumes walking. "Tell him he's welcome back anytime. Just him. I could use a friend around here."

I bite back an equally snarky retort. As much as sparring with Cadence comes naturally, it is not helping my case. Instead, I say, "Fine, you want to play dumb? Go for it. Get it out of your system. Say whatever you like. But I know deep down you're horrified by what happened yesterday. You dread the thought of touching that barrier again, of coating your fingers in its filth. So don't. Stall. Tell Maryam you can't do it after all. Run away—this city is big enough to find somewhere to hide for at least a few days, right?"

She flips her hair, but her hand trembles.

"I'll—I'll get Ash to send Ravel back for you. If anyone could sneak you out of the city, he could. And I promise I won't say a word about any of this. You can tell everyone you changed your mind. Say you had a plan to save the city, but it didn't work out, or even that everyone was already dead by the time you got here, or—"

"I'm exactly where I want to be." She flounces onto her throne with a nod to Maryam.

"Problems, dear?" Maryam coos, draping herself more artfully over her own ornate perch.

"Nothing I can't handle." Cadence kicks a knee over one arm of her only slightly less ostentatious chair and tries to look comfortable. "So, what's on the agenda?"

Maryam clicks her tongue. "You're going for awe and adoration, dear. You want them trembling with frustrated desire, not barely suppressed amusement. Try again."

Cadence scowls and waggles her dangling foot, though the angle has to be cutting off her circulation. "I'm good."

Maryam lifts one flawless shoulder in the most delicate of shrugs. "As you will. Just try not to fidget in front of the help."

And Cadence doesn't, feigning indifference as one supplicant after another grovels their way through the receiving chamber. Her lips get whiter and thinner, her face more flushed, her fists tighter, but that leg stays rebelliously cocked as gravity and her own weight gouge divots into her ribs and calf.

Lucky me. I don't even need to harass her. She's miserable enough, if far too stubborn to admit it.

Given the circumstances—and the dreary repetitiveness of the reports—I even risk wandering away for a bit. There's not much to see in the upper reaches of Refuge. Dual-band supervisors, division heads, and superiors divert themselves in private quarters or stalk around harassing the single-band drones, who are otherwise hard at work or obediently resting on their respective floors. Though, as it turns out, there is quite a bit less obedience behind closed doors than I had been led to believe. But the ranks of workers are thin, more rooms empty than not, except on the lower levels where people are crammed into the shared dorms of re-education centres.

Whether they're there due to reprimands—some failure of duty or diligence—or just being held in a convenient pen for the Mara's snacking needs, it's hard to tell. Some faces are familiar. Ange's people, most likely. Or maybe I had seen them dancing in Freedom. But something back up in the little throne room plucks at the strained edges of my attention and drags me back to Cadence's side.

At first glance, I'm not sure what it could have been. Another overdressed figure cowers at Maryam's feet, babbling of the difficulties his division is in, if only the mayor could see her way to—of course, he doesn't mean to say that she doesn't provide for them, but—no, no, he is more than capable of continuing, if she would perhaps—

Boring. Utterly unremarkable. There have been hours of these meetings, and they all go the same way. Division heads or supervisors bring a complaint couched in flattery, a petition for more supplies, a cringing and blame-shifting apology for not meeting targets. Maryam smiles wordlessly until their sputtering peters off. Then she makes her demands.

In this case, it's more patrols—though the head of the enforcers protests that he has too few to draw on, that it is impossible, between the heightened frequency and so many prisoners to guard, not to mention the outside sweeps—really, there is hardly anyone left, surely those at least could be—

And that's what must've caught my attention: *sweeps.* They're rounding up all the survivors, the ones whose ancestors never fled to Refuge, generations of hardscrabble outsiders from the crumbling streets of our drowned city. The ones who never learned to live under Maryam's iron regulations. And yet, even counting the packed prison dorms, Refuge's population still seems far too thin.

Either the rest of the survivors are holed up somewhere Maryam's enforcers can't reach, or the Mara's hunger has grown beyond even my fears. For every soul the dream-eating monsters devour, their need grows. Unchecked, that growth will be exponential. And there is no one here who can stop them except Cadence.

"I'm busy," she yawns. "Besides, I have more important things to destroy."

7

BROKEN

MARYAM WAITS UNTIL all her supplicants have cleared to walk Cadence back to the barrier. Come to think of it, it's odd she doesn't just cancel her meetings since running Refuge can hardly matter anymore.

Cadence snickers. "Stupid. Of course it matters. People still have to eat and stuff. You're so short-sighted. We see the bigger picture. Getting rid of the Mara is just one part of that."

"You do know she literally sacrifices people to them, right?"

"I'll take over, dear." Maryam flutters her fingers. "Welcome back, my child. If only you hadn't avoided this little chat in the first place. We could have saved so many lives together."

"Stop talking to her like I'm not here." Cadence glowers.

"I understand you have a connection to my boy," Maryam continues talking over her, unconcerned. "So you will have some familiarity with what it takes to lead."

"Um, gross?" Cadence interrupts. "You should probably know that neither of us is Ravel's biggest fan . . ." But she backs down under Maryam's slow blink.

"You're young. You especially, dear. Your other self perhaps understands a little better. But you, you oversimplify, clinging to the myth of a simple world. Heroes and monsters who never change sides, never blur the boundaries. We all do silly things when we're young . . ."

The mayor trails off, her satisfied smile wobbling. "Well. I hardly remember anymore, you know. We become different people over time, and the girl I used to be—oh, she was a silly thing. She thought she was saving the world too. Sacrificed everything she had and ever loved to save it. But when you sacrifice yourself, who's left to finish the job you started?"

"Is she done yet?" I yawn noisily to cover the prick of her barbs.

Cadence smirks.

"Yes, you can't help that arrogance any more than I could, can you, child? Is the other one complaining? Competing for your attention? Consider why she feels the need to stop me from explaining. And you, darling, you should listen. The woman you are becoming will surely have greater need of what I have to say than the child you were."

"Enough of that." Cadence stomps. "Do I look like a child? What about this power that you want so much seems *childish* to you?"

Maryam reaches to pat her cheek. "Adorable. I can see why you indulge her, darling. But sooner or later, you'll need to stop playing games and seize the reins. As endearing as children can be, it takes an iron will and a heart of stone to care for them. To provide. To stop the monsters at the gate and make a safe, healthy home."

"Is that what you think you're doing?" The words spill out too fast, goaded to fury despite myself. Despite the fact that she can't hear my protests. "Providing for 'the children?' By slaughtering their families? Kidnapping them? Stealing their childhoods and their memories alike? Turning them into spiritless drones who can do nothing but obey? Is that what you were doing for me—us? Providing? Caring for us?"

Cadence trembles with fury. This is it. This is the turning point. I finally broke through the shield of her stubbornness, and now—

But the light in her eyes trickles away, her expression smoothed over by a dull, heavy blankness.

Something's not right. It's not like her. She shouldn't be able to just switch her emotions off.

Even I can't tamp them down that fast.

Maryam laughs and takes Cadence's hand, guiding her step by step to the edge of the barrier. "That's right, child. Just like that. There is no rush to grow up. No need to let the other one complicate things."

And Cadence doesn't resist, doesn't recoil, as Maryam guides her hand to the barrier. Her fingers stutter on the broken patch from yesterday, skating off the hard surface until they reach its edge and dip below. Her fist closes. Her face knots with effort—but not disgust.

"Stop it!" I shriek. "What are you—"

The wriggling strands snap and crumble to dust.

Cadence totters, catches her balance, and reaches for the barrier again, this time without Maryam's guiding hand. She shows no sign of revulsion or fear, only a dreadful exhaustion. She has changed, as if yesterday had never happened. Is Maryam meddling with her memories somehow?

"That's right, dear," Maryam coos. "Just like that. You're doing the right thing. Completing your purpose. Saving us all, just like your parents wanted."

The patch of still, cracked deadness on the surface of the barrier grows—a double handful, then twice that again. Maryam props Cadence up as her knees sag and her lips pale. It's hurting her, draining her to damage the barrier like this—and that gives me hope.

Maybe there's still time enough to stop this.

"I won't let you," Cadence groans, her hand slipping from the slick surface, this time without the strength to tear strands free. "You can't stop me."

"No one will stop you, child," Maryam soothes. She lets Cadence slump to the floor and moves to summon the guards waiting around the corner. "You've done very well."

And I've failed entirely.

I don't know what she's done to Cadence or how. And without knowing, how can I hope to reach Cadence, to change her course? But there's still some hope—the damaged barrier has not yet fallen. Everything rests on Ash, now.

"You might as well give the poor dear a break, darling," Maryam says. It's eerie the way she keeps addressing me while looking at Cadence. "You can't change her mind—and this is hard enough on her without you making it worse. At least let her enjoy the time she has left."

I don't like the sound of that at all.

I would shout at the mayor, try to persuade even her to change her course, if she could only hear me. But with Cadence losing consciousness, there's no one to give my words voice.

Fear and frustration boil inside me—and then outside, rippling the air with near-visible waves of pressure.

Am I imagining this? Hallucinating? Or, I don't know, overlaying the dreamscape somehow?

But Maryam's diaphanous layers of gold and glitter are fluttering in an impossible breeze. Her lips part around teeth bared in a predatory smile. She's thrilled—or furious—but in either case, very much aware of my presence.

I scream, leaning into the rage. But the full force of my fury makes itself felt as little more than a breeze.

"Fantastic, darling." Maryam beckons her suddenly jumpy guards to pick Cadence up off the floor. "I'm impressed. Truly. But be warned—I won't allow any interference. You will permit me to put things to rights before I go."

The air stills. Before she goes? Goes where?

Maryam laughs, sends her guards on ahead with Cadence, and turns back to the barrier. I remain, watching. Cadence is out of reach for the moment. I can't do anything to change her mind while she's unconscious. Her dreams, if she even has them now, are closed to me. But Maryam . . .

I'm curious. However devious and manipulative Ravel might be, he's clearly nothing compared to the lethal intellect of the woman who made him.

"I'm not dying, if that's what you hope." She casually reaches out to stroke the cracked patch where Cadence has ripped life away from the barrier. "But I am old. You've seen it, I think? The ritual? The Mara, draining and renewing this form, along with our contract? I could have sworn I felt you there with me, darling.

"But perhaps you have not yet realized what is to come. I have raised and sheltered generations at unimaginable cost. I have made sacrifices you can't even begin to imagine. And now, at long last, my suffering is so very nearly at an end."

She falls silent, seemingly mesmerized by the sickly churning of the still-living portion of the wall. It's horrible. I can't imagine spending a moment longer near it than necessary . . . but I don't leave.

I should. Cadence is still unconscious, so there's no real point in waiting around. I need to check in with Ash. And, although I don't need to sleep, exactly, the dreamscape seems to offer a sort of rest. Too long away and I feel its pull. It's getting harder to think clearly, harder to focus, to care, even.

Still, I wait, hovering in the nowhere-that-is-everywhere, narrowing the bulk of my attention to this one terrible spot in case this mother of lies does or says something I can't afford to miss. And my forbearance is rewarded.

HISTORY

"**H**AVE YOU GONE, darling? Will you not stay and listen to an old woman's sad tale?" Maryam's voice drops to a clipped whisper. "Quickly now, and plainly, before we attract the wrong kind of attention. This barrier is coming down. I will not allow you or your little friends to stop that. But when the monsters finally go, it is all but inevitable that I will, too.

"If you are listening, if you have any power, any way to communicate, any way to outlast the end of this city and regain what you have lost, use it to help the ones who are left. Believe me or don't, but I've protected as many as I could for as long as I could in the only way that I could. I think you know we've reached the tipping point. Passed it. The cost of survival keeps going up, the lives saved fewer by the day.

"Before there is no one left, I must break what I have built. But the children who make it to the other side will need a leader to guide them, to provide shelter and sustain them. Stay out of my way until I've done what must be done, and then send for help if you can. If it comes to that, even my dissolute and irresponsible Ravel could be of use.

"Understand, I do not ask this as a favour. Hate me if you like. Fight if you must, knowing it will only increase the suffering in the end. But give the innocents what help you can, when it is over. Don't let my sacrifices be wasted."

She raps the dead patch, sighs, and turns her back on the barrier. I watch her go, speechless at the audacity.

She expects me to clean up her mess? To wait in the shadows while she breaks everything she can get her hands on, and then pick up the pieces?

And the worst of it is: of course I would. I'd do anything I could for the survivors—except there won't be any. She doesn't realize, or doesn't understand, that bringing down the barrier will only make things worse. Instead of just her tower, her city being wiped out by monsters, it'll be the world.

Maybe it's not just Cadence I need to break through to . . .

I hesitate on the edge of reality, ghosts or nightmares trembling at the verge of my awareness, and peer through the phantom walls and floors as the golden woman ascends. She's human, though it's an easy fact to forget. Maybe she does care in her own twisted way.

And maybe that's the problem. Maryam cares too much and too narrowly. She cares only about those she calls her 'children,' the helpless, mindless drones trapped in here with her, suffocating under the weight of her rules and regulations. She has stolen so much from them. From me, come to that. And for those weighed down by the burden of her repressive love, she'll sacrifice the whole world. Whether that is a metaphorical or a literal sacrifice doesn't seem to matter to her in the slightest. And, insanely, Cadence has chosen to be on this madwoman's side.

I'm desperate for some good news—but when I move to step across the boundary between real and other, the air thickens as if dozens of reaching hands snatch at me, pressing, warding me off. I struggle against my ghosts, careful not to look into their faces, helpless not to. Their features waver, despairingly human one moment, distorted and empty-eyed the next.

Ange has not yet joined them, and that gives me both comfort and the strength to shoulder the nightmares aside and drop into my field of wildflowers, snow-capped mountain peaks springing up to hide the horizon. Instead of the ocean, a clear pool. Instead of trees, reeds rustling in a gentle breeze. Warmth and peace and . . . no Ash.

Still, he is on the road and has every excuse not to be here yet.

There is much to love about the dreamscape, not least of which is the absolute control it affords me. It's easier to bend it to my will when I am alone, when it is simply a matter of creation and not a contradiction of another's will. I quiet my racing heart and even out my ragged breath with no more than a thought. When a golden flower catches my eye, I merely blink and it is blue, or pink, or gone in a satisfying puff of petals. I frown at my reflection in the water and change it, making the skin even, the eyes wider, the hair longer, shinier.

After the infuriating helplessness of the waking world, it's refreshing to spend time in a place where every whim is instantly fulfilled. When the gentle loveliness of my sheltered meadow becomes dull, I replace it with a storm at sea, the waves crashing around and then over me. When the noise becomes too much, I sink below the surface and whirl dizzily on the currents. After a time, the press of the water is suffocating, so I dismiss it, walking through the weightless fronds and past a very surprised octopus squirming in midair.

But the ocean is alien at the best of times, and without Ash, it only brings back unsettling memories, so I wipe the slate clean and loll around on candy-coloured clouds in a comfortably featureless space, toying with transparent models of turbines and irrigation lines, solar cells and planting rods, wondering if I've understood the function well enough from those brief glimpses in Under and Nine Peaks to tweak the forms with any success.

Maryam's words are still worming their way under my skin. Just suppose we stop her—dismantle her whole toxic system—how will we survive? What will it take to clothe and house and feed whoever's left? Do we try to march them all through the mountains to Nine Peaks and turn them over to the elders? Maybe send them on ships to the mysterious island Ash hopes holds his long-lost parents? Or—if the threat of the Mara is removed, the barrier broken—what would it look like to start over right here?

It may be crumbling and toxic and flooded and monster-overrun, but it's *home*. And if I feel that way, maybe other survivors will, too. So I shift the fabric of reality, weaving a city out of sand and twigs, fitting together simple devices from the imaginary rubble to churn water from the streets and warm the patched and rebuilt towers.

The occasional surprised-looking seagull coasts through with a disgruntled squawk to let me know I'm doing creation wrong, but after a time I reach that slow, empty point between yesterday and tomorrow where I am renewed. It's like sleeping with my eyes open. Everything goes pale and insubstantial.

And then I'm back at sea. Or—not quite. Standing on a tree-lined bluff overlooking a rocky shore, peering out over a dark, angry sea—and a ship tossed in a storm.

"Finally," a girl says from behind me. "He said I had to stay behind since we couldn't reach you. Ghost, I mean. We didn't expect it to happen so fast, but he said there was no time to waste. That you needed to know we found them. He insisted."

Her voice is faint, the vision slipping in and out of focus. These waves aren't nearly as tall as the ones I conjured on the other side for my own amusement, but they're ten times as terrifying. That fragile-looking shell they toss so easily is all that provides scant shelter to Ash and, presumably, his other friends.

"Is this enough?" the girl pants, her face strained but vaguely familiar. "This sort of thing isn't my strong suit. We weren't even sure I would be able to reach you through this forest. But Hatif thought it could be connected, even though we've come so far. He said it's all one forest."

The familiar whorls of the forest's gift shift under my hands like threads. There's an eerie sensation of being caught in a web, gossamer threads spanning out to form a massive, intricate fabric spread across more land than my mind can encompass; grand trunks and knotted roots the elephantine beacons of a vast city, brilliant with the churn of life; the tiny organisms in the soil beneath infinitesimally tiny, mere pinpoints in the web, but every part of it dancing with the secret language of the trees. All one forest indeed.

I shake the overwhelming vision off. "You're one of Ash's squad."

She frowns. "Aleya of Spectre. Or—you'd better call me Min. Ghost says you're not her, not Cady. Not one of us."

Am I supposed to be bothered by that? She seems like she's focusing too hard to be snide, but maybe she's just gifted. She looks a little like Ange, now that I think of it—and feels just as reassuringly dauntless.

I don't usually like people on instinct, but in less fraught circumstances, and assuming she didn't mean to sound quite as dismissive as she had, I might enjoy spending time around this razor-sharp girl. I tear my gaze from her back to the ship. "How long?"

"I can't hear you. Pull from your end, or—" Sweat beads on her forehead.

The landscape around us wavers, flickering in and out. I press both hands into the satiny surface of the forest's gift, wrapping my fingers around the anchor to strengthen the unseen bridge between us, drawing on the vast forest's energy.

Rain lashes down, though I don't feel its sting. The wind whips the trees and hurls spray deep inland. Lightning splits the sky. A hollow roar shakes the very air around us.

"How long will it take him to return?" I shout.

She winces. "Too loud. I can hear you fine now. Crossing shouldn't have taken long. Storm came up out of nowhere."

The rain seems to move in sheets, snatching the ship from sight one moment, parting around it in a glimpse of surging waves and dipping mast the next.

"They'll be alright. It's a boat." Boats are meant to go on water, right? It's lasted this long. Min's—oh, forget it. If Ash called her Aleya, I will too. *Aleya's* long, dark eyes are narrowed against the storm, strands torn from her tight knot whipping in the tempest. She makes a low noise that I choose to interpret as agreement because the alternative is unthinkable.

"You're really ahead of schedule, finding the ship so quickly. You can't have spent hardly any time searching.

And if the crossing was supposed to have been fast, then even with the storm, they can't have far left to go, right?" I'm babbling as if I can drown out the storm with just words. "Plus, it's an island. That means there can only be so much land on the other side before you hit more water. So they'll be back by tomorrow, probably. And then you'll need some time to travel south. But if your gear is in good condition, that's, what, only a few days tops?"

"No. There's no way we can keep up this pace. They will reach the island today." She swallows hard. "They will. It's not far from the mainland here. If it were clear, you could see the opposite shore. Even with the storm . . ."

I nod encouragingly, stomach churning with sick fear at the way her voice has gone low and cold.

She continues, "The island is vast. They will have to travel for some time on the other side. It could take a few days, maybe more. It wasn't possible to load the bikes, send them over. Putting aside whatever time it takes to petition for help—and assuming Ghost can even convince them to send anyone—that's up to a week before we can expect to hear anything. And from here, it's another few days' travel at least to reach you. We'll have to work our way back east to the main route before we can head south and then back out to the coast."

She tears her gaze from the sea, fierce. "You stall for a week at least. Could be two, maybe three. You hold it together until then. Understand?"

"That's too long. The barrier—it's already dying. They're killing it, inch by inch. I don't know how long we have—"

She turns back to the storm, teeth gritted against its force, forehead knotted. "So slow them down. We'll help, but there's only so much—"

The rain parts, but the surface of the waves still boil. The ship tips up at an impossible angle, a dark mass clinging like tangled seaweed to the opposite end. A strand whips up, coiling. The clean line of the hull buckles.

Aleya spits a low string of curses and pulls power from the forest, fraying our connection. It pools in her free hand, flame-bright as she takes aim at the attacking sea-monster— and the storm closes in.

We can't even see the ship, much less coordinate some kind of counterattack.

But I felt the way her magic drew from the forest, saw the way its light flew to her hand without dimming the whole. I have an idea.

I dig my nails into the anchor-knot and let all of the panic and fear and horror and rage boil up and out in a wordless plea. There's a wavering too-full moment where it seems like the forest's bridge linking Aleya on the coast with the otherspace of the dreamscape will blow apart, but it bears the sudden load. Aleya rocks on her heels as a tunnel of force blows through the rain and the waves, pushing the storm aside in a narrow channel.

I barely manage to clamp down in time, denting the now half-submerged ship's side but not piercing it. Tentacles flail at the sudden jolt, making the ship groan.

But it doesn't slip free.

I'm beyond communicating, lost in the vast web of power. Aleya doesn't wait for instruction. She sights and shoots between one heartbeat and the next. The compressed dart of liquid light disappears into the tangle of coiling arms and sends them whipping free with an ear-splitting screech.

"Don't stop," she says, cold and quiet, her voice reaching me on a separate wavelength from the injured monster. "Whatever you're doing, don't stop until I say so. They're not clear yet."

But already my grip is slipping, vision flickering with exhaustion. The forest's strength is endless, but mine isn't. Raindrops splatter through the space I can't quite keep clear, the wind battering it, warping it enough that Aleya's next shot slaps harmlessly into the waves.

Tentacles reach, taking fresh hold of the ship. More than half of it is below the surface now and dipping further with each wave.

It's too distant to make out the features of those clinging to the exposed deck, the ones torn away too blurred to identify. All I know is Ash is somewhere out there, and his friends with him. The only people in all the world who I could have hoped to receive help from.

And there is nothing I can do but watch as the sea closes over their heads.

In the moment before I lose my grip on the forest's power entirely, it's clear the ship is gone. There is nothing left but a single, massive tentacle curling against a scorching flash of lightning. The storm crashes down once more.

Aleya leans into the nearest tree, both hands clawed into the trunk, clinging to the forest's bridge as desperately on her end as I do from mine. She doesn't have to say a word. I know that look. That horror. That despair.

The wind slaps loose strands of her ink-dark hair against her wet face, gusts of rain narrowing the entire world to the cold emptiness of this desolate shore, concealing the wild, heartless sea.

And then we're no longer alone.

Eyes in the waves, and teeth. A darkness reaching, uncoiling across silt and stone to the edge of the trees, splintering trunks and flattening brush beneath a weight never meant for the crushing gravity of land.

Aleya meets my eyes wordlessly. Then she lets go of the tree.

The bridge unravels, the waking world slipping through my fingers no matter how I clutch at the forest's gift, both of us cut off from that deep well of power. I drop to my knees, gasping amidst the revoltingly cheerful meadow of the dreamscape, warping it to an ashen wasteland before I hit the mud.

Maybe she let go to free both hands to fight. That must've been it. I was just reading into that final look.

She didn't send me away out of pity. Out of anger. Out of grief. She turned to fight, not to spare me the sight of one more death. She did. She's like Ange, I know it—she wouldn't give up. Aleya. *Min.*

I fix my gaze on the mud, refusing to look up, to check the horizon for one more ghost. Or for a dozen.

Min—and Ash. Aleya and Ghost, and the others, besides. Who did he say he was taking? Not Steph . . . of course not Grace, Grace is safe for a little longer. Was it the wiry, hyper boy I'd met so briefly in Nine Peaks, or the huge one? Hatif, that was the redhead, the other dreamweaver. He was on the ship, right? And—and . . . who was the last?

Two to a bike means four? Was it six or four in the end? Maybe four (four dead), four dreamwalkers, one on the shore and three in the waves, in the (four dead) only three, and I never met—I don't—Aleya and Ghost (is Ash? Ash is dead? *Ash* is—)

Stop it.

Stop. Focus. Say their names. Aleya and Ghost. Ghost and Hatif. Hatif and Banshee—*oh no, oh, Grace, no, it's—*

Stop.

Breathe.

Grace is safe, it's just Banshee and Ghost, and Banshee is (four dead), her sister is . . . and the boy, the other boy, that's Rei—was it Rei? Was Rei there too or just—oh, Hatif, and now Aleya, Min-called-Aleya, who could have been a friend, and now—

I can't. I can't even remember all their names, never mind their faces, and now they're dead (four dead and a ship's crew besides) and I can't look up and I can't—

And in another place, Cadence's eyes open on a bright, clean room. She doesn't know Ash is—her *friends* are . . .

I have to tell her. I have to. Don't I? Does it matter? Will it even change anything?

Will it change everything?

9

HEARTBREAK

GRIEF IS IN the mind. I can order the tears to dry and the shaking to stop. I can stand tall and spin serenity around me with no more than a thought, at least in this place where thought is all and creates all.

But grief is also in the body—even an imaginary one. The shuddering, gulping loss still drags broken nails across the inside of me, scratching and plucking and rasping an endless refrain of all that has been ripped away.

But even the relentless intensity of grief grows dull after a time. It backs into a corner and lets the mind slowly start to churn once more.

I can't wait that long—I have to push with all my might to make the space to think. And what I think is this: *Ash isn't coming back.*

It's a while before I can scrape together enough space for the next thought.

It's some time after that that I'm able to get back to work. But if Ash isn't coming back, he is definitely not bringing an army. There's no one on the other side of the barrier to send help. And while some part of me would like to curl up in the dreamscape and let the world burn, it's mostly the same part that I've backed into a tight corner and walled up deep inside my mind to keep Victoire company, so that's fine.

In fact, everything (*not everything, never again*) is fine (*four dead*) because Ghost (*not Ash, please not Ash, not—*) just gave me what I needed (*four dead, four is only the beginning . . .*)

One death for many, isn't that the devil's bargain? Maryam's bargain—and Ravel's?

I did not choose this sacrifice. It's not my fault.

But perhaps it is mine to use. One death for many. The one death that matters. The one death that will reach Cadence, that will change everything.

One death to save the world.

In the end, I don't even have to say it. She knows as soon as I shoulder between the ghosts, oh so careful not to look at their faces. As soon as I break through to the waking world, she *knows*.

"You're lying." Her face crumples. "You're *lying*."

"I didn't want this. You know I didn't."

Cadence's fists ball around the sheets, trembling as if she's a heartbeat away from throwing the covers over her head and turning her back on it all. "It's not real. You're making it all up."

So I show her, letting her, for the first time, inside a memory only I hold instead of the other way around. Knowing what's coming doesn't make it hurt any less. If anything, my dread colours each moment, weighing down the sky, darkening the sea, sharpening the rain.

"You're lying," she whispers, hopelessly, when it's all over.

"My imagination isn't that good."

She lets out a shuddering breath, curling into herself. "You couldn't even remember their names."

"They were your friends, not mine."

It is a cruel thing to say. I didn't mean to be cruel.

"Banshee. Hatif. Maybe Rei or Qareen if it was six after all. If Mogwai and Dybbuk stayed behind, that leaves Qareen. And Rei is"—she lets out a harsh laugh that ends in a sob—"Rei's the pretty one, the little hyperactive one."

"Aleya, Banshee, Qareen, Rei, Hatif and—and Ghost." I say it out loud for her, and for me, to silence the shrieking voice and those broken nails walled into one corner of my mind. Four—or six. "Aleya. Banshee. Qareen. Rei. Hatif. Ghost. I'll remember."

She nods, scrubbing the back of her hand across her face. "Min, and Jess—Jessica, really, I'm pretty sure. And Orisa, and Ajay. And Liam. And—and—"

"Ash."

Her lips wobble and her nostrils flare. She ducks her head to hide a fresh wave of tears. "And Ash."

"Min. Jessica. Orisa. Ajay. Liam . . . Ash." (*Four dead, or is it six dead, oh*—) But we don't even have time left for grieving properly because—

"What's wrong, sleepyhead?" Maryam sweeps into the room and perches on the bed, pressing Cadence's chin up with sharp nails.

Cadence slaps her away. "Leave me alone."

Those mesmerizing golden eyes narrow. The mayor's knuckles ripple once, talons tapping against her breast and stilling almost immediately. "I can see someone woke up on the wrong side of the bed. Hormones, dear? I could solve that for you if you like."

"Out."

The shriek makes Maryam jump.

"Just a suggestion. It's up to you, of course." She pats Cadence's knee under the blanket, a quick, hard tap. She's up and away before Cadence can lash out. "Take the morning off. Get some more rest. Save your energy for our work later."

Cadence tumbles out of bed to slam the door after her, leaning into it long after it's latched as if bracing against attack.

"She didn't sound like she was planning to return," I say carefully. "We have a little time."

"I don't want to talk to you." Cadence's voice is muffled, hair tangled and stuck to the damp mess of her face.

I'm too numb to feel sorry for her. Or for myself, for that matter. And this is too important to wait. "Tough. It's time to grow up and deal with reality. Mom and dad are dead. Now Ash is too. And instead of fighting the literal monsters out there killing people, you've been collaborating with the enemy to unleash the worst of the bunch on the world. You want to be the one in charge? Fine. I never really wanted the job anyway, or that stupid body. It's yours. Enjoy. I don't care about the magic, either. Keep it. Just stop using it for Maryam."

Cadence blinks, red-rimmed eyes startled. "You're not mad at me?"

"Furious," I say tonelessly. "Incandescent with rage. But not for stealing my life. For all I know, it really was yours in the first place. Want to avenge our parents? Cool. Do that. But stop living in the past and do it right."

She draws a deep breath as if to protest. I hurry on before she can get a word in.

"Killing that possessed monstrosity of a barrier was a bad idea when we were a kid. It's only gotten worse in the meantime. If you need a goal, maybe try taking down the Mara? You know, like we were going to do all along? If that's not enough for you, I wouldn't be averse to cutting Maryam off at the knees either."

She giggles. It's so unexpected I lose my train of thought, which only makes her laugh harder.

Then, as if the memory crashes down on her at the same moment it does me, she chokes on a sob and slides to the floor. "He's really gone? They all are?"

"I think so." I don't see how they could have survived those waves, even if they weren't infested with sea monsters.

She nods, drawing her knees in and resting her cheek on them. "Okay. That is—It's my fault, isn't it?"

"It's not that simple—"

She snorts. "Whatever, stupid. I get it, okay? You can back off now. I'll handle things from here."

"...Just like that?"

She gets to her feet, holding onto the wall as if the floor is likely to slide out from under her. "What did you expect, fireworks?"

Well, yeah. Or something. "If you're not working with Maryam, it's no longer safe to stay here. What do you think about Sam and Lily's old place, for now? Just until we figure something better out."

"Nope." Cadence wanders into her closet.

"I know going outside is risky, but it's also harder for Maryam's enforcers to track you down out there. It's not like she'll just shrug and find something else to do when she finds out you've left."

"I'm not leaving." Dressed, if haphazardly, Cadence heads down the hallway—and passes the turnoff for the elevators.

"It's not safe. Maryam's not likely to take no for an answer. If you won't help her, she'll do whatever she can to make you. And it might not be the best idea to explore the limits of her capacity to make you suffer, you know?"

Cadence strolls into the audience chamber and steps over the grovelling toady of the hour to get to her throne. "No one's making me do anything, thanks."

Maryam graces her with a brilliant smile and keeps it in place until the room has cleared. "Feeling better, dear? Anything I can help with?"

Cadence scowls. "The other's being more of a pest than usual today. And I'm bored—I don't see why you want me to sit in on these idiotic meetings. They're all the same: blah blah, under-resourced, staffing shortages, rising vacancies. Blah. They whine and beg. You smile. I yawn. They leave."

"You of all people should know information is power, child." Maryam stretches. "But I'll admit it does grow tiring after the first few decades."

Cadence rolls her eyes.

Maryam laughs. "Why don't you tell me what you'd rather be doing?"

Cadence raises a scarred hand, waggling her fingers. The barrier-burned pattern ripples on her skin.

Maryam's smile stretches a little wider. "If you're feeling up to it, I don't see why not."

FROZEN

IT'S A DESPERATE gamble, but when has Cadence ever wanted to do things the easy way?

I'm afraid to ask what she has in mind for Maryam and the enforcers tasked with clearing their path. But I have to admit there is a certain genius to luring them so far away from the mayor's sumptuous apartments. No one's going to come looking for them all the way down here, not for a good long while. And every hour Cadence can manage free from pursuit is precious.

Cadence walks a step behind Maryam, a bland expression fixed on her face. The guards range ahead. I peer past to get a better look at whomever it is they're so careful to send scuttling. Are there more people lurking down here than before? Where have they been hiding? And, most important of all: who are they?

There are three main possibilities. Now Ravel is gone, I have to assume Freedom is no longer operating and, with the nightly revels shut down, his people would either have returned to the mundane business of masquerading as obedient drones up in Refuge or, if they burned that bridge, sought out shelter in the surrounding maze of abandoned service corridors and concrete-block storage rooms, transit tunnels, and other forgotten corners.

But there's also Ange's network of survivors from the deep tunnels. Ravel managed to help some across the barrier to safety.

More were slaughtered by the Mara in those final hours before Cadence betrayed us. I'm pretty sure more than a few of those who remain are imprisoned in Refuge's retraining dormitories right now, but the numbers still don't add up.

Which brings me to the third possibility: that some of the survivors from outside of Refuge and the underground warren it presides over have given up trying to cling to life on the streets, especially with enforcers on the hunt, and have migrated down here. The Mara haunt these upper levels, but they rarely venture much farther below the waterline, after all.

I don't think anyone's ever really monitored the total human population in this city of nightmares. Maryam would know the count for Refuge, of course, and presumably, Ange must have had a sense of how many people she protected, but outside—who knows? A few dozen families? A few hundred? It's hard to imagine more, given the impossibilities of scrounging sufficient supplies from the crumbling buildings or growing much worth eating amidst the toxic fumes.

But without losing track of Cadence and whatever she's scheming, it's hard for me to properly investigate all the nooks and crannies down here. With no one left to meet up with in the dreamscape (*four dead, Ash, oh please, no*)— with no reason to spend my nights in that place, maybe I can try to get a more accurate count. Without Ash, (*four dead*) there is no real chance of saving them. But even so.

Although, once Cadence gets away from Maryam, I guess I'll be busy keeping an eye on her while she sleeps and sounding the alarm if anyone gets too close.

Cadence frowns. "Creep. Don't watch me when I sleep."

Maryam glances over her shoulder in question. "The other one giving you trouble again, child?"

"Nothing but," Cadence says. "She just doesn't know when to quit."

"Nice." I gather my awareness in and focus on the few dozen or so feet between Maryam and her perimeter of enforcers.

"Keep up the act. Do you want to, I don't know, work out some kind of signal for when you're ready? Or I can update you on the guards' locations as we go? The room they just cleared is pretty big, and the corridor beyond kind of runs sideways along it for a bit. At the next turn, I think they'll be far enough to have a hard time hearing anything, if you're ready. I'll say when they turn the corner, and then you can knock her out or whatever—Okay, now!"

Cadence snorts and keeps marching along behind Maryam without breaking stride.

"No problem, there'll be other chances. I mean, we're getting a little close, but I'll keep you posted. There's another bend ahead. And if you want to send a signal without Maryam knowing, just, um . . . scratch your ear, okay?"

Cadence lifts a hand, examines her nails—and then drops it to her side.

I narrate every turn and choke point the enforcers pass, but Cadence doesn't even hesitate to consider her moment, much less signal the start of her attack. And then she's standing at the end of a tunnel bisected by the long arc of the barrier, reaching out for the frantic churn of the still-living portion.

This is not happening. "What are you doing? You can't risk—"

She flinches at my shriek.

"Problem?" Maryam's studied casualness does little to hide the fanatical gleam in her eye.

Cadence shakes out her hand. "Cole's a little shriller than usual. Really won't take the hint."

She reaches again.

She's acting as if nothing has changed. As if Ash and very nearly all of her old friends didn't just lose their lives trying to stop this from happening. As if—*six dead*—as if the news hadn't affected her at all. Or as if our conversation had never happened . . .

Cadence raises shaking hands to her head, hunching over.

"What is it?" Maryam is oddly gentle. She puts her arms around Cadence as if holding her up instead of holding her in place. "What's wrong?"

Cadence blinks, her pupils jittering as if searching for something in thin air. "I don't—I can't—" She shakes her head. "It's nothing. I just . . . I don't know. I thought I'd forgotten something. Or lost something. It's gone now."

Maryam pats her shoulder. Cadence gives her a fragile smile—and stabs her hand wrist-deep into the barrier, tearing a handful free and letting it splat on the floor. She steps into the mess even as it shrivels to dust to seize a double handful next.

This isn't . . . It's not an act. It's not some plot to goad Maryam into complacency so she can escape. It's—she's—

I scream, pushing the sound out in waves of force that rock Maryam on her sparkly heels and flatten Cadence's choppy hair against her skull. Her eyes widen, her lips pinch, and the next squirming fistful of shredded souls and gold dust she raises above her head, brandishing her grisly prize in midair.

"Stop trying to control me." She cups her hands together to catch the dust as it decays. "You can't stop me. Even with whatever this new trick is, I won't let you. Stop it. Go away."

She blows, sending the lifeless residue out in a cloud as if throwing it in my face. I blow back, first gleeful, then sickened at the way it clings to her skin. She doesn't even try to wipe the gritty film away, just turns back to her task.

"I'm not sure she understands, dear," Maryam says from some distance, having retreated quickly to avoid the worst of the mess. "Why don't you keep up the good work, and I'll have a little chat with the other one, see if I can't make things a little easier for you?"

"I don't like you talking to her." But Cadence keeps tearing at the barrier, crouching to reach closer to the floor.

"You're doing such a good job," Maryam soothes. "Almost done here. I'll just go make sure the next patch is clear for us while you finish up."

Cadence nods, white-lipped, tearing wriggling threads free by the handful.

Maryam crooks a finger and cocks her head then turns on her heel and swishes out of view.

Despite myself, I follow.

"I did tell you," she says over one elegantly lifted shoulder. "You can't stop us. I'll admit I was a little worried there for a moment, but you really can't reach her anymore, can you? She is frozen in time. You've moved on. You're a future she will never touch, and nothing you say or do can change that. You'll only make things harder on her, poor child, with your stories and your pestering and your delightfully refreshing little breezes."

"What have you done to her?"

She wanders deeper into an adjacent, pipe-filled space, turning sideways to keep from smudging her dress on untold years worth of grime. "You'll wear yourself out fighting her, you know. Though she's not quite as strong as I hoped. It's a shame I wasn't able to get my hands on any of the adults. Or even you, when you were still useful. Are there many like her, do you know? Is she strong for your kind?"

Her manicured nails hover over the patch of barrier that cuts us off from what would have once been the far wall. Her lilting tones flatten. "Never should have built this so big. If I had known how much work it would be to break it, I would never have tried to surround so much of the city. Let that be a lesson to you: don't ever let your dreams run away with you. Of course, if I had known the future, I might never have tried walling us in to begin with."

Cadence's energy is flagging, her nails ragged from tearing at the barrier where it bisects the walls, and floor, and ceiling. And on the other side of one of those walls, the mayor of the Towers of Refuge sighs and gives the sickly churning mass a rueful look.

"You're still there, darling? Of course you are. What else do you have to do? Pester that poor child? Don't you see it's hard enough on her as it is? We all must play our part.

These ones provide shelter," she flutters her fingers at the barrier. "Well. Provided shelter. I was the architect, the maker of the plans and the one who brought them to life. Now my time, too, is nearly at its end. And when that child has finished destroying this foolish shelter—and not a heartbeat before—she will be freed from her work as well."

Maryam rolls her head, loosening her shoulders. "You're the lucky one, you know?"

Cadence stretches, runs her fingers along the ceiling where it meets the rough, cracked surface of the barrier, searching for any squirming signs of life she might have missed. Then she scrapes down the seam of the wall, across the floor, and back up, leaving a thin trail of blood. The red stains lose colour, leaching to a sickly yellowish tone as the stone-hard surface pulses to life in the wake of the tiny drips and blotches.

On our side of the wall, the undamaged section of the barrier churns faster, glimmering with a ruddy light for just a moment. Maryam covers her mouth, eyes staring, taut golden flesh taking on an ashen cast.

She whirls and dashes back to Cadence, snatching her away from the barrier. They land in a tangled heap on the floor, Cadence trembling with exhaustion and confusion, Maryam's brows knotted. She almost looks sorry.

But all she says is: "Don't feed it, dear."

II

ALLIES

"**H**OW COULD YOU?" I clamp down on the urge to scream in frustration. I'd nearly burst trying to hold it in until she was alone again in her room. "I thought you understood. You agreed—you said you would handle it."

"I think I'm handling things pretty well," Cadence says, peeling off filthy clothes with hands made clumsy with exhaustion. "Not my fault I couldn't fin'ish today—no one told me blood could undo my work."

"That's not—what about Ash? And—"

"What about him?" She examines her cracked fingertips and frowns. "I know he didn't want to be left behind, but it's not like it's my fault. I begged mom to let him come."

"What are you talking about? Ash is *dead*, Cadence. Your mom has nothing to do with it."

She shakes her head. "You're wrong. Ash is fine. He's at home training with dad's second-best blades. He's gonna grow up big and strong. He promised to practice every day. When dad gets back, bet he'll even help him train so next time he can come, too."

She grins, miming a swipe with an imaginary blade. "I'm still gonna be better, of course. Betcha he's so jealous. But I would've brought him if it were up to me. I'm generous like that."

She frowns at her fingers again, muttering, "When did this happen?" She licks one and grimaces, spitting.

I gag. "Don't do that. There's probably still—" The thought of the dusty grime that had been alive and squirming in those hands not an hour ago makes me queasy. "Ugh. Just don't. You need to—"

"Stop telling me what to do. Go away. I don't know you. Go away or I'll tell mom and dad on you."

What is going on? Her—our—parents have been dead for years.

"No, they haven't," she shrieks, launching herself out of bed. "Stop saying everyone is dead! I don't like you. I'll tell if you won't leave me alone. I'll tell on you."

Did Maryam do something to her? Was it the barrier? Or is she doing this on purpose?

"Go away," she swats at the air, chanting: "Go away, go away, away, away."

She's acting like a kid. And talking like one. And— "Cadence, you're scaring me. This isn't funny. Ash died yesterday, and you're playing games. It's not okay. And it's not bringing him back."

"Ash isn't dead. Stop saying that. Stop saying everyone is dead."

Maryam appears in the doorway as if summoned. Which, based on the amount of yelling going on, is probably the case. "What's wrong, dear? Who's dead?"

Cadence stops cold. "Who are you? Where's mom?"

Maryam blinks. And smiles. "Your mother is busy with her mission, remember? When she's finished, she'll come back. That's why you've been doing such a marvellous job helping out—so your parents can return sooner. But why aren't you in bed? You should be resting."

Maryam straightens the rumpled bedding and pats it invitingly.

"There's a ghost saying scary things." Cadence sits obediently. "She won't leave me alone."

"Oh, well, we can't have that." Maryam strokes Cadence's hair and tucks her in like a sleepy toddler.

"Those pesky ghosts are always getting in the way, aren't they? Let me think. How about a send-the-ghosts away ritual?"

"Bad idea," I warn. Maryam's rituals generally boil down to some variation on monster summoning. "Cadence, I don't know what kind of game you're playing, but you need to cut it out before you make things worse."

She whimpers, scrunching lower under the covers. "It's yelling at me again."

Maryam cocks her head. "Is it? What a naughty little ghost. Okay, let's try this."

She makes a sort of triangle shape with her thumbs and first two fingers, peering through the window at Cadence, and waggles her remaining fingers while solemnly intoning, "Bye bye ghostie, fly away home."

Cadence giggles and copies her.

"Did it work?" Maryam whispers, fluttering those long, elegant fingers in midair as if feeling for ghosts.

Cadence bites her lip and scans the room. Her chin drops. "It did! The ghost is all gone!"

"Are you serious right now?" My frustration escapes in a puff of force that ruffles Cadence's hair, making her squeal, and sets Maryam's glimmering chains and baubles jangling.

She puts a protective arm around Cadence. "Oh well. It wasn't a very strong ritual. How about I set up a better one for tomorrow? We'll chase that ghost of yours away, don't you worry."

"But it won't let me sleep," Cadence whines, cuddling closer. "I want you to get rid of it tonight. I can't rest if you don't."

Maryam's lashes sweep in a slow, languid blink that ought to send any sane person diving for cover. She'd said Cadence was 'frozen in time,' but this is more like regressing . . .

"Please?" Cadence wheedles in the same strange, babyish tones. "Make it go away now, okay?"

"As you wish, dear."

Maryam must have been planning for just this moment because she has hardly ushered Cadence to her seat in the golden audience chamber when the enforcers show up. There are six—two to each prisoner.

The enforcers are, of course, fully masked and uniformed. Anonymous in their sameness.

The prisoners are not.

All three are grimy and, I suspect but am not equipped to confirm, reeking. One is draped in a threadbare worker's uniform without hood or mask. Another is barely dressed at all in a skimpy costume from Freedom, the sort of thing that was never meant for prolonged wear. The last clutches the rags of a dark cloak over once sturdy fabric. She's one of Ange's, I'm almost certain of it.

The armed escort seems to be there mostly to keep them upright and moving. The prisoners shuffle, heads down, faces slack. Drugged, most likely. But there's no time to worry about them, because I'm pretty sure I know what's coming next. And if I can't get Cadence to stop it somehow . . .

But no matter how much I yell or plead or invoke the names of the lost, Cadence just shakes her head and stops her ears and huddles into Maryam's shadow.

"It's still bothering you, isn't it?" Maryam says sympathetically, motioning to the enforcers.

The first pair haul the uniformed worker forward, pushing the ashen-faced man to his knees at Maryam's feet.

I shudder. "You know what this is, Cadence. You were there with me when Ravel did this. When he made me be a part of sending—sacrificing—lives to the Mara. You don't want that. You don't need to be a part of that. Don't do this—"

Maryam guides Cadence's unresisting hand to the head of the first victim. Cadence pales but repeats the words without faltering, intoning the ritual sacrifice that summons the Mara. And they come, their greasy malevolence slicking the air around me.

I am compressed, suffocated by their massing. They're ravenous, so empty there is a weight to their presence, a kind of hollow suction that tears at the fabric of the world.

I don't have a choice. I flee to the other side of the tower, stretching my awareness to watch, helpless, as the worker's terrified eyes hazily find Cadence's. Powerless, as she blinks back startled tears and completes the ritual. Despairing, as the empty body slumps at her feet and the Mara pulse, momentary satisfaction at the kill instantly engulfed in yet greater hunger.

An expression of such horror, such anguished guilt crosses Cadence's face that I dare to come nearer and plead with her again. She can say Maryam made her do it. A memory lapse, a drug, some kind of hypnosis—she can't undo what has been done, but she could stop it from happening again—

But when Maryam asks her with a knowing look if the ghost has been banished yet, Cadence hesitates.

"Will you help me take down the dome?" She juts her jaw mutinously.

"Of course, dear," Maryam says. "As soon as we deal with your ghost problem so you can rest."

And at the same time: "Of course not," I say, ignoring the filthy press of the Mara, that gnawing hunger that tears at my edges, seeking to draw me in. "Never."

"The ghost won't leave me alone." Cadence looks at the second prisoner, the dancer, and then at the body at her feet. "It won't let me rest."

Maryam gestures to the enforcers. The body is dragged away—they don't bother lifting it. The next victim is hauled into place. He's sweating, mouth slack and drooling. His pupils jitter, tiny amidst the panic-stretched whites.

He is fully aware of what's about to come.

"Don't," I whisper desperately.

Cadence studies the man's face before positioning her hand so she won't have to see it as she feeds him to the monsters.

This man would have seen Ravel offer sacrifices to the Mara in Freedom's ritual Exchange, maybe even seen me at Ravel's side, pointing out the next victim, my hand feeling the warmth leave a human form as the monsters sucked it dry. He had probably seen the Mara take lives unoffered, too. They stopped waiting for sacrifices to be presented some time ago.

None of that knowing seems to have made a difference. He manages a single, strangled cry as Cadence completes the ritual. I fight to keep my place as the Mara surge, again snatching the merest taste before being overwhelmed by a new surge of hunger.

"Will you help me?" Cadence says again, staring into the middle distance. She wipes her hand slowly on her thigh. "Will you help me end it?"

"I promise you, the barrier will fall." Maryam wraps long fingers over Cadence's shoulders from behind. "I will not leave you until it is destroyed."

Cadence shudders.

"Mom and dad would hate this." I don't truly remember them, not like she does. Or did—her memory is clearly confused unless this has all been some elaborate scheme. "They wouldn't have wanted this for you. They wouldn't want you to dirty yourself like this."

"What do you know? You don't know anything about them. You don't care about them. You don't want to save them like I do—"

"Cady, they're dead. Finishing their mission can't change that."

"You're wrong," she shrieks, shaking Maryam off and stepping over the prone form at her feet.

The waiting mass of the Mara roils with hunger—and pleasure at her misery. They're—I think they're feeding off it.

"The ghost," Maryam murmurs, beckoning the enforcers.

One pair circles wide around Cadence's raging to collect their burden. The last two start forward with the final victim, but Cadence stomps up and shoves them back to the far end of the room.

"Wait," she growls. "I didn't answer yet."

"Did we solve your ghost problem after all, dear?" Maryam trills.

"I don't know, did we? What do you say, ghost? Are you finished? Or should we keep going?" Cadence grabs the Underfolk woman by the collar, pulling so her head tips back. "There are more where this came from."

"You don't mean that. You don't want this." I can barely force the words out. The pressure in this place is crushing, the darkness heavy and thick around us, just waiting, practically salivating in anticipation of another meal. The only thing that keeps it at bay seems to be Cadence's turmoil—and mine.

The growing weight bearing down on me isn't just my imagination. It's not just a natural side effect of the Mara's concentrated presence, either. Not entirely. They're . . . they're feeding off me right now, off the horror and fear and anger and need to stop this. And as soon as I am aware of what's happening, the drain intensifies, each new dimension of horror giving them more purchase on my soul.

I can't afford to run away, to give up. But if I stay . . . I don't know how long I can endure before there isn't anything left of me.

"You lose," Cadence says, shaking the last victim's collar. "Give up and leave me in peace now, and this one gets to live another day. Or stay and find out just how many prisoners Refuge has on standby."

Maryam rubs her temple. "It's late. Let's not give it too much longer to make up its mind, dear. You need your rest."

The enforcer to Cadence's left jolts and then slides bonelessly to the floor.

Cadence hisses in annoyance. "Do something about your minions, would you?"

Can't she feel it? Didn't she *know* the moment the darkness surged?

"Quickly," Maryam yawns prettily. "We don't have all night."

The remaining enforcer hurriedly dumps his prisoner and heaves his fallen comrade over onto his back, tugging mask and goggles free to expose the pearly white eyes of the Mara-taken.

"Bad monsters," Cadence grumbles. "What's the point of a ritual if you just go and take what you want on your own schedule?"

Maryam sighs. "It does rather ruin the spectacle, doesn't it? So embarrassing. They don't pull it that often on me, I'm happy to say, but I understand my boy had the devil of a time keeping appearances up. You—what are you waiting for? Clean that up."

The enforcer scrambles to drag his companion out of the room. The prisoner tries to crawl away in the meantime, squirming on her belly when she can't force knees and arms to bear her weight.

Cadence squats in front of her. "Last chance, Cole. Be a good ghost and fade into the background. We can keep this up all night."

"You know I can't just—"

She grabs a handful of the prisoner's hair and yanks. "Last. Chance."

"What is wrong with you? You're not—you don't have to—this is Maryam, somehow, isn't it? She's controlling you. She's—"

"Dream for us." Cadence draws the opening words of the Exchange out, slow and menacing.

The monsters churn with pleasure. Such a feast, this festival of lies and desperation and delicious horror. Sacrifice and a show.

It's sickening. And there is no way out, no one to come to our rescue. To my rescue, as the Mara tear at the edges of me. To the hapless prisoner's rescue, as they set their talons into her soul. No one can reach us. No one is coming to save us.

There's only me. "Stop."

"You know that's not going to happen, unless . . ." Cadence shakes the prisoner. "You go. You leave me alone and promise to stay away. And not just for an hour or whatever. We can start this all over again anytime, you know." She bends down to hiss the next phrase of the ritual into the prisoner's ear, "Your sacrifice for our freedom."

"Okay. I got it. I don't know what's wrong with you, but—"

The Mara churn in disappointment. They're not eager for the fun to end.

"Not one more word," Cadence says. "Just go."

Maryam comes up to stand with her, one hand on her shoulder, the other reaching to trace the line of the prisoner's face. She doesn't say a word.

And neither do I. But I don't leave, not yet. I want to test something. I need to know if Cadence can sense me—if Maryam can. If they can still tell when I'm around if I'm totally silent. Given how often Cadence taps into my thoughts, I'm not too confident this will work, but it's worth a shot.

"All done?" Maryam murmurs.

Cadence yawns. "Apparently." She lets go of the prisoner's hair. The woman falls with a thud.

"Delightful." Maryam stoops elegantly and strokes the sweat-slick strands of grimy hair. "But you're still here, aren't you darling? No hard feelings, you understand, but I can't have you pestering this precious child until our work is nicely wrapped up with a bow. So here's just a teensy reminder—be kind enough to keep your distance in future. No distractions or else." She tightens her grip on the prisoner, smiles. "Take her. 'Your death for our life.'"

Cadence startles. I bite back a cry. The Mara pulse with that sense of fleeting satisfaction that instantly transmutes into ravenous hunger, the sucking void of their presence so strong it threatens to tear me apart.

I don't wait for the mayor to summon more enforcers to lift the body, don't need to see the prisoner's face to know what has happened.

I have failed even in giving up, too slow to save a single life, too gullible to see through Cadence's games, too stupid to find a way through to her. Too weak to stop the Mara.

And now they know it.

ETERNITY

12

I ONLY JUST manage to escape the waking world in time. The Mara are swollen with power, insane with hunger, and enraged at my repeated attempts to stop them. I hurl myself through the waiting ghosts at the border of reality, forcing their grasping hands aside, and barely make it across without being torn apart.

The sky bleeds. The ground is scorched dust over jagged rock. The air is thick, cloying. I am alone.

My fingers press and knead the forest's gift as if it only needs the right touch to reach across the endless miles to Ash.

I haven't forgotten his death, but the instinct to look for him remains. He is gone, his body lost to the waves, the rest of him . . . I don't actually know. Lost to me and to the forest, clearly.

But maybe—maybe there is a place like this for him, somewhere. Another dreamscape more perfect even than our imagining. A peaceful eternity of pleasant afternoons in the sunlight and serenading flowers, or whatever nonsense he'll come up with.

Maybe he's with the others.

Or maybe he's just gone.

Lightning scorches the sky. The arid ground splits with a crack, flames licking up from the molten stone below in shimmering waves of heat. I hold the forest's gift out over the fissure. The rising smoke curls around it, making its whorls and knots seem to churn with fear.

It wouldn't take much. The slightest tilt of the wrist would send it tumbling into the fires below. Who needs a bridge, after all, when there is no one waiting on the other side?

I don't know why the creature I met in the forest outside of Nine Peaks gave me this—this thing. It's not like I earned it, not like I did anything worthy of some mystical token. If anything, I was acting like a whiny brat, kicking up a fuss and breaking stuff in its territory.

It couldn't have known I would go back to the city and get trapped with no other way of communicating. There is no greater plan, no deeper meaning. I'm not anyone special—unless you count especially stupid.

But when I try to drop it into the fire, the wooden knot doesn't fall. I shake my hand, but it's stuck somehow. I can't see for all the smoke. My eyes tear with the heat and grit. I start coughing and can't stop.

So I make it all go away. The smoke. The fire. The whole blasted landscape. It's all a bit self-indulgent anyway.

And in the glaring light of the sterile room I replace it with, I can finally make out what saved the forest's gift from the fire.

A thin tendril, pale green, weaves between my fingers like a set of rings. A thicker band, ashen brown, wraps around my wrist. I wiggle my fingers, and the strands move with me, warm and so soft I barely feel their touch. I poke at the satiny tendril with my free hand, and it slips free, only to latch onto my other hand.

For an instant, I'm handcuffed. Then the band circling my wrist unwinds and curls in midair, rolling itself back up into familiar curves of the knot of wood.

Or whatever it is. I'd drop it if it weren't clinging to me in the first place.

There's a gentle creaking. A forest springs up around me, obliterating my safe, sterile white room. *The* forest—because I didn't create it, and there is no one else here to bring it into being.

I even try sending it away. Nothing changes. Nothing else moves, except for the slow, soft retreat of the clinging tendrils. I drop the forest's gift as soon as it lets go, backing away until I trip over a root and landing in a less-than-fragrant pile of decaying leaves and mouldering needles.

My back thuds into rough bark. I'm surrounded by trees. And not ephemeral, spice-scented imaginary constructs of trees, either. At least, not *my* ephemeral constructs.

There is a dry rustling, laughter-like. The creature I met in the forest with Grace peers out from behind a tree, its branch-like limbs obscured by shifting layers of leaves and moss. It nudges the smooth-grained knot toward me.

"You want me to pick it up?"

It nudges it again. I flush and shift my weight, eyeing the little thing sitting so innocently on the ground. I hadn't thought about the forest *knowing* I had tried to throw it away.

"I don't need it anymore. Um, I mean, thank you. It was useful. Really. But there is no one to—I just . . . I don't need it. Thanks."

The rustling gets louder. The creature nudges the knot harder. It rolls a few inches toward me with the momentum before slowing. It rocks for a moment, then starts toward me again, curves rippling as if it's propelling itself.

"Keep it away," I scramble to put the tree at my back between us, stumbling over exposed roots and low ground cover. "That—don't let it touch me!"

The whole forest goes still, the creature putting its forelimbs up in a placating gesture. The wooden knot-thing also stops, shifting in place with a low shushing. It shuffles back a few inches and pauses, rocking.

"Has that thing been alive the whole time?" I scrub my hands against my thighs.

The thing in question wobbles timidly. The tree-creature cocks its head. The forest waits.

Eyeing the wood-grained brown skin of the creature, I have a sudden, horrible thought. "It's not—is it your baby?"

The tree creature goes stiff and then starts shaking. The whole forest follows suit, branches rustling, the little knot of wood at its feet wheeling in delighted circles.

"It's not that funny. I mean, you all look the same, so . . ."

The creature lowers itself, bringing its forelimbs close to the ground. The forest's gift scuttles back to it, tendrils lifting to twine with the tree-creature's twig-like digits. The creature draws its arm close, and the knot vanishes under its leafy garb. Then the creature steps into the nearest tree and is gone.

"Fine, whatever. I didn't want to know anyway." I kick the nearest root and jump back when it creaks in irritation. "Oops. Sorry."

I put a hand out to the trunk for balance while I pick my way around the roots. The tree pushes back.

Or rather, it sprouts leaves under my hand, the tree creature stepping out of the surface of the bark. I backpedal, arms pinwheeling, feet slipping and snagging on the uneven forest floor.

The creature waits until I've found my balance—and a new tree to shelter behind—before reaching a forelimb into the shifting mass of leaves around its core and pulling out a familiar shape. It holds the knot of wood out toward me.

"Uh, nope. You can keep it. Really. I don't want to know. Don't need it either. I'm good."

The knot ruffles and unravels a bit, like a small animal stretching.

Is—is it *looking* at me?

The creature bends and puts the knot on the ground. It wobbles a few inches toward me.

The taller being steps back into its tree and is gone, taking the forest with it. I'm back in my bright white room, every surface slick and stark and unblemished—aside from the lonely-looking bit of wood shivering on the floor.

Despite myself, I can't help feeling a little sorry for it. It was a creepy liar, of course, acting like an innocent chunk of wood all this time, when all along it was . . . Uh. Whatever it was.

Forest-monster spawn? Creature droppings? Some kind of ambulatory organ?

I shudder. The knot rocks toward me hopefully. I glare. It flattens itself in remorse.

I've really got to stop assigning meaning to its twitching.

"They left you behind, huh?"

It bobs.

"Can't you call them back?"

It wobbles.

"Were you playing dead all this time so I wouldn't freak out and throw you away?"

It freezes guiltily.

I sigh. "Whatever. You're here now. Nothing to do but—"

It's my turn to freeze. There is nothing to do. Nowhere to go; no one to see. Nine Peaks won't help. They won't even venture outside their walls to speak with me directly.

Ash is beyond helping. There is no one outside the city to look to.

And if I go back to trying to persuade Cadence to switch sides, it won't change anything except the number of deaths on my conscience—and now, hers. Not to mention the risk of approaching the Mara while they're feeding. I might not be alive in the traditional sense, but I'm not all that eager to die either.

So . . . what now?

The knot scuttles closer, nudging my foot and backing off fast. It rolls a quick circuit around me, darts in for another nudge, and backs away.

It's silly but I smile all the same. An animate bit of wood isn't the most useful companion ever. But maybe it is better than being alone.

Hang on. Perhaps I've been too narrow-minded. There's no one left to work with, but that's only if you count dreamwalkers. Of course, they are the only ones who can visit the dreamscape, cross over the barrier around the city, and, you know, actually hear me in the first place.

But there are still regular old humans all over Refuge and the surrounding areas.

They're not that useful, obviously, given they don't have any power to actually fight the Mara, but if I could only communicate somehow, get them to resist Maryam, to stall and get in her way . . . She was always so careful to make sure no one was around when she had Cadence damage the barrier. She had her enforcers chase people away so they wouldn't see her. That must mean they could make trouble for her if they knew, right?

The knot nods in agreement.

"Wait, you heard all that?"

It nods again, bobbing in place.

"And—and you agree?"

It bobs faster.

". . . do you know how to talk to regular humans?"

It droops.

"But you think I should try anyway?"

It bobs and scuttles in a circle.

"Ugh. That's a little gross."

It droops.

"Also, you need a name."

The knot tilts questioningly.

"How about 'Stupid?'"

It sags.

"Jumbles?"

It flops over.

"Twiggy?"

It flops back the way it was.

"Fluffy?"

It goes still. Then it bobs twice and scuttles in a circle.

"Ugh, really?"

It scuttles through a series of joyful loops.

"Fine. So. We need to find some humans. Then we need to find a way to, like, influence them? Or something? Push them in front of Maryam and hope they make enough trouble to stall her?"

I shove my hands through my hair. It sounds really, really stupid out loud. Where would I even start? I mean, sure there are probably a few humans around that I could look for. That one enforcer, Haynfyv. Cass's brother. He seemed like he was breaking free of Maryam's influence the last time I saw him. If he's even still alive.

Who else . . . ? Maybe that kid, Liwan. The trainee. If *he* is even alive. He was pretty beat up the last time I saw him, though. Ange would be the best to work with. If she's . . . alive. That's a lot of ifs.

But Ange knows how to get things done. And an enforcer on the inside could be useful. And I've been in Haynfyv's and Liwan's heads before, so maybe I could do it again.

Fluffy bobs happily and does a little twirl in place. I sigh. This is the worst excuse for a plan I have ever had, and that's saying a lot. As a ghost, I can't even see—or feel—threads on the other side, much less manipulate them. But what else am I going to do, play with an animate chunk of wood and wait for the world to end?

Guess it's time to go invade some dreams.

 SEEKING

STEP ONE: RECONNAISSANCE. Fluffy huddles in the crook of my arm and shivers as we shove through the growing wall of ghosts and into the waking world. Since Cadence acts as an anchor on this side of reality, I can't avoid seeing her—or pausing to watch her sleep for a few moments.

She's all knotted up under the covers, knees drawn to her chest, arms curled in close. She moans, tucking her chin, but doesn't wake.

Maryam strides into the room, blinks at the huddled form under the blankets, and turns to leave. Then she turns back, tiptoeing to the side of the bed. She leans down and brushes Cadence's hair back.

"Just a little longer," she whispers. "Just hang in there a little longer. It'll all be over soon."

The last time I saw those long, elegant fingers, they were feeding an innocent woman to the Mara. I bristle, anger pulsing out into the waking world and stirring Maryam's curls.

She sighs, her face hardening. "You know you shouldn't be here, darling. Don't make me do something we'll both regret."

I send another pulse of rage without meaning to. Her nails graze Cadence's cheek. Cadence moans and stretches.

Maryam slides off the bed and backs toward the door. I flee before I can see anything else infuriating and pointlessly distracting.

I never actually regained my powers—Cadence's powers, really, which might have been the problem all along—and whatever level of force and disturbance this current ghostly existence is able to exert is clearly far from sufficient to divert Maryam, not when there's no forest in here to share its power. Cadence has proven she won't listen to me. Or can't.

It's time to find someone who will.

I start on the roof. Though I'm not likely to find anyone useful up there, if I'm going to hunt for allies—or useful pawns, more like—I might as well be thorough. But when I reach the open air, the view is distracting for more than one reason.

The sky is empty and faded. The wheeling gulls with their sharp cries are missing. This place was the site of the first glimpse of true beauty I remember, so much so that it made it into my first imaginings of the dreamscape and coloured all those early encounters with Ash. But now the light is dim instead of brilliant, the view cloudy and . . . cracked?

When I first fled Refuge and come up here, the upper arc of the dome had seemed thin, practically invisible. That's definitely not the case now. The churning surface is milky and clotted, long jagged lines splintering across the sky.

From deep below ground, in that tiny patch of the barrier that bisected the tunnel and adjacent room they'd started in, Cadence's work had seemed incremental. She had been destroying it a few inches at a time.

At that rate, and given how quickly her energy had flagged, it ought to take her weeks, months—even years, maybe—to cover the whole surface. But the relatively miniscule damage she has inflicted at the barrier's base is clearly having massively wide-scale results. At this rate, it might not be long at all until the sky caves in on us—and lets the monsters out.

I need to hurry.

Though neither Fluffy nor I have any discernable physical form in the waking world, I still sense its concerned wriggle of agreement.

I take one last look at the damaged dome of the Mara's prison and sink below the rooftop to scour the next highest floor. And then the one below that.

The upper levels of the tower are nearly as sparsely populated as the lowest. There's little beyond a few growing spaces along the perimeter, where original window-walls have been left uncovered to take advantage of the light that used to filter through.

None of the cultivation workers are familiar to me. The occasional enforcer wanders through to intimidate the drones, but Haynfyv is the only member of Refuge Force I'm willing to risk trying to contact, and there's no sign of him so far.

I drop through Maryam's opulent suite to the floor below without pausing, catching only a quick glimpse in passing of Cadence yawning through yet another audience.

Maryam's floor is buffered by more empty space, including the under-populated superiors' apartments where division heads, supervisors, and other supposed leaders enjoy a level of comfort and luxury unknown to the drones below.

But that's the end of the easy part. The search will probably slow down from here on. There could be someone useful concealed among the workers, and there are several floors' worth of various work divisions and living areas to scout. The drones' hooded and masked uniforms make it impossible to identify familiar faces by design, though I can check the ID codes printed on their uniforms to speed things up. Assuming the codes haven't been tampered with.

The retraining floor is swamped with prisoners, so I can only hope Maryam hasn't had time to start wiping people's identities. And, of course, once I do find someone who might be useful, there's the problem of how to reach them.

I make it through the production zones, the clerical floors—including the abandoned wreck of my old surveillance division—and two residential floors before I find him on Floor 9.

Haynfyv has been busy.

He also appears to have gone insane.

The walls are covered with overlapping layers of scribbled notes—and just plain scribbles, where he either ran out of paper or stopped caring. In one corner, they've migrated to the ceiling. Bits of string and tape trail across the whole mess, in some cases sagging across most of the room like a spiders' web after being hit-and-run by a squirrel.

I pop over to inspect his neighbours' workspaces to make sure this isn't just standard procedure among enforcers. Who knows, maybe they're all trained into insanity?

But the adjacent rooms are bland, if a little grimy. There's a touch more personality in Refuge Force workspaces than most divisions', if only because they seem to have been skimming seized goods for their own use—or as prizes. The walled-in private spaces would also mean they're under less scrutiny than most workers.

Very few rooms are occupied. Most of the force must be out on patrol or holed up in their sleeping quarters on another floor. Maybe that's why Haynfyv is passed out in a corner right now—he just came off duty? But that hardly explains the state of his room.

He moans in his sleep and rolls onto his back. He can't be comfortable on that floor. Why would he sleep here in the first place?

His scribbles are almost illegible—not much in the way of clues there. Anyway, it's hard to concentrate when he's just lying there sleeping without a mask or goggles or anything to cover that devastatingly familiar face.

Maybe I'm just imagining he looks so much like his brother. I didn't know Cass that well, or for that long. He's been dead longer now than I knew him alive. So it's probably just the guilt getting to me.

But what right do I have to risk Cass's brother's life? Of all people, why would I think this agent of Maryam's twisted regime would be a good ally? And how on earth would I even go about communicating with him?

He groans, shifts, and kind of tucks his head into the crook of one arm. For such a big guy, it's an oddly cute gesture. Like a kid or a small animal snuggling in place. Fluffy wriggles, annoyed at the comparison.

"You're not an animal. And you're definitely not cute."

It huffs and gives me the cold shoulder. I go back to peering at Haynfyv's face. Maybe there are fewer lines on it? He was Cass's *younger* brother, after all. Is his lower lip fuller, or is that just the way his arm presses his cheek? Are his cheekbones a little softer? His nose broader, his chin longer?

If he were wearing one of Cass's masks, would I be able to tell the difference? I definitely can't picture Haynfyv in the flamboyantly excessive costumes of Freedom. He doesn't seem like the type with a sense of fun at all. Cass, on the other hand, he could pull a blank face when he needed to. But put Ange in the same room and he could hardly contain himself.

One of the advantages of ghostliness—I can get as close as I want, hover at whatever weird angle it takes to get a good look at the enforcer, no matter how he tosses or turns, with zero risk of embarrassment when he wakes up. In theory.

In practice, the moment he starts to stir, a wave of irrational panic has me flailing for cover—which is how I accidentally find myself invading Refuge Force Inspector 09-Hayne-05's dreams.

DREAMING 14

THERE'S A MOMENT of whirling disorientation. The waking world fades, darkness sweeping in . . . and then it's back. Only everything's a little messier than before.

Scratch that—a lot messier. Chaos has taken over. The air is filled with rustling notes and a thick web of coloured strings. I can barely move without getting tangled.

I drop to the ground and crawl. If I can just reach the nearest wall and get my back to something solid, I'll—

Wait, crawl? Since when did I have a body to manoeuvre around obstacles? I rap on the floor, producing a hollow sound and bruising my knuckles. I try to stand and get snarled in the trailing strings, setting the notes swaying and fluttering.

Then I dismiss them with a snap of my fingers, sweeping the clutter from the room to reveal bare walls and a very confused looking Haynfyv in the midst of his newly scoured personal dreamscape.

He looks from the note in his hand to the suddenly clear patch in front of him, shrugs, and pins it up anyway.

"Seriously, why?" I step closer to peer at the note. "See? Completely illegible. Meaningless scribbles."

"Illiteracy is no excuse for rudeness. Also—" He clears his throat. "You're a tad close."

"You—you can see me?"

He blinks, once, slowly. "Of course?"

"You can hear me too?"

He frowns, putting a hand to my forehead. It's warm. His hand, not my forehead. And big.

I stumble back, trip on literally nothing, and end up sprawled on the floor staring up at the enforcer. Maybe clearing the room out was a bad idea after all. Now there's nothing to hide behind.

Haynfyv follows my progress with a concerned look. "Are you unwell?"

"Are you serious? Things start vanishing in front of you, some random stranger pops up, and your first thought is *I'm the one who's sick?*"

"You are not a stranger. You are her worship's apprentice. 18-Cole-, though you seem to have taken on the moniker Cadence since your elevation. May I help you?"

So either he is super weird, or he hasn't figured out he's dreaming right now. Probably both, but I might as well test and see.

I put Fluffy down and give it a nudge. It tucks and rolls like an ordinary ball of wood at first, then ruffles itself and scuttles back, nudging my hand as if it's a game.

Haynfyv swallows hard but stands firm. From the ashen undertone to his dark, Noosh-greyed skin and the way his eyes are bugging out, he might just be starting to notice something is a little off after all. That is a good sign—maybe he still has some grip on reality.

But then he gets down on his knees and reaches out to poke Fluffy. When it bristles and backs away, he makes a grab for it, juggling with both hands to try to hold onto the rippling, twisting knot.

"Shh, easy there." His hands blur trying to keep hold of the animate tree-spawn. "It is very well made. Did you fabricate it?"

"How many machines have you seen that can move like that?"

Apparently, Fluffy is over being startled and has moved on to being playful. It unwinds several tendrils and latches onto Haynfyv. He switches over from trying to hold onto it to trying to shake it off.

I reach over and rescue him. "As much fun as this all is, I'm kind of on a deadline here."

He can hardly tear his eyes away from Fluffy long enough to frown at me. Fluffy extends a couple tendrils in his direction. He starts to reach back before catching my glare.

"Emphasis on *dead*," I say reprovingly. "Enough playing around. Here's the deal: you're dreaming. Which means we're in something called a dreamscape. Everything is only as real as you want it to be. Or, rather, as I want it to be—because you're just a human."

"What else would I be?" He raps the floor. "Solid, if you'll observe. Entirely concrete. Also, literally."

I vanish the floor under his knuckles on the next rap. He pokes his whole hand into the hole and feels around, so I fill it with glitter. He rotates his wrist, watching the tiny specks catch the light.

His imperturbable curiosity is a little freaky. If I were in his place I would be . . . actually, I'd probably be desperately trying to pretend nothing's wrong. Maybe I am making more progress with him than he's letting on? "Let me recap: nothing is real here, which means I can make anything I want happen."

I snap my fingers and the glitter peels itself from his skin and flaps around his head on jewelled wings. "Problem is, despite my awesome, limitless power in here, I currently have practically zero ability to affect the waking world. Which is where you come in. You're human. You're alive. That means you can act on the other side. And you're with Refuge Force, so you even have some freedom of movement."

Haynfyv rubs a hand over his face and mumbles.

"What was that?"

He scratches the back of his head. "Not with them."

"Who's not with who now?"

"Refuge Force. I am not currently in their employ, precisely."

". . . Is that all you have to say?"

He shrugs. "It is a complicated situation. That—earlier—in the southwest sewer channel." He's referring to the Refuge-sanctioned slaughter of the refugees Ravel and I were trying to smuggle away.

"I departed," he says. As I recall it was more like *fled.* "I have not formally returned to my position since."

"You're literally sleeping in your office right now."

"I—pardon?"

I pinch the bridge of my nose. "I don't think you're getting this. You. Are. Asleep. I'm in your dream. I'll probably be around when you wake up, too, but you won't be able to hear me on the other side. So I need you to listen to me now. Got it?"

"Hmm?" He's staring at Fluffy again. "Ah. Would you be so kind as to return my notes? I was in the middle of a particularly sensitive strain . . ."

I throw my hands up. "Fine. Sure. Have the mess back. I'm done wasting time here. This was a mistake."

I twitch the chaotic tangle of string and scribbles back into place and watch Haynfyv shuffle through the layers. So much for my plan. Maybe the sight of mass slaughter in the tunnel near the barrier broke him. Or maybe he was crazy all along.

Come to think of it, this might all be my fault to begin with. There was that time in Freedom with the Mara . . . make that two times. One of which involved his long-lost brother getting killed before his eyes. Saving me.

"Hey." I duck and squirm my way through the webbing to tap Haynfyv on the shoulder.

He peers back at me. "Hmm?"

"Just . . . Sorry. You know, if I'm, uh . . . If what I did hurt you, or whatever. And about Cass. I'm really sorry about that. I wish . . . If I could go back, if I could change it, I would. Really. He was a great guy."

His absentminded gaze sharpens. He whips around and snatches at a note, dragging a skein of string and paper free with it. "Cass . . ."

"Right. Cass. Your brother. He died, remember?"

He shoves the slip into my hand and dashes off, shouldering trailing masses out of his way. "Cass and Jer's presence preceded my arrival in the lower reaches of the complex."

". . . Jer?" The spiky scrawl on the note doesn't clarify things any.

"My elder brother. He is deceased. They all are. No connection to your concerns, as it happens."

"But Cass—"

He reaches out and taps the top-most note of a wavering stack. "Cass and Ange, Jer and Amy. Brothers and twin sisters, if the records are correct. There were rumours of an infant—"

Amy? Is he saying Lily's dad was Cass's brother? "You're talking about Ange's sister's kid? Lily?"

"It is true, then? I have a—a—"

"The word you're looking for is niece, if she's really your brother's."

"Where is the child? Is she in a secure location?"

I start to answer and catch myself just in time. He's finally focused and tracking with me. Family seems to be the key to getting his attention. If I can just frame what I need from him through that lens . . . "As far as I know, she's safe—for now."

He peers at me through a snarl of threads, tracing one absentmindedly. He plucks a note from its far end and shoves it at me.

"You. Why do so many of these lead to you?" he murmurs, looking back to the looping, interwoven tangles.

It is oddly like dreamweaving, now I think of it. If I let my eyes drift off focus as I turn in place, the notes clump together in patches like people, strung together with the threads of connection and longing, desire and aspiration, hate and lust and all the other dreams.

If I could read Haynfyv's scrawl, what would these clusters of notes tell me? But maybe I don't need to read them to find out.

"Hey." I wave in his direction, setting off a bouncing, fluttering chain reaction. "What's with the notes? And the strings? In your, uh, office, or whatever. That room where you're sleeping right now. You covered it in notes and string too. Why?"

He runs a hand along one of the strings and raises his eyebrows. "Is it not evident?"

". . . Sure."

"Then why did you enquire?"

"I was being sarcastic. Obviously."

He laughs as if this is somehow clever. Infuriating man.

"It is a component in my investigative procedure. You know, very few of the force's inspectors do any genuine investigation in the course of their duties. But in my research, I was fortunate to come across many traditional techniques that are no longer covered in training. While consoles and surveillance feeds have their uses, the tactile nature of this"—he twangs a string—"is invaluable for mapping relationships and possibilities, as well as established evidence. Though, ordinarily, there is no need for such a complex web. You said 'for now.'"

"Huh?"

"You said my niece was safe 'for now.' That implies that she will not remain safe. Explain."

Ah. There it is. I duck my head to hide a satisfied smirk. "That's why I'm here. I need your help."

He nods impatiently. "You already stated that. Your explanation is inadequate. Elaborate."

It is going to be a lot for him to take in. Maybe I should break it down, ease him into it.

On the other hand, time is limited. "The barrier around the city has been keeping the Mara contained for generations. Maryam is working with Cadence to destroy it.

I can't let that happen. But since I can't actually do anything in the waking world, I need you to stop her."

He raises a finger. "Two questions. One: you are Cadence, are you not? Personnel code 18-Cole-, intake registration Cadence Cole, progeny of unregistered and presumed unaffiliated adult male and female posthumously coded as XF-Cole- and XM-Cole-. And two: how does this affect my niece?"

Fluffy wriggles out of my grasp and goes tumbling off into the tangled threads. My arms are too light in its absence. Empty. Is it terrible that I don't actually know Cadence's parents' full names? It doesn't feel terrible. Just . . . hollow. "Not Cadence. Just call me Cole. And if you don't help me stop the Mara from getting unleashed, Lily is going to die. Everyone is going to die."

"'Just Cole' in the manner in which I could be referred to as 'just Hayne?'"

"Huh?" I just said the world is ending and he's puzzling out naming conventions? "What about 'Lily is going to die?'—and you are too—isn't connecting?"

He shrugs. "Precision in language is vital."

"I'm not playing word games with you here. I'm Cole. We've met—you keep getting in my way. I'm trying to save the world. Things happened, and now I can only talk to you when you're asleep. Cadence is the one collaborating with Maryam. She's got issues. You know what—just forget about her. She's not important right now. Focus on Maryam. She's trying to destroy the barrier around the city. If she does, the Mara escape. If the Mara escape, their food supply will no longer be limited to this city. The more they eat, the stronger they get and the more they need to eat. That is not going to end well. You will die. Your dead brother's kid will die. Everyone will die. So you are going to stop Maryam."

He snaps his fingers. The crisscrossing web of string poofs out of existence. The notes flutter to the floor. He frowns and shoos them into neat piles. Fluffy, suddenly visible in the mostly empty space, wriggles with delight and bowls into a pile, setting its contents flying.

Haynfyv takes a deep breath and tears his gaze from the creature. "How?"

"I don't know, okay? I didn't make it. It's just like that."

He waves away my grumbling. "Not that . . . creature. How am I to stop Her Worship?"

I flick a chair into existence so I can slump into it. "Maybe start by dropping the honorific? And that's really your first question?"

"You have provided a plausible account for the evidence available. I am aware of no reason not to proceed on a provisional basis with the thought experiment. Based on the premise you have established, what would you suggest to be an appropriate response?"

I pause to untangle his language—a little too 'precise,' if you ask me—but since he seems to be headed in the right direction, I'm not about to argue. Especially because he's not pausing to leave me an opening.

"You have made the assumption that I am capable of taking some action which would prevent the mayor from irreversibly damaging the dome surrounding the city," he continues. "This further presumes that she or her agents have the knowledge and capacity to enact significant damage against said barrier. And you have additionally and tangentially stated that I am asleep and currently dreaming your existence, this space, and our conversation. I have now sufficiently tested this hypothesis. This space does not respond in accordance with natural law. I require additional information to examine your other assertions."

"Huh?"

"How do you envisage me preventing Her Worship the Mayor of the Towers of Refuge from injuring the barrier? Your response may but will not necessarily touch on her nature, plans, and abilities, the nature of the barrier itself, and the nature of the Mara or other elements of the city, given the time available. As we are operating under the premise that I am asleep, please also consider that I am unlikely to remain so indefinitely."

"Uh . . ."

He snaps his fingers again, summoning his own chair into existence, and peers down his nose at me. "In other words: talk fast before I wake up."

Fluffy wobbles over, rolls twice around his foot, and subsides.

Did—did it just cuddle up and fall asleep on him?

"Tick-tock," says Haynfyv.

I swallow a frantic giggle. He wants to know how to stop Maryam. He wants me to tell him. Because I showed up disrupting his dream and asking him to stop her—so of course, he expects me to have some idea of what to do. Of course he does.

I wish Ravel were here. Or Ash. Or Ange. But it's just me.

And there is no time to waste. The sky is cracking, and Cass's Refuge Force brother wants to know what I expect him to do about it. Not to mention, if I'm not convincing enough, he might decide I'm making all this up in the first place.

So how do I figure out the right direction to push him toward, convince him it's the right thing to do, and motivate him to get moving?

Ravel's cocky smirk floats to the surface of my panic. Ravel, the master manipulator. Ravel, who built his own realm out of nothing, always knows how to pull the exact string to get people to follow him.

Just . . . channel Ravel.

I paste on my best attempt at a suitably devilish smirk. "Here is what I need you to do."

15
INVESTIGATIONS

AYNFYV UNFOLDS HIMSELF with a groan. Fluffy gives me a mental nudge, probably wanting to know what happened to its comfy napping spot. But for our plan to work, the inspector has to wake up.

Now I just have to hope he remembers what to do next. It probably wouldn't have occurred to me to worry if he hadn't brought up the possibility. But now his claim that humans don't usually remember their dreams, if they're aware of them at all, is all I can think about.

Everything hinges on my ability to communicate through dreams now. If Haynfyv starts acting on our meticulously plotted plan, I'll know it's worth trying to turn more agents to my side. On his own, there's only so much he'll be able to accomplish. But if I can start building the resistance one by one, there's at least a chance I'll be able to raise enough forces to keep even Maryam at bay.

Unfortunately, Haynfyv isn't exactly racing to confirm my success. We agreed he would send a signal after waking up so I'd know our plan was on track. He graciously called it my plan, despite suggesting most of it. But all he's doing is yawning and staggering stiff-legged from one end of the room to the other, peering at his notes.

Anytime now would be great. Really.

He tears a shred of paper free and crumples it in a ball, tossing it in a corner. Fluffy wriggles as if it wants to give chase.

The inspector rubs his eyes, nods, and scribbles something illegible on a fresh bit of paper. He wanders over to a different wall and tacks it up.

If I had a stomach on this side of reality, it would be sinking. Where is his sense of urgency? Stopping to play with his notes wasn't part of the plan.

Haynfyv rolls his shoulders, making his neck crack, leans over, and rummages through the nest of blankets and balled-up bits of paper in the corner. He comes up with a slightly crumpled mask and smeared goggles. They get a frown and a painstakingly slow and thorough wiping with a blanket corner.

I'm ready to scream by the time he ambles out the door, as neatly uniformed as he can manage. He raises a hand in greeting to the enforcer coming down the hallway but says nothing in passing. Which is good, in that he didn't start babbling all about his crazy night, but also devastating.

He's either messing with me or has forgotten all about our conversation on the other side.

Fluffy rumbles in concern. Now what? Should I assume he's just unusually dense and find someone else to try again with? What if he remembers everything, he's just not on my side? Maybe he's headed to Maryam to report me like a good little enforcer . . .

But when he reaches the elevator, he heads in the opposite direction of the mayor's apartments. This is more promising. We agreed that he should investigate the underground perimeter of the barrier to start with. That way, he could establish the truth of what I told him while also looking for ways to slow or counteract Maryam's activities.

The floor display ticks down as my hopes rise. He forgot to signal me, that's all. He got too excited about investigating and dashed off, expecting me to figure it out. He already signalled me and I just missed it.

I get the sense the inspector thinks I'm a bit of an idiot. He was probably being clever, subtle, in case of surveillance. We really should have agreed on a specific signal ahead of time. I assumed he'd just wake up and start talking to me, but of course he realized that would be too dangerous.

Or he was embarrassed. Not everyone is used to talking to invisible people, after all. Fluffy rumbles agreement. Of course that's it. He wouldn't want to go around looking like he was talking to himself. He's probably waiting until he's beyond the reach of Refuge's surveillance so he doesn't get scooped up and sent off for retraining.

But the numbers flicking by on the display slow and the car stops too soon with a groan and a slight but unnerving bounce. Haynfyv's mirrored goggles reflect the doors sliding open on an unfamiliar floor in Refuge instead of the semi-abandoned underground.

Here, the lights are bright and the hallways freshly painted in lumpy, bland neutrals. Two enforcers pause mid-pace and scramble to snap their goggles back down and straighten their masks. Haynfyv gives them a nod. They bristle, moving to fill the hallway. He taps the code printed near his left shoulder, denoting his rank. They exchange glances and move aside.

Haynfyv marches past, turns a corner, and repeats the whole process, finally facing down a third pair of Refuge Force guards on either side of a windowless door. This time, when he points out his code—which apparently comes with a relatively high level of clearance—the guards fail to move aside.

"Sorry, Inspector," one says, shifting his weight. "This one's under special orders. No visitors but Her Worship and Her Worship's Hands."

Her *what?*

"I do not 'visit' prisoners," Haynfyv says crisply. "I interrogate them."

"Not this time," the other guard says with satisfaction. "This time, no one goes in except the mayor or the apprentices. And you don't look near strange enough to be either of those kids."

The first guard nods. "It's the uniform, see? The boy never would wear a uniform right, and we hear that new girl, she dresses up all fancy like Her Worship, even though she ain't got the—" he sketches curves in the air, smirking.

Haynfyv makes an impatient motion. "I have no—" He pauses, repeating the gesture. "No *current* interest in a discourse on dress-based signifiers of authority. Neither do I intend to entreat you to act counter to Her Worship's instruction. I merely wish to look in on the prisoner to ascertain her condition for the purposes of reporting her welfare and readiness for interrogation to Her Worship. I repeat: I will not enter the cell. I will not be visiting the prisoner. Now, open the door and stand aside."

"Now, I don't know about—oof." The first guard's elbow in his side obscures the rest of the second enforcer's sentence. There is a brief scuffle and some low grumbling to the effect of "just 'cause he's not Her Worship don't mean he can't make life difficult." It ends with both junior Refuge Force members standing to one side while Haynfyv and Ange stare at each other through the open door.

She's alive.

I hoped—but just because her ghost hadn't yet taken up residence in my nightmares didn't mean she wasn't long gone. And now she's here, in the flesh. For a little longer.

Her bruises are livid, but she unfolds to her feet with no sign of stiffness. Haynfyv holds up a hand, palm out, to warn her against approaching. He shoves his goggles up on his forehead and nods, maintaining ferocious eye contact, but says nothing.

She blanches. "You're—you are, aren't you? Cass's—?"

Haynfyv takes a step forward, and the second guard lunges to grab his arm.

"Hey, you said you weren't going in—"

"Sorry, Sir, but he's right," the other chimes in, moving to block.

Ange springs with a shout, taking the distracted enforcers off-guard. But Haynfyv sets his feet and fills the doorway.

She runs into him shoulder first and bounces backs. "Why? Aren't you here to—?"

He shakes his head, still silent. She takes another run at him, and this time he catches her and holds her in place until the guards take over and wrestle her back to the far wall.

Ange is alive. Ange is safe and alive and *here.* Safe-ish, anyway.

I throw myself at her—and flinch away from a sudden sizzle of pain.

What was that? And how? I don't have a body. I barely even exist on this side of reality. So how on earth did I just get *burned?*

And why is this pain so familiar?

"Thanks for the assist, Sir," the first guard says, panting with the effort of holding onto a furious Ange despite his partner's help, not to mention being a good head taller than her. "I don't suppose you'll need to mention this in your report?"

Haynfyv takes a step back, peering not at the embarrassed guards with their spitting, kicking prisoner, but at the edge of the doorframe. Ange must have given him more trouble than I realized because his fingers seem to have dug in and gouged little holes where the frame meets the wall. He peers at his dusty fingertips, fitting them back into the divots. When he removes them again, there's a glimmer of metal beneath. Gold. Layers upon layers of thick gold wire mesh are embedded in the wall around this cell.

Fluffy squirms unhappily, but this is the best news I've had since Haynfyv woke up. That much gold means Maryam's trying to keep her alive. Granted, it's probably also meant to keep me out as well as the monsters. But if there's one thing my miserable upbringing in Refuge equipped me with, it's resistance to the typical dreamwalkers' gold allergy.

The door closes, hiding Ange from view. Now that I know it's there, I can perceive the cell as a sort of dead space. While most of the upper floors of Refuge have some gold content, the mesh there is thin and sparse.

Those walls and floors are nearly transparent if and when I want them to be. Ange's cell appears nearly opaque, even when I focus. It burns when I press up against it. But it can't keep me out.

The pain is astonishing but fleeting once I've crossed over. Alone, Ange looks exhausted and more injured than she had let on. She draped herself across the narrow cot at the far end of the room in such a way as to be able to roll off and to her feet at a moment's notice, should the door open again. But her eyes are closed and her breathing shallow.

Still, the Mara didn't get her. And Maryam hasn't executed her. Yet.

"I don't suppose you can hear me?" No response.

It was a long shot. I shouldn't feel so flattened by her lack of response. Nor should I be this thrilled when her eyelids snap open. She stares right at me. . .

Making me all the more crushed when they flutter closed again. I shouldn't be. She's not dreamwalker-kind, to hear me when she's awake. I'll just have to wait for her to fall back asleep now, that's all.

I drift closer. Her breathing is even, if alarmingly shallow. Are her ribs cracked? Is she sick? She doesn't look flushed . . .

She doesn't feel warm, either, when I float right through her and bounce off the outer wall with a sizzle.

Ouch. But it's worth the risk of a fleeting burn to talk to her again. I lean in—in—

And get another stinging swat from the wall as I slip through again. Why can't I reach her dreams? What's wrong with her? Or me?

The air stirs in the cell, ruffling her dark hair. She jerks up on her elbows, scanning the room with too-bright eyes. Maybe she does have a fever. But she wasn't imagining that disturbance.

I think . . . I think that was *me*.

So I do it again, reaching for the deep, nagging frustration of powerlessness, a simmering rise that boils over into a wave of force that stirs the fabric of the waking world around me.

That's all it does, though. No matter how hard I bear down, without the forest's vastness to draw on, I can summon little more than a breeze.

Ange shuffles over to the cell door, feeling around its edges for the source of the breeze. She frowns and works her way along one wall to the cot then back around to the door again, inspecting floor to ceiling for signs of a vent.

By the time she completes a third circuit of the room, her lips are blue and her hands are shaking. Sharp spots of colour blossom in her too-pale cheeks, highlighting glassy eyes. She shivers, tossing for a few moments on the hard cot. Then she goes limp.

She's worn out. She needs her rest and time to recover. But her world isn't the only one on the verge of ending, so I slip into her dreams.

16

FURNITURE

ASS IS WAITING for me. His eyes are flame and his hands ice.

Behind him, Ange whirls across a patterned carpet in a pool of light, laughing. She looks younger, healthier. And much, much happier than I've ever seen her.

Around the perimeter of the carpet, there are just a few simple but curiously elegant pieces of wooden furniture. A chair, all sharp, clean angles. A small table, the lovingly oiled grain gleaming. A spindly standing lamp—the source of the light. An open shelf, holding just a few boxy, unfamiliar objects.

There's also music—faint, intricate, and equally unfamiliar.

I can barely hear it out here in the darkness, out on the edge of the horizon where Ange's ghosts wait. Cass isn't the only one here. He's just the only one I recognize.

He visits my nightmares, too.

"I need to see her." I put a tentative hand on his arm. It burns. I knew it would. "I need to speak with her."

Cass's shade shakes his head. The flames flare brighter.

"Please. I have to—"

"Leave," he rasps, barring my way. Smoke curls from between his lips. "You have done enough. Leave her in peace."

I take both scorching hands in mine and look the phantom, or memory, or nightmare, or whatever it is full in the face, despite the heat and the brilliant darkness. "I'm sorry. I can't fix it.

I can't bring you back. I probably can't even save her. But I need to talk to her. And I'm not waiting for permission."

Then I push past the resistance at the borders of her inner world.

"Took you long enough," she says.

My Ange. Tired, tough, unbending leader of the Underground, Ange.

She looks around the furniture-strewn, lamp-lit room with its lilting soundtrack and huffs.

"Sorry. Apparently, I've been feeling nostalgic." She waves a hand. The unfamiliar room is replaced with the makeshift infirmary in the tunnels below Refuge—or, at least, a reconstruction of how it was back before that space was destroyed. "Better?"

"You were waiting for me?"

She shrugs. "It was always a possibility. I'm assuming you're here for real this time, but I've been wrong before. So? What did I miss?"

Fluffy takes that moment to tumble out of my arms and scuttle its way over to Ange. It nudges her foot.

Her nostrils flare. "What is that?"

"It won't hurt you."

"That is not what I asked." She scoots Fluffy away with her toe. It squirms, chortles, and wobbles back to where it started.

"That's Fluffy. It's—I think it's the forest."

"The—"

"Or part of the forest, anyway. It might be tree-creature spawn, or just, like, a part of the tree creature that moves on its own, or . . . I don't really know, actually. The forest wasn't super clear about it."

Ange leans over and pokes Fluffy doubtfully. Fluffy lifts a silky twist and pokes back. She shrugs and allows it to clamber up her arm then onto her shoulder, where it amuses itself by winding tendrils into her hair. "What else did I miss?"

The answer is long, involved, and occasionally teary. More on my part than hers, though she does mist up briefly when I confirm her sister and niece both made it out of the city safely and currently are being looked after in Nine Peaks.

She keeps circling back to the other survivors, frustrated and disbelieving when I insist I don't know exactly which refugees Ravel managed to haul across the border. Not as many as were slaughtered by the Mara or captured by Refuge's enforcers, I know that much. But she keeps coming up with new descriptions to try to jog my memory. Do I recall one with this nose or that hairstyle? Did I notice if—?

It's okay if she wants to play guessing games, though. Almost anything would be okay. She's alive. She can talk to me—though, of course, there's no guarantee she'll remember anything we've talked about when she wakes up. Haynfyv doesn't seem to have been able to.

"You're being too rigid about that." Ange digs a hand into the concrete beneath us, tears out a chunk of it, and crunches it in her fist.

She's been much faster to grasp the possibilities of the dreamscape than Haynfyv. Although, maybe she's just more inclined to think the world should bow to her wishes in the first place.

"Pay attention." She holds up the resulting gravel in cupped hands. "I'm you in the dreamscape. The gravel is information—what you experience, what you say, what you do. Hold your hands out, together, like mine."

She pours the gravel into the bowl I make of my upturned hands. "You're Haynfyv in the dreamscape. Now spread your fingers."

The pebble-sized bits of concrete patter to the floor, leaving me with gritty hands covered in dust.

She taps my palm. "This. Haynfyv just woke up. He can't hold onto everything, but maybe a bit of what you gave him sticks. Make sense?"

I shrug. "It's possible, I guess. It's not like I know how any of this works either. But if he's trying to act on—on—" I hold up my palms in illustration.

"Information dust? Dream residue?"

"Uh, sure. That. But it's not enough. Even if I can get a little bit of information to stick after he wakes up, and after you wake up, and after—I mean, there's only so much time, right? Say I could talk to even a dozen different people while they're sleeping; get them to remember a tenth or a hundredth of what I tell them. It's not enough to really make a difference."

"So you're going to give up? Fine. Go wallow somewhere else." She dusts her hands off and gets to her feet. The room warps dizzily around us.

"What was that?"

She shrugs, looking away. "I thought you were leaving. Because you can't win against Maryam and your evil little twin. Boo hoo."

"I'm not going anywhere. Not right now. Stop trying to distract me."

Ange reaches up and kneads Fluffy, who rumbles in pleasure. She starts working its tendrils free of her hair, still without looking at me.

Strange to be the one pushing her instead of the other way around. "You're sick, aren't you? What did Maryam do? Are you dying?"

She rolls her eyes. "It's hardly that bad. I'm just a little feverish. You're lucky there aren't purple sewer rats dancing on the ceiling right now."

I can't stop myself from looking up. Ange coughs a laugh. Then she heaves a sigh—and finally meets my gaze straight on.

"You've got to stop worrying about all the things you can't control, kiddo. So everything's not going your way. What else is new? Do what you can while you can. Run into a wall you can't walk through? Turn and look for a corner. Haynfyv can't follow simple instructions? Maybe he's just unusually dense. Or, maybe, you've got to hustle and get a few more pawns out there wandering around and making trouble."

The room stretches and sags around us. Ange kneads her forehead. "Speaking of which, I'm not the most useful person to be hanging out with at the moment. Not much I can do to help the cause from the glitter-goddess's prison cell. Why don't you toddle off and see if you can't nudge a few more players to action while I get some rest?"

It can't be a good sign that even in her dreams, her eyes shine with fever.

"I'm getting you out of here."

She waves a limp hand. "Not a priority. You've got the world to save, monsters to destroy, and baby doppelganger to put back in her place. I'd get on that if I were you. Speaking of which—"

If I hadn't spent my relatively brief working career as a drone in the surveillance department, the list of names and locations she rattles off would be utterly useless. As it is, more than half are scattered across the warren of underground service corridors, abandoned halls, hidden rooms, and half-drowned tunnels below Refuge that I never really did learn to navigate.

Here's hoping being able to pass through walls will speed up my search because Ange has clearly given me about all the help she can manage. Her words slow, her movements growing more and more lethargic. Her dreamscape is melting, fading by the minute.

Fluffy strokes a gentle loop against her sadly but uncoils when I reach for it. Ange moans at its absence, but even here, her eyes have drifted closed. Her body floats limp in the now-formless void.

Her ghosts have drawn near, too, groaning and shifting uncertainly, flames guttering. Ash's memory snags at my sleeve in passing, but it takes no effort at all to shake him off. I push through the boundaries of Ange's shrinking inner world and out to the other side, where her body shivers on a thin cot in a cold cell.

And there's nothing I can do but leave her there to suffer and fight for survival. At least for now.

17
LIWAN

HAYNFYV HAS WORKED his way down into the tunnels much farther than I expected. Is he headed straight to the damaged spot in the barrier I told him about? Does he remember he needs to watch out for Maryam and her guards? Or is he just going about whatever he originally planned for today, and it just so happens to be investigating the maze of semi-abandoned spaces down here?

It would really be useful to know how much he remembers—not to mention how typical or not his reaction will prove. Refuge runs in shifts, so, in theory, it should be possible to dream-hop at all hours—if I can find more people to work with in the first place.

I need an army, but not just foot soldiers. Captains. Generals. If I just throw people in Maryam's way one by one without a plan, she can get rid of them without lifting a finger. I'll need the kind of people who can gather and motivate others: strategists, and those skilled in frustrating Maryam without getting silenced, permanently. I need *Ange*—but she's in no shape to help.

Did Ravel ever struggle with finding the right people? Did he have to save his energy and study his targets to figure out what lever could move them? Or did he just naturally draw everyone who crossed his path into his gravity? He had always made it look so effortless . . .

Maybe I shouldn't be so frustrated with Haynfyv. He's slow, and not very communicative, and was working for Maryam up until . . . Actually, it is possible he's still working for her. In general, he seems to be a pretty devoted rule-follower. But last night, he'd also proven insightful when he hadn't been distracted by the wrong details. Even if he is useless awake, maybe I can pick his brain when he's asleep and use that intelligence to my benefit.

That said, he has already proven somewhat useful. He led me to Ange, after all, although that wasn't part of the plan. He also had a list of suggestions for me. Who might be useful based on their role, or background, or record of behaviour, where to seek them out.

His and Ange's lists overlapped on more than a few counts. One possibility isn't far from here, so I leave Haynfyv poking around a dusty mechanical room two tunnels and a half-dozen turns away from where he should be investigating and start a search of my own.

Since Refuge's training—and retraining—dorms seem to be crammed full of prisoners, I tamp down any hopes of finding anyone useful left free in the Underground. The Mara have been pushing deeper than ever before in their growing hunger and strength. Even if a few of Ange's people had managed to evade Maryam's raids, they'd have had the monsters to contend with.

I push my awareness out to its limits, peering through doors and walls and floors to inspect every corner, checking behind every caved-in ceiling and hidden space in the walls for signs of life.

I would never have found them if I had to navigate on foot—yet another advantage to being able to walk through walls. I knew Cadence always had it good. Except for the whole, you know, being powerless to actually *do* anything part.

The survivors are mostly young. In Refuge, I'd expect to see them on the Training Floor or apprenticing in work units. Some bear the ruddy, acid-etched marks of a childhood spent in the corrosive smog of the city, while others look less worn.

Those ones would have found shelter earlier in life, either with Ange's people deep underground or when they were ripped from their families by Maryam's enforcers. Liwan, as I'd experienced so vividly in his very nearly deadly nightmares, was one of the latter.

There are a few older adults in the group as well, probably Ange's people. They look vaguely familiar—maybe from the parade of artisans, cultivators, and engineers she subjected me to while I was recovering from saving Freedom? At the time, I thought she was trying to nudge me into choosing a work division Under-style and hadn't paid that much attention. But now, I have to figure out which people are worth trying to reach when they fall asleep.

Liwan is a given—he already has a little cluster of eager followers emulating his prickly determination. Not that I'd actually use a kid like that as a soldier. Besides, he's still limping from the damage he took at the hands of the Mara the first time they tried to take him. I just need to test if there's some kind of extra connection between me and those I've previously dreamwalked with, back when that wasn't the limit to my abilities and the sum of my existence.

I didn't notice it so much with Haynfyv or Ange, but Liwan has a kind of shine to him, like the light is brighter just where he is, his edges sharper. His eyes are dark, not molten gold, and his movements tight and reserved, not extravagant, but there is something of Ravel's larger-than-life feel to him.

I drift closer. A little too close. When another boy fumbles a jar, Liwan lunges right through me to catch it before it can shatter on the dusty concrete. It's awkward for me but not useful in any way. There is no brush of illuminating threads, no dizzy tumble into his inner world. I'll have to wait for him to fall asleep to talk to him.

In the meantime, I should check on Haynfyv's progress before trying some of the other leads he and Ange suggested. And soon, it'll be time for Cadence to tear away a few more chunks of the barrier. I should be able to watch from a distance.

As long as I don't speak to her, I don't think it'll be a problem. Other than the part where she's steadily working toward the end of the world, of course.

Fluffy tugs at me, making one of its odd rumbling noises.

"What? There's something here you want?"

It wriggles.

"I don't suppose you can be more specific?"

It flops over and lets out a sort of puff.

"I'll take that as a no."

Maybe it's bored. Just in case, I pause to scan the hidden enclave once more. This time, a few others stand out to me. Maybe it's just a trick of the light down here—spliced wires and ancient equipment making it flicker and pulse. Or maybe Liwan isn't the only one with a little extra shine.

Two of the girls and one of the boys seem just a touch crisper. It's barely noticeable, not as pronounced as with Liwan, but they seem more vivid. And the teens aren't the only ones who glimmer no matter where they go. One adult woman, showing a pair of kids how to position a growing lamp over a box of seedlings, and an older one, scolding her trio of charges as they play around with the ingredients for a meal instead of mirroring her efficient movements. And one of the older men, quietly showing a pair of intently focused girls how to run a freshly repaired wire to a dark bulb.

Liwan first, when they sleep. Then I'll try contacting the adults.

"Satisfied?"

Fluffy rumbles contentedly.

"Well, as long as you're happy."

I find another three adults and five teens with that extra little spark that may or may not mean anything at all before I have to check on Haynfyv. There are more clusters of survivors hiding in remote corners of the tunnels than I expected. Even pushing the limits of my perception, I can't finish exploring in time. And what I really want is to go back to Ange and find her awake and well enough to boss me around. But Maryam will be bringing Cadence down to chip away at the barrier any minute now, and . . .

It's not like I can stop her dragging the trapped fragments of stolen lives from that filthy wall, nor to protect Haynfyv if he stumbles into their path. But I can't just stay away and pretend it's not eating at me, either. By the time I finish wrestling with myself, it's too late.

Haynfyv is mid-argument, insisting that he is on a legitimate investigation and outranks the pair of enforcers doing their level best to shoo him away. Maryam, Cadence in tow, is catching up quickly. The guards tasked with clearing her path get more physical the nearer she approaches, concern with failing her overruling their trained respect for superior officers.

"Wait, isn't this the one that was demoted?" They crowd Haynfyv back toward the nearest doorway.

He retreats into a torrent of increasingly large and obscure words that all come around to meaning "yes, but," while backpedalling.

Maryam glides around the nearest corner and laughs. "How delightful. I had thought you dead, but here you are after all."

Three pairs of knees hit the concrete. Her guards stammer apologies, which Maryam ignores on her way past.

"I seem to have overlooked your last few reports, Inspector. Perhaps you could bring fresh copies in person?" She doesn't turn to look at him in passing.

I have a feeling that Haynfyv's usefulness isn't going to last much longer, even if he shows up at her feet in an hour, paperwork in order and all accounted for. Which isn't likely to happen, since he's been holed up in his room obsessing over connections between people he really has no business knowing about.

Cadence wanders after Maryam, yawning.

"You're . . . You seem familiar." She squints at Haynfyv.

"Inspector 09-Hayne-05," he rattles off without elaborating.

She blinks sleepily and trails off down the hallway without further comment. She has met him, of course. Maybe he just never made much of an impression?

There's no particular reason she should think anything of this encounter, either. So as long as he can steer clear of Maryam, he'll be okay.

"Surveillance worker 18-Cole-," he murmurs.

The guards wince.

"I wouldn't call her that to her face, nor to Her Worship's, if you know what's good for you," one says, making shooing motions at Haynfyv. "Now clear off. Her Worship wants this area cleared."

Haynfyv shrugs and heads down the hallway in the direction Maryam and Cadence have just come as if heading back to Refuge. But when the two enforcers race off to resume their efforts to clear Maryam's path, he turns around and stares after them.

"Cadence Cole," he says, holding up a pinched hand as if pushing a pin into a board. He repeats the motion with his other hand. "And Her Worship. In the tunnels . . ."

Is he starting to remember? Or is it just his compulsive need to investigate the mysteries that surround him that sends him pacing with soft steps after Maryam and her entourage?

But there's no time to worry about the fate of one dangerously curious man just now. I watch Cadence tear her first handful of the day free from its writhing body. Maryam has her working on a fresh section on the opposite side of the subterranean maze. Apparently, the mayor's not concerned about cleaning up the tiny patches where Cadence's blood recharged the surface yesterday.

There's something about that scene—a nagging, plucking sort of thing at the back of my mind—but I can't quite grasp hold of it yet. And the sight of the shattering sky pushes it out of mind entirely.

After Cadence tears a second double-handful free from the barrier without showing signs of slowing, I shoot up through all the hidden layers, and further, through the cloying, dense fog, to the topmost levels of the tower where the air is almost clear—and the view of the barrier is unobstructed.

It shudders with every blow, fresh cracks splintering across the increasingly opaque surface. Its churning oscillates between sluggish and frantic. Cadence has destroyed hardly more than a single wall's worth at its base, and it's already looking like this?

I have no way of knowing how thick the barrier is or how much of a crack the Mara need to escape. Maybe they're squeezing out into the open already?

I wonder . . .

Unlike me, the Mara can manifest a sort of physical presence. As far as I know, that's a new trick of theirs, though, a sort of power-up skill. Originally, they weren't embodied any more than I am. So there is no reason they couldn't squeeze through the tiniest of cracks in the barrier. And if there's no reason they can't escape right now, then is there anything keeping me here?

I waft into the air, higher than Refuge's roof, higher than I've ever been. The crumbling, smog-choked city spreads out below me, the barrier close enough to touch.

So I do.

THE PAIN IS a living thing; it ferrets out every corner and stabs deep with red-hot pokers.

I can't escape. Frozen in mindless agony, nearly beyond thought, melting into—

Fluffy rumbles.

I gasp. Saltwater floods in. I choke and flail, bubbles of precious air escaping until they run out—and, lungs burning, tongue coated with brine, I remember I don't need to breathe.

But I do have a mouth. A face. A whole body, even, as solid and warm and living as the dreamscape's altered reality can make it. Fluffy nudges my cheek, threading worried tendrils into my hair. Cool water surrounds me, pushing away the overwhelming memory of that fiery pain.

"You brought me here?"

It snuggles into the curve of my shoulder, all but purring.

"So I'm gonna go out on a limb and assume the Mara aren't getting out just yet, either." I try for flippant and barely muster 'shakily jaunty,' but since there's no one to hear but Fluffy and the forest that inexplicably surrounds me, despite the fathoms-deep saltwater, I guess it doesn't really matter.

The tree creature steps out of the nearest trunk and holds out a forelimb to Fluffy. Fluffy rumbles a warning and nestles in closer. The creature emits a rumbling of its own.

Fluffy squirms—rather ticklish, given its current position—and reluctantly extends a tendril toward its . . . parent? Main body?

The creature vanishes Fluffy into the depths of its rustling coverings and subsides into a tree. I throw myself after it, flailing through the water.

"Where are you going? Give it back!"

I dig my nails into bark seconds too slow to snatch the trailing edge of the tree-creature's garb and bring down my fist in frustration. But before I can make contact, the tree is gone, along with the whole forest. I'm floating in cool water, nothing but indistinct specks eddying in the dimness as far as I can see.

There's a long slow moment where nothing happens. Nothing at all. Time just . . . goes. And then I blink and lift my head, and the water rushes away to be replaced by a rolling meadow ringed by snow-capped peaks that screen the haunted horizon from view. And at their feet, the sleeping forest.

When I step into the shadow of the trees, there is awareness, but it is not awake. Not at first. Then it shakes off its drowsiness and gathers itself to meet me. My heartbeat is loud in my ears, the blood rushing, heat rising to the surface. Not fear, not exactly, nor shame, but a sort of breathless blend of anxiety and regret and growing frustration. Moments later, the familiar treelike creature emerges from the nearest trunk and pauses, catching my gaze and reaching back to pat the bark reprovingly.

Though I feel suddenly lighter than I have since before Ash's ship went down, I am not in the mood to apologize. "You try getting jerked around by everyone and everything at their convenience. See if you feel like being gentle and patient."

It backs against the tree, disappearing into it inch by inch.

"Okay, okay. I'll stop battering the trees if you stop forcing me into stuff."

It pauses, half submerged in the trunk.

I sigh. "I know. You pulled me out when I got stuck in the barrier, didn't you? Thanks. And sorry. I'm just . . . tired of screwing everything up."

The creature slips serenely out of its tree and holds Fluffy out to me.

"I can take it?" I reach—

The creature draws back. Fluffy squirms.

". . . Or not? Why did you give it to me in the first place? And is it, like, offspring, or . . . ?"

Fluffy and the creature—the whole forest, for that matter—give off a sigh. I flush again, embarrassment narrowly outweighing frustration this time. Then Fluffy is in my arms, and the forest is at my back, and a wall of ghosts is all that stands between me and the void.

Cass's shade stares at me, his mouth working wordlessly, the dark hollows of his eyes lighting with flame one moment, almost human the next. The child-form of Suzannah Bell writhes at his side, flickering to the broken, aged corpse I first knew her as and back again. Behind her—no. I don't want to see the others. I can't.

The forest insisted I rest. It saved me, though I still have no idea why it bothered—or how it was able to pluck me from the treeless wasteland of my city. But I have work still to do there. So I close my arms around Fluffy. Then I shoulder my way through the ranks of ghosts to the waking world.

The sky is still splintered, milky and churning. It hasn't fallen yet. And it will have to fall for the monsters to break free. After what that barrier just did to me, damaged as it is, I'm pretty sure the Mara can't escape yet either.

So I fight back the only way I know how: through the living. First Haynfyv, and then Liwan, and then a half-dozen others. I race from one dreamscape to the next and back, pushing myself and each one of my potential soldiers as hard as I can to make it in time. , Despite Refuge's mission to train the impulse out of us, everyone dreams. The moment they fall asleep, I'm there.

So many have unformed inner landscapes, their focus flitting from one half-developed scene to the next, unable to carry on a conversation long enough to be of much use. The bright ones are easiest to connect with, easiest to persuade. In the waking world, at least to my perception, they stand out just slightly. But their inner worlds are crisp and deep, their awareness and interest in my intrusion keen. The boy I know as Liwan is one of the brightest.

Kelvin Lee dreams in the past tense. The ghosts of his family inhabit that same smog-choked corner of a crumbling tower I remember from the first time I walked in his waking nightmares. 12-Lee-01 was a trainee who would never make it to worker much less floor supervisor or superior. One of Refuge's many victims stolen from the streets and destined for a life of mindless servitude—or, more likely, an early death by Mara. He hadn't taken very well to brainwashing.

"You're the one who saved us," he says, as the memory of his mother sweeps up a black-haired infant. His father ushers her and the smaller boy out of the dim but well-kept room. "Well, not them."

"I won't hurt them." I can't, even if I wanted to. They're only memories.

He shrugs. "Habit. I find it comforting for them to stay in character. It's less creepy than having them freeze or fade out or whatever when I stop paying attention."

He knows they're not real, then. "How much do you understand?"

"Not enough." His jaw is set, his eyes bright. He comes closer. "You came back."

It's not a question. I shake my head. "I just needed to see something. I'll go now."

He steps in fast, wrapping his hand around my forearm. He's at least a few years younger, a good head shorter, and probably still suffering from the aftermath of the brutal injuries inflicted by the Mara before Ash tore him from their clutches. All the same, the fierceness of his stare and the sharpness of his grip freeze me in place.

"What do you need?" he says. "What can I do? Tell me."

I swallow. If he were even just a few years older . . . but he's not. He is a child, still, for all that he suffered. For all his will to fight. "Stay low. The deeper, the better. Keep an eye out for Refuge Force—they're hunting further every day."

He eases back, eyes narrowing under dark brows. "There's more, isn't there? You wouldn't have come back just to tell us to hide."

Each day a troublemaker like him continues to draw breath is a miracle, not that he wants to hear it. I'm still a little in awe of his mutinous resistance to Refuge's mind-numbing training regime, though it had drawn the very nearly deadly attention of the Mara. Though Ash had snatched him from their jaws, this boy's defiance must have drawn the authorities' attention because I remember him there with the other prisoners when Ravel and I had broken them free. "Why didn't you leave when you had the chance?"

"I stayed to fight," he says without inflection, but behind him, the echo of his mother peers around a half-closed door, his younger brother tucked close to her side. She shakes her head sadly.

Liwan follows my gaze. He swats the door shut. "Made it as far as the tunnel's end with the others. That guy with the crazy glowy eyes was taking people across, right? But I didn't want to leave. Not yet. Not if . . ." He rubs his hands on his thighs, fingers clenching. Looks up. "The other two might still be here, you know? What if they're—" he gestures at the ceiling.

My heart stutters. I'd skimmed past those eerily silent halls at the top of the tower in my search for soldiers. I'd tried to forget those still, small bodies in their rows of cots, the machines wiping away their pasts while moving their skin and bones forward, bringing them to readiness for the trainers. We weren't supposed to remember the lost families. The stolen siblings. But it seems Liwan has never forgotten his.

"You can't save them," I say. "They might not even be there. You should have left when you had the chance."

Cracks splinter underfoot, climbing the walls and spiderwebbing across the ceiling. Fine dust sifts down in a gritty rainfall. But all Liwan says, through gritted teeth, is, "You didn't."

He's so obviously desperate for a mission, for any way to fight back. Scrabbling to survive for another week instead of striking back at Refuge and the Mara isn't enough. I don't blame him. He's too young to be a soldier in this war—though, give him a few years and he could have been an excellent one—but now he knows I'm here, knows there's a bigger battle raging, I don't think I'll be able to hold him back. Better to try to channel his efforts than have him running around on his own making things more complicated.

Besides, I can't afford to waste days and nights searching for the perfect allies. There's too much at stake. We have to act now if we want to save Ange.

When I track down Haynfyv to set it up, he insists we need to focus on the bigger picture. Saving one human shouldn't be a priority when there is so much more at stake. But her connection to his brother, to his—and her—niece, is enough to convince him to help with the plan.

He brings the expertise needed to orchestrate a jailbreak. Liwan supplies the muscle, promising to marshal a willing squad for the adventure. I dart back and forth, clarifying plans and carrying messages and repeating, repeating, repeating instructions in the hopes that at least some of all this effort outlasts the waking of my forces. Though I brave the sting of the gold-lined cell to enter Ange's dreams and bring her up to speed, I can't get her fever-ridden mind to focus.

Finally, I've done all I can.

Ange shivers, lids fluttering over glassy eyes. I tell her to hold on. She doesn't respond.

Higher in the tower, Haynfyv stretches, putters around his room, and wanders off with no discernable sign of purpose or urgency. It's not ideal but, by this point, it is expected. He already played his part, helping refine the plan and hammer out the workings of Refuge Force and their high-security prison area.

If we're really lucky, maybe the faint echoes of his dreams will nudge him in a useful direction during today's meandering. Either way, it's up to the Underfolk now.

Liwan bounces out of bed and enlists more helpers than he can manage in "his" scheme to break into Refuge and free the prisoners. It doesn't take him long at all—he seems to have Ravel's effortless ability to draw people to him. It's amazing to watch. And also terrifying.

I really hope I'm not about to get a bunch of kids captured—not to mention killed.

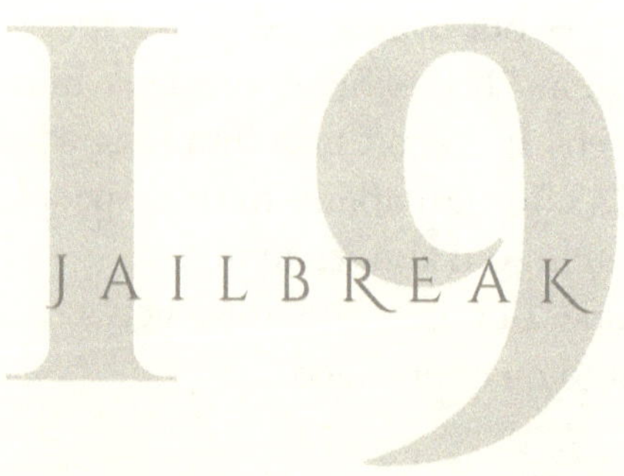

JAILBREAK

THE FIRST SIGN that something's wrong is more felt than seen.

It's as if a background hum cuts out, just for an instant. I never would have noticed it but for the shock of its absence. Now I'm aware, it's the work of a moment to trace the sensation back to its source: the damaged barrier is churning with incredible agitation.

Am I out of time? Is this it? Maryam wins?

But when I race to check the patch Cadence had been chipping away at most recently, there is no new damage and no one to be seen. I hate to leave Liwan unattended—not that I can do anything but bear silent witness to his mission—but I need to know where Cadence is. What she's *done*.

I let the anchor of her body reel me back, but she's up to nothing more troublesome than yawning through an unremarkable meeting in the mayor's audience chamber, far from the barrier's surface.

The arcane shiver comes a second time.

Neither Cadence nor Maryam reacts. They don't seem to even be aware of the disruption to the barrier's energy, never mind have caused it.

Is this some kind of delayed reaction to their work? Or is someone or something else manipulating the undead dome?

Fluffy nudges me. It's right—there's nothing I can do right now either way . . .

And then it registers: this boring meeting, like every other boring meeting. Maryam's daily chore of receiving reports and petitions and issuing new orders. Cadence's insolently pointed lack of interest. Totally unremarkable—except that this report is about a sick prisoner. Some inspector is reportedly agitating for her to receive treatment. An inspector who has no business visiting the prisoner and indeed has been flagged for ignoring a summons to report to the mayor's chambers. Would Her Worship like him brought up immediately or simply detained until further notice?

It's Haynfyv. He must have remembered just enough of what we discussed in the dreamscape to send him poking around Ange's cell again. Now the eyes of Refuge are going to be on her—just in time for Liwan to trot into the middle of a trap.

I drop through the floor faster than thought. Maybe I can catch them before they leave. Maybe—maybe there's still someone asleep in that hidden corner of Under, someone I can try to pass a message through. Send a warning, even if it's just a vague sense of unease by the time the messenger wakes. Something, *anything* to stop them—

But Liwan is already out the door with a half dozen of his young friends, sneaking through the underground maze toward the stairwell. They seem to have worked out a complex system of hand signals since I last checked in. Although, based on all the whispering and elbowing, it's not clear if anyone actually remembers what all the signals are for. Liwan pauses to give a muted scolding on the importance of stealth. One of the older boys challenges him, setting off a brief scuffle and a new round of hushed negotiations.

What was I thinking? These kids aren't trained for this. If they were a trainee squad from Nine Peaks, maybe they could pull this operation off. I can definitely envision Steph orchestrating a successful rescue mission. Ash could have, too, of course. Or whoever it was in charge of Spectre squad. But this rag-tag little crew can't even hold it together long enough to make it into enemy territory, much less infiltrate a top-security zone and pull off a jailbreak.

Thank goodness Liwan isn't stupid. Any minute now, he's going to call it off.

Only, through some combination of dumb luck and Liwan's whispered threats, that doesn't happen. His pack wanders wide-eyed through the wreckage of what were once Freedom's halls, giggling about rumours of what was supposed to have gone on behind the heavy wall hangings. A couple of the older ones exchange glances and blush, evidently well aware.

They edge up to the door at the base of the stairs, pale and jittery under their dark hoods. Liwan motions them back, reaching out to tap the handle as if it might burn him. When it doesn't, he swallows a sigh of relief, eases the door open and waves the others through.

They climb, single file, pressed against the wall as if hoping to blend into the shadows should a door unexpectedly open. But no one does, and they advance one floor, two, nearing three—

And the barrier shivers.

I gasp. Liwan freezes. He whips around, raising a finger to his lips.

"What?" one of the youngest whispers. "We were being quiet."

Liwan hisses and brandishes the finger. The kid glowers, his neighbours twisting to give him reproving looks. A girl who looks about the same age nudges him crossly.

Liwan shakes his head and turns to continue his climb as if there's any way this gang of amateurs should be allowed to keep going.

But his reaction—that was just a coincidence, right?

"Did you feel it?" I murmur.

"Who said that?" Liwan stalks back down, glaring. "What about 'shut it or we'll get busted' isn't getting through to you?"

Blank stares. Shuffling. Craned necks, as each one eyes his or her neighbour suspiciously for the source of their leader's anger.

"We're not going another step until I get an answer." Liwan eyes each of his underage soldiers in turn. "I mean it. Talk. No, don't talk. Just put up your hand. Or I'll call this whole thing off."

"Perfect." I squeeze Fluffy in delight. "Do that."

Liwan glances behind him. There is nothing but the opposite wall of the stairwell. ". . . Cole?"

Wait, can he—? "You can hear me right now?"

He scrunches his face, straining. "Well, yeah. Barely. But yeah. Thought you said you could only talk to me when I was asleep?"

This opens up a whole world of new possibilities—ones that I can explore just as soon as I save these young idiots. "Apparently not. Listen carefully. I need you to turn around and go back down these stairs. Fast. But quiet. Stop at the bottom. I'll make sure the coast is clear."

"What happened?"

"It's not safe right now."

He scowls, twisting to stare up at the dim glow of the nearest landing. "But if you can look ahead and tell us when it's clear to move, why can't we—"

"Just get these kids back to safety."

"But what if—"

"No. They're not ready for this. Take them back. Now."

Liwan's expression turns mutinous. "We made it this far. I don't see any reason to turn back." He gestures to his worried-looking wannabe army and starts back up the stairwell. They don't move to follow.

"You—you can't all hear me, right?" I ask. Haynfyv never seems to, but maybe he's just unusually dense . . .

A couple of the kids get a pinched, listening sort of look, but none respond. Liwan shakes his head and keeps climbing. The others exchange glances and shrug. Apparently, no one's willing to be the first to turn tail and run, despite their leader arguing with thin air.

"I wasn't trying to criticize you, okay?" I call after him.

Liwan starts up the stairs to the next floor. Only two flights to go before they reach their destination.

"Look, it wouldn't matter if you had the best-trained team in the world. Everything Haynfyv told me is useless. The shift patterns have changed. The enforcers will be paying extra attention to Ange. She's—she's not even there anymore, okay? They took her away for treatment. You'll be risking their lives for nothing."

Liwan rolls his eyes.

I dig desperately for something that'll scare him into submission, finally landing on: "If you want to be Marabait, there's easier ways to do it. Look, you know what it's like. You barely survived their last attack. You want to risk that kind of slaughter again for no reason? It's not just your life at stake. If you don't call this off right now, you're responsible for whatever happens to them."

That's a lie, of course. He wouldn't be here if I hadn't pointed him in this direction in the first place. I must've gone insane there for a moment, willing to use even these kids to feel like I could make a difference. But now—

The barrier shivers.

Fluffy pokes me, trying to get my attention. But I can't worry about that. There has to be something I can do, something I can *say*, to stop Liwan. To save them. "You might not be the first to get sacrificed, you know? You'll get caught, all of you. They won't kill you right away. They won't need to. You're just a bunch of kids.

"No, first, you'll be rounded up and stuffed into the training dorms. You hated it there, remember? Even before it was a literal prison. Some of you will get sick. Too many people, too little space. You'll be starved because there's no sense wasting resources on prisoners.

"The waiting will seem endless. And then an enforcer will come. Maybe he'll take one or two at a time. Maybe more. They'll hold you in place. But you won't struggle. You won't be able to. They drug you first so you can't move. You can't fight, not for yourself or for the others.

But you'll be aware. You'll watch, helpless, as the Mara suck them dry, one by one."

He misses a step, cracking his shin against the sharp-edged concrete.

It's working.

I lower my voice; slow its pace to a death-march. "And then it'll be your turn. And you'll go peacefully. Silently. You won't fight. They won't let you. I've seen it. That is what's waiting for you, if you don't turn back. That's what you're leading them into."

Liwan closes his eyes, nostrils flaring, lips pressed into a pale line. That got through to him. That nightmarish vision of his future. I didn't even have to make it up. The truth is terrifying enough.

But he picks himself up, waves off the others' concern, and continues on, one floor, and then another, pausing to let each of his foolish little soldiers catch their breath before continuing.

The barrier shivers once more. Fluffy squirms. And Liwan and his team climb past the floor Ange is being held on.

"We're not the ones who should be starving," he breathes. "It's time to stop feeding the nightmares."

He's headed to the training floor. The dorms that have been turned into more holding pens for sacrifices to the Mara. He was never planning to try to reach Ange from the start.

If I weren't so horrified, I'd almost be impressed. "You're making a mistake. I understand wanting to save them, I do, but it's hopeless. There's no point—the Mara will take them either way."

He keeps climbing.

"You don't get it. Everyone will—" I choke on the truth. Everyone is going to die. Everyone. If I can stop Cadence and Maryam from destroying the barrier, it won't stop the Mara from devouring every living soul within it. If I fail, everyone in the city still dies—and soon after, everyone outside it, too.

Liwan and his friends aren't going to survive long no matter what happens. Neither is Ange. Or Haynfyv. Even the best-case scenario at this point is nothing more than me stranded in a city full of ghosts.

But for some reason, I can't stop yelling at them, trying to persuade them to turn back. I don't want them to die. I know it's pointless, absolutely the wrong thing to focus on, but I can't stop—

The barrier shivers.

Fluffy—did that stupid thing just *bite* me? But there's no chance to scold the treespawn because deep below and halfway across the city, a familiar voice rings out with cocky self-satisfaction.

"Miss me, flame?"

20

RETURN

E SHOULDN'T BE here.

I would tell him that if I wasn't in such a rush to put him to work.

"They're almost there. Hurry!" I dart in circles as if it'll nudge him to greater speed.

"Not quite the greeting I was hoping for. I've come a long way to see you, you know?"

"What about 'innocent kids are gonna get killed' aren't you getting right now?"

"All work and no play," he sighs. "Darling, you're no fun at all."

"Less talk. More running."

"I would never." He grimaces in exaggeratedly fastidious distaste.

At least he's moving in the right direction, I guess? He's the last person I expected to save the day, but when he stepped through the barrier calling my name, he opened up a whole host of new possibilities. Better yet, for some reason he, like Liwan, can hear me on this side of waking. Maybe it's something to do with exposure, tuning into a new frequency, or just latent talent. Doesn't really matter; the important thing is getting him to Liwan in time to get those kids out alive. Grilling Ravel on what on earth he's doing back here can come after.

Refuge's increased patrols mean I have to stick with him and sound the alarm whenever enforcers are about to cross his path if I want to keep him from losing time trying to avoid them. When he hits the base of the stairs, I risk spreading myself thin to scan for Haynfyv, but he doesn't seem to be in range. Hopefully, he's off poking around some abandoned corner and staying well out of trouble.

Liwan has only one floor left to climb, while Ravel's just getting started. There's no way he'll be able to catch up in time. I yell at him to go faster anyway.

Then I leave him behind to yell at Liwan. "They're right on the other side of the door, you know. You won't even make it one step without getting caught. Look, why don't you wait for a shift change, at least?"

He pauses, reaching for the door. "Changed your mind about us?"

Ravel is moving faster than I expected. If I can just stall Liwan a little longer—"Hey, it's not like I want you guys to get caught. If you're sure you can't turn back"—he jerks his head, a definite no—"okay. Have it your way. You're only making things worse, but I get that you don't see it that way. So, fine. I'll help."

He flattens his hand against the door and leans his head against the frame, listening.

"What, don't trust me? I mean, it's not like I can see through walls or anything. You probably know best after all. No need to listen to useless little old me."

He frowns at my sarcasm but says nothing, which is the right choice since there really is a guard—actually a pair of guards—stationed on the other side of the stairwell door, more to monitor the elevator directly across from it than anything, but I'm sure if a bunch of kids come storming out under their noses they'll feel obligated to react.

Ravel's getting close. Life on the outside must agree with him. I'm impressed by his stamina. He's catching up fast; I just have to hold out a little longer against Liwan. "You remember the layout, more or less? It's changed.

They've knocked out some of the inner walls to make bigger holding areas. Besides, there was so much damage from before. When the Mara slaughtered everyone, remember? Which is what you're leading these kids into. Just in case you forgot."

Too far. He reaches for the door handle.

"Sorry, sorry. But listen, my point is you've got to make it down this hallway, around the corner, and half that distance again before you even reach the nearest door to where they're holding the prisoners. That's"—I run a quick tally: four guards, two on each set of doors, plus another two patrolling the perimeter, but I might as well tack on a few more for good measure—"Eight, no, ten enforcers to start with. I assume each of your little soldiers is capable of taking an enforcer or two out on their own? Before any can sound the alarm?"

Ravel has just two floors left to go. If he could risk calling out to them without being heard, this would all be over. Just a little more—

Liwan looks over his shoulder, flashing a sign at the determined—and scared-spitless—kids lined up behind him. Then he shoves the door open with a yell, diving at the pair of very surprised-looking enforcers on the other side.

"What was that?" Ravel pants from two dozen steps and a landing away.

I cringe. Two of ours down already. A pair of enforcers down, too, surprisingly. Liwan is sharp—he went after the weapons first. Armed, his forces could be in better shape than I anticipated. But there is no time for them to experiment with the unfamiliar tools, there's little enough combat skill to share among the lot of them, and they're rapidly losing the element of surprise.

"Cole?" Ravel calls. "Tell me those brats didn't just—"

I summarize the situation. Three down, now. Our remaining wannabe soldiers have pinned the second pair of guards by sheer strength of numbers, but just piling on is a losing strategy. These enforcers are only temporarily incapacitated, and more are on their way, racing from posts around the perimeter of the floor.

Ravel slows, stops, and leans against the nearest wall. "I know you don't want to hear this, flame, but I can't help them."

"Don't be stupid. Of course you can—you're almost there. There's still time—"

"You're not thinking straight. Right now, no one here knows I'm back in the city but you. It's not worth losing that advantage to save a few dumb kids."

I hate to admit it, but he's right. He can cross the barrier without suffering harm. He can take people across. He can hear me, even when he's awake. Who knows what else he's capable of? Plus, he knows *everyone*—and everyone's weaknesses—and has underground networks that stretch across the city, from the heights of Refuge to the outer fringes of the streets. He might even be Maryam's weakness. He's offering to do what he can for the city—and even if he weren't offering, I might be able to use him. I *will* use him in whatever way I must.

Right after we save Liwan and his overeager pack of idiots. "Follow my orders exactly."

"Are you sure? This is what you want?" The fine tendons in his hands are ridged with tension.

Why has he returned? For the sake of the city? To save his people—the same ones he manipulated, even sacrificed, to seize and hold power? As part of some devious plot to gather even more power in the midst of chaos? Is it complete arrogance—or delusion—to think that he could have come back for me?

In the long moment I hesitate, caught up in Ravel's inimitable capacity for creating drama and confusion, Liwan crumples, winged by an enforcer's shot. They haven't even made it past the first corner yet, and four others are down on his side. The first two fallen enforcers are being used for cover to trade fire—one of the girls has figured out how the stolen weapons work—while another has been captured but is still upright. Mobile cover for a suicide run toward the corner where the remaining enforcers are sheltering. But this floor has a full loop or rectangle of corridors around the perimeter. The first side to realize they can just sneak up behind their enemy's backs will win.

"Get your hood up," I order Ravel, barking the orders to keep panic from choking my voice. "Turn right as soon as you get through the doorway and break for the corner. The shooting might stop if the enforcers are surprised enough, but don't count on it. The faster you run, the less likely you are to get shot."

"You're putting a lot of faith in my lung capacity, darling."

"Go. Now."

Shockingly, he does, bursting up the remaining stairs and through to the hallway with a shout. Immediately turning away from the stunned faces of enforcers and Underfolk alike, he vaults the bodies strewn across the floor and sprints for the far corner.

He makes the turn without getting hit, only to backpedal at the sight of a door guard staring back at him. "Now what?"

"Don't stop. Get over there before he thinks to shoot!"

Ravel puts his head down and charges as the hapless enforcer fumbles for a weapon. Apparently, he wasn't wasting his time in Nine Peaks—he has the guard disarmed and on the floor before I get a chance to issue my next set of orders.

"Good. Shoot and keep going."

He doesn't hesitate, discharging the weapon without a flicker of remorse. Enforcers' arms are meant for suppression, not lethal force. At least, they should be within Refuge's walls. So there's a good chance he knew the guard would survive. Probably.

Armed, Ravel makes short work of the single guards stationed at the doors along the far hallway, but the next bit will be trickier. All remaining enforcers have clustered at the end of the fourth stretch of hallway, attacking the three kids still laying down fire. Ravel will have to take most of them out alone. If they notice him coming down the long, unprotected stretch of corridor behind them, there's no way he'll be able to avoid taking fire himself.

I might be able to do something about that. "Liwan, you're doing great. Help is on its way."

He blinks, struggling to focus, fighting the compulsion to lie down and sleep. One arm dangles limp. His leg drags on the same side.

"Final push, now, hard as you can," I order. "If you can just keep the enemy distracted for another minute, it'll all be over."

The kid beside Liwan takes a shot to the head and drops without a sound. I swallow a sob. He nods to his one remaining soldier, an older girl. "Pick it up. No surrender."

She bares her teeth and reaches for the newly orphaned weapon, squeezing off shot after shot with her free hand.

On the opposite side of the tower, Ravel pulls his hood up further and peers around the corner.

"Coast is as clear as it's gonna get. Just go!"

An enforcer falls to one of the Undergirls' shots. She's firing with both hands now, wildly. Liwan leans heavily against a downed enforcer, wheezing as he pulls the trigger.

Ravel rounds his third corner and sprints toward the remaining cluster of enforcers using the fourth for cover. He raises his weapon. It's not made for accuracy over large distances. He'll be halfway down the hallway before it's safe to get off a shot. But Liwan and his young soldier are hanging in there, drawing all the guards' attention.

Until their efforts backfire. A lucky shot drops another enforcer, who falls back, a dead weight against his fellows. Only three are left standing now, two trading shots with their attackers, one struggling to drag the fallen out from underfoot. He turns—and catches sight of Ravel.

Ravel's shot drops him before he can raise the alarm, but the body falls against the remaining enforcers. They twist to look.

Ravel takes another out before their first shot is fired. It's down to a one-to-one faceoff; Ravel barrelling forward while the last remaining enforcer braces himself behind his fallen comrades for the shot. He can't miss, not at this range. The Undergirl is cautiously advancing from the opposite direction, but she's moving too slow. If anything, she'll be in the perfect position to fall under the enforcer's next shot after he takes out Ravel.

Liwan is in no condition to help. He limps in completely the wrong direction, working his way toward the opposite corner.

The last enforcer aims. Ravel yells, squeezing off another shot. It misses by a hairsbreadth.

The elevator chimes.

SMUGGLING

THE SOUND OF impending rescue distracts the last remaining enforcer. His shot goes wide, grazing Ravel's elbow. Ravel jumps, squeezing off the decisive shot from above as he hurdles the barricaded enforcer and keeps right on going.

Reinforcements have arrived. Ravel might catch them off guard enough to get a shot or two in before they overwhelm him. The girl is likely to take a shot in the back if she doesn't stop gaping and find cover. Liwan—he lunges out of sight just as the first enforcer steps out.

Huh. Maybe that kid has better instincts than I've been giving him credit for. But the stunning effects of even a glancing bolt are catching up with him. He staggers, leaning into the wall for support.

Ravel can't be far behind. Already his steps weave, one arm hanging limp, and he didn't even get properly hit. Doesn't stop him from taking out the first enforcer, or the second, who had foolishly poked his head out to stare slack-jawed at the mess of bodies.

The rest of the reinforcements must decide they need a better strategy than hop-out-and-see-what-happens. The door starts to slide shut, bumps into the prone form of the fallen enforcer, and hisses open again.

Ravel stares. The Underfolk girl flanks him, levelling her dual weapons. She blinks. Her arms fall to her sides.

In the distance, Liwan hits the locked door to the prisoners with a strained cry. He sags, wheezing, pulls himself up, and hits it again. Muted cries and thumps filter through from the other side.

But in the open elevator car, all is silent. The only Refuge Force members it brought, out cold on the floor, stunned by the stolen weapons turned against them. And, on a wheeled cot, a silent form, still but for the faint flickering of her eyes behind closed lids, lost in fever dreams.

Ange. Here. No wonder those enforcers had been so inept. They weren't reinforcements; they were interrupted in the middle of a prisoner transfer. Which means—yes, there. A bare three floors away and closing fast, a second car full of the expected reinforcements.

"Stop staring," I order Ravel. "There's more on the way. Take cover—"

He grabs the Undergirl by the elbow and shoves her into the open elevator car. She protests. He reaches down and hauls on the enforcer blocking it from closing.

"You don't have time for that! Liwan's too far away to reach you in time. And the rest—there's no way you can load them all in and get clear before reinforcements arrive. Just take the stairs!"

"How long?" Liwan, overhearing, calls from a corridor away. He hits the door in front of him again and then turns his weapon on the lock, firing twice, barely reacting when a bolt ricochets into his shin.

"What are you doing? There's no time—hurry!" He won't make it through another skirmish, not on his own. He needs to get out of here.

Ravel kicks the enforcer's legs out of the path of the elevator's sliding door and steps over the body. He puts an arm out to hold the girl back and calmly presses the button for the lowest floor the elevator can reach.

"You wouldn't. Don't you dare—" The mechanized doors slide shut on my protests.

Moments later, the locked door in front of Liwan cracks. The whole latch mechanism falls out, smoking. Prisoners stream through, bowling him over. He curls up, covering his head.

In the distance, the elevator chimes again. The doors slide open just as the newly freed prisoners round the corner. Enforcers start firing into the crowd without even stepping out of the car.

Ravel abandoned them. Abandoned us. He is using the distraction to escape with Ange.

Prisoners scream and fall. The lucky ones flee back the way they'd come or past in the opposite direction, forgetting or unaware the floor is a closed loop. Some few, probably devotees of Freedom, correctly identify the unassuming door across from the elevator as the way out and risk the dash for the stairwell.

Liwan pulls himself up, sways, and leans into the wall for balance. He glances at his cracked and overheated weapon and heaves an endless sigh.

"Of all the stupid, reckless, pointless—" I start.

"Jealous," he wheezes, hobbling toward the screaming and ignoring the prisoners desperately fleeing past him to nowhere. "You want in, huh? Too bad. 'S my party."

For a madman on his last legs, his eyes are surprisingly clear. He even smiles faintly. "That was a good trick. At the end. Surprise attack. Who?"

It's not worth the risk, blowing Ravel's cover. Not even after his latest betrayal. Liwan doesn't have a chance making it out of here safely. I tell him so.

He nods, still painfully shuffling toward the enforcers. "'S fine."

"It's definitely not. You know how many of yours made it out? One. No one's coming to save you. You risked it all, and for what? How many of these prisoners are going to be walking around free by the end of the day?"

He leans so near the corner he could reach around it if he wanted to. Head down, eyes closed, sweat standing out on his skin. "You'd have risked us. For one."

"If you'd just listened to me, everyone would be safe right now!"

"No." He lifts his head. Pushes away from the wall. Sways. Pulls himself straight. "No such thing. My choice. End well."

He throws himself around that corner, shouting orders with a ferocity that belies his gasping faintness only moments before.

The enforcers haven't even bothered stepping out of the elevator. The only escape route off this floor is the stairwell door across from them. All they have to do is sit tight, safely ensconced in steel, and fire straight across the hallway.

For every prisoner who makes it through, a half dozen slump to the ground or lose their nerve and run screaming past into the closed loop of the floor. But in less than a minute, Liwan has rallied a handful of prisoners and sent runners to herd the stragglers back for a mass push to escape.

The Refuge Force reinforcements aren't prepared for organized resistance, not after how easily the prisoners scattered under their first blows. Volunteers risk themselves to build a barricade of unconscious bodies, angling in toward the exit. There are only a few weapons on the rebels' side left intact and still loaded. Every shot is a precious chance for another knot of prisoners to break for the door. Liwan insists on staying behind, one of the last left upright, wedging himself against the fallen to shoot for as long as he can cling to consciousness.

It's all so pointless. Everyone he's trying to save is doomed. Maybe not here, not today, but soon. Then again, so is he. And if I had any way to save him from falling in this moment, I would.

Instead, all I can do is tell him he's doing great; he's saving them all. I count the escaped prisoners off for him, one by one, inflating the numbers to the point where he laughs, blearily. Thankfully, he slumps into unconsciousness before the next car full of reinforcements arrives.

Then I abandon him to his fate. If he was willing to sacrifice the few days or weeks of freedom he might have held onto to give these prisoners his share, the least I can do is make good their escape.

When I catch up with him, Ravel isn't impressed. "Ange is in bad shape, flame. Don't you think you're asking a bit much? Hard enough to vanish one dead weight into the ether, never mind a whole straggling band of useless drones."

"More than half of them are yours. And Ange's. Handle it. Quickly."

"Yes, darling," he huffs. "I'll see about rescuing the whiny dancers, too, if it'll make you happy."

Ugh. I think I preferred "flame" as his pet name of choice. I have to assume he doesn't realize he's imitating his mother. Unless . . .

Fluffy nudges me. If I had a neck right now, the hair would be standing up on the back of it. There is no way he has been working for her this whole time, right? No reason for him to rescue Ange if that were true, for starters.

"Who's nearby?" he asks, interrupting my examination of his recent actions.

"No one. Obviously."

"Okay. Well, *obviously*, I can't just keep pushing this thing." He gives the wheeled cot an unnecessarily hard shove with his one good hand. "We're running out of clear floor. Neither can I carry Ange while racing around rescuing ragtag bands of prisoners after getting *shot*, although I do very much appreciate your superhuman assessment of my skills. Find me the nearest muscle, and I'll see what miracles I can pull off for you."

His whining is eye-roll-worthy. They barely winged him. But he has a point, much as I hate to admit it. His quick thinking has gotten Ange this far. Or brazenness—come to think of it, I'm not sure it even occurred to him that diving into a Refuge-controlled elevator to steal an unconscious prisoner could backfire.

With my luck, if I tried it, some surveillance drone would notice and lock the car down between floors. I'd be left to stew until Refuge Force could collect me at their leisure. But of course, he gets effortlessly delivered to the lower levels, complete with a handy wheeled cot to save him breaking a sweat no less. And now he wants help?

Too bad for him. He's only skirting the wreckage of Freedom's halls right now. While the former club is technically below ground, it's really only in the topmost layer of the labyrinthine underground sprawl. Most of the people who know how to survive down here also know to hide in the far reaches and are nowhere near . . .

Except for Haynfyv, who doesn't seem to be aware of the concept of hiding.

I can't believe this. Ravel's inhuman luck strikes again. "What are you doing down here?"

Haynfyv pokes at a shred of flocked velvet, shining a lamp into the chamber half-hidden beyond its drape. He shows no sign of having heard me. Which is typical. But just because I can't boss him around doesn't mean he can't be useful.

It's a slight diversion, but Ravel is willing to risk it once I explain.

"Message from Her Worship," he calls, making his way across the pitted floor of Freedom's purple hall, wheels squealing and skidding in the debris, as if there's nothing at all unusual about the missing heir to the throne turning up in an abandoned club with an unconscious prisoner in tow.

"Where have you been?" Haynfyv towers over Ravel. "And isn't that—"

It's a good thing Ravel has so much practice acting the arrogant and entitled brat. He talks over Haynfyv's protests, issuing commands and immediately swishing off as if he's certain they will be obeyed, all without giving away the slightest shred of information about his own plans.

"What happens when he runs into a dead-end?" I say. "You're not worried he'll question his orders and end up handing Ange back over to Refuge?"

Ravel snorts. "Not likely they'll let him leave. 'Specially not with Ange in tow."

They? I could have sworn he just sent the inspector into an abandoned corner out near the edge of the city. Maybe there's some secret enclave of Underfolk near there that will intercept him before he gets stuck. As it is, I have no idea how the bumbling inspector has escaped capture this long—he seems to keep forgetting that he's technically in trouble.

But I'll let him go for the moment. I need to focus on rounding up the straggling prisoners and smuggling them away to safety before Refuge Force catches up.

In the end, Ravel keeps me too busy arguing about if we really need to save yet another batch of escaped prisoners, or if I couldn't be happy with just the ones we've managed so far—*darling, flame, now be reasonable*—to grill him on just what brought him back to the city. Or rather, who.

RESURRECTION

"**Y**OU COULD HAVE said something."

I don't mean to whine. It's embarrassing. Besides, it's not like I had a moment to spare to deal with the shock even if he had spoken up when he first returned.

And what I really mean to say is—what I really *want* to say . . .

But there are no words. Stunned tears obscure my attempts to express how—how *grateful*—

"I know," Ash says quietly. "I'm sorry it took so long. We can talk later. Right now, it looks like you have other things to worry about."

But Ash is alive.

And here. With Ravel. And not just that, but also with Ange's sister Amy, and her . . . Actually, I'm not entirely sure what Sam is to Amy, but Lily treats him like a father.

I could strangle Ravel for that—if I could actually lay hands on him right now. He had no business bringing a kid back to this place, and he knows it. For that matter, Ash knows better, too.

"Everyone's a critic." He grimaces. "But you're right—Lily shouldn't be here. Problem is, by the time we realized she stowed away, it was too late to turn back. And it's not like we could just leave her to fend for herself on the other side.

I laugh. And then sob.

Ash is alive. Ash is alive—and here. And—"What about the others? On the ship with you? And Aleya, is she okay too?"

He hesitates, his expression clouding over. "Later. Right now, you've got to do something about Ange."

"I can't. Go ahead and try, if you like. She's too sick to get any sense out of. She needs medicine. Someone here must know where she kept stuff in Under. Or—Ravel, what about your connections? Can you get her what she needs?"

Ravel glowers. He's been leaning in a corner staring down his nose at everyone and doing a poor job pretending my reunion with Ash isn't driving him wild.

"You're the one who brought him here," I remind him. "You can live with the results. Or we can fight about it later if you want. But right now, Ange needs your help."

"He can't save her," Ash interrupts. "She's too far gone. They don't have treatments that can bring her back. You're the only one who might be able to manage."

"Me? I don't know what—"

He holds his hands up, stopping my protests. "You're her only hope, C. Just because you don't know how to help her doesn't mean you can't. Dreamweavers heal. She's beyond human medicine now. So it's you, or nothing."

"But I'm not—I can't—"

"Cole." He brushes Ange's hair aside, wincing at the heat burning her up from within. "You don't have time to wallow. It's your choice. If you want to save her, you're going to have to skip the identity crisis and just *try*. I can come with you, but I can't do it for you."

He dismisses impossibilities so easily. Magic, healing, my absolute failure to learn or reclaim the dreamweavers' power that I only ever borrowed temporarily anyway . . .

I mean, sure, I can dreamwalk now, but isn't that because I only really exist in the dreamscape to begin with? And I've already wasted more to try to save her than I can afford. More time, more lives, more energy. The smart thing to do would be to let her go now. To let this fever take her unawares, instead of dragging her back to face the coming horrors at my side.

I'm not that strong. "Ravel, you're in charge of treatment. Get her help." If I'm going to do this, I might as well stack the deck in my favour. He'll make sure she gets the best medicine available, while I do . . . whatever it is I can.

"He's right, you know," Ravel hitches an insolent thumb in Ash's direction. "We don't have anything that'll save her."

"You heard her." Ash drops to sit on the floor with a wall at his back, frosting over with mist. To me, voicelessly, he says, "Won't do much good, but it doesn't hurt to keep him busy."

Ravel snorts, apparently well able to hear both of us from the other side now. "Whatever, glitter boy."

But Ash is already gone, his body protected behind its silver shield, the rest of him brushing by to burrow into Ange's feverish nightmares. I follow him into the dark.

He finds me there, takes my hands, presses his forehead to mine in the crushing turmoil of Ange's fractured inner landscape. We anchor each other, space flexing and warping around a core of solidity that starts with the merest brush of fingertips and grows, moment by moment, inch by inch, into an island of our own making.

"Good." Ash backs off to where we can see each other without going cross-eyed. "See? You're better at this than you think. Now let go."

I shake my head, gripping tighter as his fingers relax.

He winces. "Ouch?"

Our bubble of stability wavers, stretches as he steps back, and firms up again without popping. "Good," he says. "Just like that. You're you. I'm me. We're safe. We're together. Now: where is Ange?"

I swivel, peering into the chaotic mess around us. Senseless shapes form, waver, and fracture into a new cycle of growth and decay so fast my head throbs. "I can't see her. I can't see anything."

"Then don't look. Feel. Where's Ange, Cole?"

I ease a hand up against the seam between us and the madness beyond. It crackles against my skin. I skip back, curling my injured arm to inspect the damage.

But there are no burn marks, no shredded flesh. The skin's not even red.

Ash sighs. "Is that your hand?"

Does he think I hurt myself? I hold it out to show him the unbroken skin.

"Ange doesn't have time for you to play games. Is that your hand? Is this mine?" He waves and then snaps his fingers.

A tree branch sprouts in place of his forearm. The twigs rustle, dropping a leaf. As it drifts down, the branch is replaced by a fish, silvery tail merging into the warm brown of his elbow, fins fluttering and mouth gaping. It blinks stupidly at me. I blink back.

Then it's gone. Ash pinches his fingers at me in imitation of the fish's gasping mouth. "Glub glub. Fish. Tree. Arm. Focus, Cole. Now: *is that your hand.*"

"You could've just said, 'Hey, stupid, we're in the dreamscape,' if you were in a hurry," I grumble. "Fine. This isn't my hand. This is an imaginary construct of a hand that I associate with myself. Happy?" I pinch my fingers back at him.

He grins. "Nah. That's your hand, silly. Doesn't matter if it's also a fish, or a tree, or a pirouetting pink bunny rabbit. You're you. I'm me. Now: where is Ange?"

I rub the furrow between my eyes, pressing against the growing ache. "You know, seeing as how we're in just a bit of a hurry, it would be great if you tell me what you know and we could get on with it."

He shrugs, spreads his hands. "Where's Ange?"

I turn my back on him. Stare out into chaos—and it starts to click. There's still no pattern, nothing solid or stable or real in any sense, but why should there be? It's not a landscape from the other side, mapped and bordered and pinned down with all the usual rules like gravity and time and space. It's the dreamscape. Ange's dreamscape. In which case, she can only be—"Out there, right? All around us."

I reach toward her—and Ash is there to stop me, pulling me back before I can break the surface of our little island.

"You won't find her like that. She's not herself right now. Or rather, she can't hold herself together. So you'll have to do it for her."

Huh? "How?"

"How should I know? I'm just a dreamwalker, C. I don't work like that."

I scrub a hand over my face, letting my head roll back. "Great. I'm powerless and you're clueless. This is going so well."

I wish Cadence were here. But this time it's just me. No snarky last-minute tips. Ravel's cocky attitude won't get me anywhere either, not when there's no one here to manipulate into doing my work for me.

So instead, I try to imagine a me that knows what she's doing. How would I help Ange if I had a dreamweaver's power back and the skill and wisdom to use it properly?

I take a deep breath and dive out of the bubble of safety, leaving Ash behind.

It's like plunging into a pile of those stinging bushes back by Nine Peaks. Warping unreality nips and rasps at the edges of me. I grit my teeth and do my best to go limp. After a moment, it's less painful and more simply . . . overwhelming. Too much input, too fast, changing too quickly to track.

So I stop trying.

One part of my brain laughs at the fact that my answer to "What would (ideal) Cole do?" is apparently "Surrender and go limp," but the rest of me is feeling out a new way forward. When I just let it all wash over me, the tsunami of chaos starts to sort itself into . . . I don't know, exactly. Not yet. Patterns, maybe? No, not that structured. More like contrast. There is form and formlessness. There are things that snag at me, that send a jolt of electricity through me, and things that I instinctively know to let slip by.

And then, without quite meaning to, my fingers close on a single incandescent strand of sparking energy—and the universe turns inside out.

23

H E A L E R

A MIRROR-SMOOTH obsidian ocean reflects an endless sky shot through with shimmering starlight threads. I stretch and spread my fingers, trailing them through the strands, breathing through tens of thousands of memories and imaginings, longings and fears.

This is my friend. This is the path and the form, the real and the reflection, the past and the future. This is *Ange*.

And she's dying.

I can feel it: a twist to the strands, a snag of the weave here, a drifting apart of her fabric there. There is a hole in the midst of her, growing. Tarnishing her light. Draining her energy. Her dreams are fading, gossamer-thin, her fears growing heavy and coarse, future unravelling . . .

I have no business seeing so much of her so deeply. Just the memory of Susan's healing makes me wince, that horrifying moment what seems like an eon ago. Back when I first reached Nine Peaks, the way she reached into me and laid me bare. How can I do this to Ange? But if I turn back, I may never find this miraculous space again. If I don't help her now, there is nothing in her future but death.

To make it all worse, she's not afraid. If anything, more threads than I'm comfortable with draw in that very direction. She's intimate with death, both familiar and desirous of it. It's laced through her past, woven through her present, a horror that became an obsession that became a soul-deep longing.

It's Cass's ghost, waiting for her on the other side. It's the family she barely remembers, the spectre of a sister she feared lost, fleshed out with the bodies of all those she watched fall to the monsters over the years, stone-faced and broken-hearted. It's the peace at the other side of her long battle to sustain life in the shadows.

I'm not sure I should take that away from her.

I'm not sure I can.

So instead, I knot those dark threads back into the still-living fabric of her, twining them with the beautiful and the ugly, the parts I have no right to see. I fill my hands with the fraying strands and weave her anew, using every last bit of heavy, misshapen fear and envy and hate and mad, driven obsession to bridge the hole in her fabric, looping in strands of courage and selflessness and humour and love to strengthen the weave, binding her together again.

My fingers slip. The pads are worn raw, knuckles knotted and aching, wrists burning. Sweat drips into my eyes and my arms shake from exhaustion. The threads—no, the unravelling—fight me, wrestling away from my grip.

But if Ange's selflessness, her drive to rescue, to protect, to rebuild, is the brightest and strongest part of her, I must be the opposite, made all of hunger and need and selfishness. I fight the void trying to swallow my friend with anger and spite and sheer stubbornness. I refuse to let her go. I refuse to lose her here and now.

And if a strange strand or two readies itself to my hand, a brighter thread slipping unexpectedly between my fingers to strengthen the weave, well, who has time to worry about the source or think too hard on where the love, or hope, or sacrifice forming that vibrant cord might have come from?

Weaving a life back from the edge is a battle longer and harsher and more exhausting than any I've fought. But finally, moments and millennia later, Ange's fabric is messy and knotted and uneven—but it is whole once more.

I pull free, fingers numb, vision cloudy, knees trembling. The inky ocean below rises to meet me, closes over my head, pulls me inside out, and then flicks me back into realness again.

"Not bad." Ash takes a sip of tea and leans back in an overstuffed and improbably frilly chair.

Ange extends a floral teapot toward me. A delicate cup appears in my hand.

Fluffy reaches out a curious tendril to tap the china, setting it ringing with a high, pure note. I jolt, suddenly aware of the treespawn's presence. Did it just appear out of nowhere? Or was it with me all along, so silent and still I forgot it was there? The forest's gift nudges me playfully, which answers nothing.

Ange pours without meeting my gaze. "Two sips, and then back to work. So much to do and so little time left."

I collapse into my own cloud-soft chair and start giggling at the tall white furry ears twitching on her head. She snaps a disc open to display what looks like a small, round, hand-held clock and frowns at it.

"The mad tea party." Ash tips a tall, much-patched hat in my direction. "It's a fun one. Pops up in fever dreams more often than you might think."

That cuts my manic giggling short. "She's still feverish?"

He puts down his tea with a sigh. Reaches over and places a steady hand on Ange's shoulder. "We'll be taking our leave now. Don't rush yourself."

Her ears quiver, her sharp expression going vague. "Oh dear. So much to do. So much to do."

"Not for you. Rest."

She nods, reaching out to take a small frosted cake from a heaping platter on the table. I don't know where the teapot went.

I'm still looking for it when Ash yanks me out of Ange's dreamscape.

"Took you long enough," Ravel says, kicking at Ash's knee and cursing when the silver mists shielding the dreamwalker stop his foot in midair.

Ash stretches, unfolding in a single graceful motion. With the wall at his back, it brings him nose to nose with Ravel.

Ravel's golden eyes narrow, his lips thinning. He bristles, elbows out, as if it'll make up the difference in height and breadth. Ash is solid in a way Ravel could never match even with a lifetime of training exercises.

Ash yawns, casually sidestepping his would-be rival.

Ravel whirls—and catches sight of Ange. "You—you really—"

She's still unconscious, but her colour is better, her breathing steady, even the hollows beneath her eyes less shadowed.

Ash feels her forehead, takes her pulse, and shrugs. "Seems on the mend. Good job, C."

"Why isn't she awake?" I try for diffidence and end up sounding strangled. "She's supposed to be healed."

"It's a miracle you brought her back at all. Looks like she can take it from here."

Lily chooses that moment to invade her aunt's sickroom, barrelling into Ash with a happy shriek. Ravel rolls his eyes. Amy sidles in after her, murmuring vague apologies without looking up from the dusty concrete.

I tune out the rest. Or, more accurately, all the squealing and bouncing and attempts to calm the kid down just kind of fade out for a bit. I don't leave, not yet, but I'll have to rest properly soon. I used up too much energy helping Ange heal. I need what passes for sleep.

But for the moment, I let the world drift by without me in a kind of ghostly catnap.

Reality reasserts itself like a slap in the face. "Don't," I gasp.

Ravel and Ash freeze. Amy looks up anxiously, but at a wave from Ash finishes herding her daughter through the door.

"What's wrong?" He scans the room.

I leave them behind, racing through walls and ceilings. "It's Cadence. She's—"

"Messing with the barrier, huh? Don't worry, it's not like it's going to fall today or even tomorrow," Ravel says unexpectedly in the distance.

I pause, even though that's not it. Call back, "You knew?"

He shrugs. "Could feel it on the way through. Or hear it? It's like the vibration has changed. Like it's screaming at a really high pitch or shaking super fast."

Shaking—or shivering? All those disturbances yesterday . . . "That was you?"

Ash quizzes Ravel on his impressions of the barrier and attempts to estimate its remaining lifespan. I only half listen in while speeding up into Refuge because what I just felt wasn't Cadence chipping away at the barrier.

"Try this one next, dear," Maryam murmurs, swaying down a line of cots.

The bodies are stretched out, restraints pulling their wrists and ankles against the edges. Liwan isn't the only one stirring, or I'd have been wondering why she bothered tying corpses down. The effects of the enforcers' bolts are wearing off, suppressants working their way out of the unconscious prisoners' systems and giving the effect of bringing them back to life. For the moment.

Cadence touches the arm of one of the first girls to fall during Liwan's ill-fated rescue mission. Her eyes flicker behind closed lids, head rolling as she struggles toward consciousness.

"Good. Just like that." Maryam folds her hand over Cadence's, pressing with slim golden fingers that urge Cadence's deeper, nails denting the skin. "Anything?"

Cadence scowls. "Not much. Stupid kid, just along for the ride, I think. That one was the ringleader, but . . . there's something more . . ."

She frowns at Liwan. He cracks an eyelid, finds her face, and squeezes his eyes shut again as if he'll be able to get away with faking unconsciousness now.

"Soon," Maryam says, following Cadence's gaze and tightening her grip. "Finish up here."

The Undergirl moans, sweat beading on her skin. Whatever Cadence is doing, it's hurting her. And then it's not. The body goes limp, mouth falling slack, chest deflating.

Maryam releases her grip on Cadence, makes a fist, and pounds it over the stalled heart. A gasp lifts that sunken chest and another. The girl's eyes flutter open for just a moment before rolling back in her head.

"Mustn't waste them." Maryam beckons Cadence over to Liwan. "Not now."

I draw a breath to beg, to throw myself at Cadence before she can dig her claws into Liwan like she just did that helpless girl—and swallow the protest unvoiced. Maryam isn't killing them, not yet.

Or rather, she's not letting them die so easily. Prisoners have one use to her: as fodder for the Mara. Sacrifice the troublemakers to protect her precious drones. Though she'll happily torture him, she's not going to throw away Liwan's life to no purpose. Not unless I do something stupid and force her hand.

"She's found a way to communicate," Cadence says, eyes closed, fingers digging in. "She is stirring up resistance against us. This one could hear her in his head."

Maryam smiles. "You are there, aren't you, darling? Naughty child, up to all kinds of mischief. I do wish you wouldn't."

"Please—" I start.

"Ah." She holds up a finger. "I really wouldn't. You'll spoil the show. If I have to waste these on a silly punishment, they just won't go as far, will they? And we've been working so very hard on a wonderful surprise for our favourite monsters, haven't we, dear?"

"Dinner and a show," Cadence recites in a monotone.

"So toddle along without a fuss, won't you darling?"

I can't help it. I really can't. The air stirs, tugging at sleeves and hems, tossing Maryam's glamorous curls and ruffling Cadence's ragged locks. But that is as far as it goes, my fury good for little more than a light disturbance.

Maryam cocks her head. "Refreshing. I'll allow it this once. Now, off you go."

And I do, before I can damn Liwan and the other prisoners to an earlier death than they've already been slated for. I storm back to the depths of the Underground and rein in my frustration just enough to call a council of war.

As Ange said: so much to do. And so little time left.

24

ABANDONED

FIVE DAYS. THAT'S how long my city has left.

Ravel thinks the barrier will hold that long, maybe a little longer, if Cadence keeps up the same pace. But she and Maryam aren't the only ones we have to worry about. Ravel left his little flock of refugees in Nine Peaks to bring me a warning: the council has finally decided to treat our situation as the threat it is—by wiping out the city before the Mara can be unleashed on the world.

"Can they do that? What happened to 'we're not warriors' and 'we don't have an army?' They won't risk people on a rescue mission, but they're fine with helping out when it comes to a massacre?" I'm not yelling—but only by the barest margin.

Fluffy shivers. Ash leans away, wincing. Ravel rubs his forehead.

"It's bad timing as much as anything," Ash says. "They've found some way to channel natural forces from a safe distance. Maximum damage with zero exposure, or so the elders seem to think. They have to protect Nine Peaks either way, so why not send the fires here instead?"

I picture flames leaping from a cargo trailer as faceless soldiers drive through the mountains, and shake my head. "It doesn't make sense. How can they attack us from so far away? For that matter, if the elders can pull off something of this scale, how are there any monsters left?"

"Does it matter?" Ravel says. "We're on a deadline. Let's get to it already."

"Even if you can smuggle a few more refugees out before the attack, even if you could get hundreds clear, it's only a matter of time before the Mara—" I start, and then we're off again on another round of your-plan-is-worse-than-my-plan.

Ravel refuses to accept that I can't leave. He claims to have come all this way just to warn me of danger without realizing there isn't anything I can do about it. Even if he stays lucky enough to always keep one step ahead of the enforcers patrolling every possible route out of the city, it's not like I can hitch a ride out with him. If he returned to extract more refugees in a bid to grow his support base up in Nine Peaks, that at least would make more strategic sense. I could definitely see him fighting for a seat on the council, happily undermining one of the elders to nab their spot. But he seems to understand, at least, that none of us have much of a future anywhere if the Mara get free. No point jostling for power in the meantime.

Ash is struggling with reality in a different way. If anything, his grip on it seems to be slipping. His story about the shipwreck sounds like something out of the dreamscape, courtesy of Ange's fever, no less. Underwater kingdoms and chatty sea monsters feature large. That, plus his insistence that Nine Peaks' attack involves powers far beyond any I've ever heard of our kind channelling, makes me wonder if whatever happened after his ship went down knocked a few screws loose. Or all the screws. And there's no possibility of help from an army of dreamwalkers—he never even set foot on the island.

Which means it's all up to me now—not that I have any idea what to do. If the Mara are unleashed on the world, everyone dies. If the barrier goes down, the Mara will be unleashed.

When will the barrier be sufficiently damaged for the Mara to escape? Unclear. Ravel estimates a week. Since he seems to have some uncanny affinity with the filthy thing, let's go with that.

So I have maybe a week to stop Maryam and Cadence. But—bonus problem—they seem to be planning something big for tomorrow. Sounds like a mass sacrifice of prisoners, including Liwan, but why now? Is Maryam doing it to mess with me or to manipulate her people in Refuge somehow? Is she simply trying to be more efficient in feeding the Mara, or is she scheming something more?

Meanwhile, Nine Peaks is planning something big in five days, according to Ravel. Some kind of attack they think will wipe out the city. Something to do with fire . . .

Which, theoretically, could be an improvement on letting everyone get slowly eaten by the Mara, except that both Ash and Ravel think that Nine Peaks' attack runs the risk of destroying the barrier, too. And now we're back to everyone dying horribly in the very near future.

I'm tempted to get someone to knock Haynfyv out so I can lay it all out for him and see if my chief strategist can come up with some kind of useful plan. But the inspector has been locked in another room to keep him from wandering back to Refuge, and Ravel and Ash are fully engaged in picking apart each other's admittedly impractical schemes.

Which, unexpectedly, gives me an idea. An amazing, brilliant idea that will save everyone—for approximately two days, at least. Maybe longer if I play it right.

"SURE, I'M IN." Ravel radiates pleasure at being the central character in this little charade.

Ash isn't pouting, exactly, but he doesn't like my plan one bit. "You're not the best liar, C. And even if you can convince Maryam you've switched sides, I really don't think she can help you."

"That's what I need Ravel for," I repeat. Again.

I wouldn't bother trying so hard to convince him, except I really need him to sit tight and stay out of the way for this to work. All this persuading and manipulating is exhausting—I don't know how Ravel does it.

Ravel preens. Ash rolls his eyes.

I sigh. "Ravel needs to be there to stall her long enough to listen and to corroborate my story. Otherwise, she'll just start feeding people to the Mara to shut me up before I can explain."

"I don't see why I can't—" Ash starts.

"You would just be one more hostage to use against me." I'm proud of how well I keep the sick, wobbly feeling that idea sets off out of my voice. "Ravel might be the only person she *wouldn't* sacrifice on a whim."

"Mommy dearest," Ravel agrees wryly, ignoring that "might." Along with Maryam's history of abuse and neglect. Not to mention her refusal to acknowledge him as a son.

Lily's presence turns out to be useful—she is not about to let Ash go off on adventures without her, and he's not about to bring her into the monsters' den. So Ravel sets off alone to save the world.

Well, not quite. But if he can help me persuade Maryam that Nine Peaks' betrayal has forced me to her side, united against a common enemy whose attack might just be turned back by a stronger barrier, there is a chance I'll be able to buy us all a little more time.

Or that was the plan. But although, as Ash pointed out, I am not a terribly accomplished liar, Ravel is.

"I'm back." He lounges against the doorframe, two fingers raised in a careless salute, ankles crossed, both singsong tone and insouciant stance calculated for maximum irritation.

One of Maryam's eyebrows arches in mirror image of his. "Oh? Had you gone?"

Cadence rearranges her skirts as if acknowledging his presence is entirely beneath her.

Ravel's lips stretch in a brief, humourless smile. "I see you missed me, mother dearest."

The temperature in the room plummets, but all Maryam offers in return is a slow blink.

"I assume you're here, too," Cadence says to me, examining her nails. "You do realize, even if he's speaking on your behalf, the same terms will apply?"

I have rehearsed what I want to say next, trimming and shuffling the order of the words to get the highest impact bits out before they can drag someone in to feed to the Mara.

But before I can get a word out, Ravel says, "Flame isn't here today, dead girl."

He strolls up to Cadence's throne-like chair and braces one hand against its tall back, leaning in, almost nose-to-nose with her. She refuses to flinch. Maryam watches without expression. What is he—?

He inhales and wrinkles his nose. "Do you smell something? Smells like . . ."

Cadence's eyes widen, her own nostrils flaring as if checking for the odour of decay. It's almost endearing how good he is at getting to her.

Ravel pulls back, fanning himself leisurely. He turns to Maryam. "It's okay. You don't have to expose your soft side in front of the help. I know you love me. Why else would I go to such lengths to infiltrate the enemy camp for you?"

Another slow basilisk blink.

Ravel pulls an exaggerated grimace. "Oh no, you didn't think I had gone and deserted you? Oh dear, how embarrassing."

"Are you done yet?" Cadence snaps, apparently, recovered enough to bristle at being ignored. "You can skip the games. I've already told her everything."

"I'm sure you thought you did, dead girl," he says without taking his eyes off Maryam. "But mother dearest knows me better. She knows I would never desert her."

Maryam extends a hand, chains and bangles chiming. He leans over it in a mannerly kiss. She slaps him.

His knuckles whiten. "Or perhaps she knows me best of all. Knows I'm a survivor." He levels a white-rimmed stare at her. Smiles, all teeth. "Knows I will do whatever it takes to win."

Maryam's laugh is low and rich with scorn. "Perhaps. But I rule here, and you waste my time with childish games."

He bows. "If my lady mother wishes brevity, she shall have it. As I have said, I infiltrated the enemy's stronghold, a torturous journey of many—" he breaks off with a cough at the warning lift of her finger. "Ah. Well. The enemy is distant but strong, as you had feared. But not so distant that they haven't heard of the Mayor of the Towers of Refuge, nor so strong that they do not fear her. They intend to attack first, to pre-empt the threat before Your Worship can bring their stronghold under your gracious rule."

His antics would be more amusing if I could see where he's going with this. He was supposed to be the mouthpiece, nothing more. His travels were proof my story was true, not part of some long con.

Right?

"Her people cannot attack," Maryam says evenly, flicking a glance at Cadence, who nods. "Their representative foolishly bargained away that right for her freedom. Even if they had not, my enforcers will take them the moment they cross over, their powers weak and useless."

"Their power is unfortunately very much greater than my lady mother has anticipated. They have no need to send soldiers to be captured. Instead, they send fire from the mountains to shake the very foundations of our city."

What is he doing? He was supposed to hold the nature of the attack in reserve, a bargaining chip against the lives of Liwan and the other prisoners.

"Impossible," Cadence scoffs. "You forget I know those old fogeys. They can do no such thing."

"Can't they?" Ravel says, holding Maryam's gaze.

She doesn't respond to his challenge, or Cadence's. Her gaze drifts to the ceiling, vacantly canted toward nothing of interest that I can make out.

Ravel looks momentarily disconcerted. Whatever it is he has been planning, it's spinning off course by the second, and I can't even yell at him about it with Cadence listening in.

My frustration stirs the air. Maryam's focus snaps back to this infuriating boy she has created.

"It is possible. What proof do you bring me?"

He shrugs. "You'll have to take my word for it."

Cadence snorts. "Dream on."

Maryam simply holds his gaze. "And?"

He spreads his hands. "And I hear dead girl has been chipping away at the only thing that protects us from our enemies, so I thought I better come home and help shore up the walls, so to speak."

"I am not—" Cadence starts.

"Is that all?" Maryam interrupts. "You heard about a plan to attack us and came back to help defend your home? This is the story you wish me to believe?"

"Would I betray my darling flame for anything less than the utter destruction of everything I have built and stand to inherit?"

And even now, I'm not sure if he is really doing this, really turning on me and throwing his lot in with her, or if he thinks this absolute mess of an improvised audience will actually turn out better than the version we rehearsed.

"He's lying." Cadence hops out of her chair to jab a finger into his chest. "She's here. I know she is. I don't know what game you're playing, Cole, but it's not going to work. I won't let you screw things up. Not now. Not ever."

Ravel grabs her wrist with one hand, her chin with another, and squeezes until she yelps. "You took her away from me, dead girl. Made her little more than a memory. She's gone, and all that's left is trash without the wits to know it's rotting. So I'm telling you: go rot quietly in the corner and let the adults fix the mess you've made, hmm?" He shoves her, turns, doesn't even flinch when she hits his back with impotent rage.

"Sit down," Maryam says. "I have indulged the both of you enough for today. We have work to do."

"No," says Ravel.

"No?"

"You will not treat me like this child. You will not dismiss or ignore. You will take my warnings seriously, and what's more, you'll follow my lead. This is my time now."

25

USURPED

I GASP. CADENCE'S jaw drops. Maryam cocks her head, eyes narrowing.

"I see. You wish to give your poor old . . ." she omits the word *mother* with a faint smile. "Well. You propose to give me a break in my decrepitude to take my mantle upon yourself, is that it? Leave me to enjoy my twilight years without the relentless burden of responsibility?"

She stands, gesturing to the chair she just vacated. "By all means, then: show me how you lead. You will sit in my place, rule in my stead. You will keep this child in line, choose the sacrifices and see the Mara fed, monitor the condition of the dome and turn back any attack. What, did you think I would recoil in horror? That I would refuse any respite extended me?"

Ravel offers her his arm. When she takes it, he ushers her to Cadence's chair and waits until she is seated before arranging himself on the foremost throne.

"I understand you have your uses," he says to Cadence. "You may stand in the corner until you're needed."

She sputters, looking to Maryam for support that fails to come.

And still, I hold back. Has he betrayed me just as she did, or is it all a trick? Ravel grew up under Maryam's thumb, knows her better than anyone. He must have seen this would be the best way to gain control of the situation.

He hasn't shredded our plan, merely tweaked the details. He's going to pull it off after all, going to save Liwan and the other prisoners slated to die today, and then the barrier, and then, maybe, just maybe, the world.

If I'm a little jealous, a little irritated at having my role in this triumph erased, that's just the cost of using others to get the job done.

Ravel goes about taking up the reins of power and reorienting Maryam's domain around himself. His manipulation is masterly, his orders hardly distinguishable from the mayor's own at the first. Tedious to watch, but I just have to remind myself how delightful it will be to have a front-row seat to Maryam's face when his deception finally comes to light.

Really, this is a win for me. Even as little more than a ghost, powerless to affect the waking world, look what I've accomplished, the forces I have brought to bear, the last-minute rescue I've orchestrated—

"Dream for us," Ravel says with unwavering confidence, his hand firmly planted on Liwan's sweating forehead.

Liwan, who Ravel was only supposed to have summoned to be sure he was still alive. Liwan, who is little more than a child. We're meant to be protecting him. Even Ravel, veteran of many ceremonial sacrifices before he mended his ways, knows better than to risk . . . than to risk—

The ritual completes. The monsters come. The prisoner falls.

One more hollow husk to join the growing heap, Cadence and Ravel working side by side through the ranks of the prisoners as the Mara feast on the lives of innocents offered up to sate their monstrous hunger.

Roaring fills my head, drowning out stammering protests, pleas for forgiveness, attempts to keep count (*four dead, five*) and dawning realization that I had never even bothered to learn all their names (*six dead and Liwan makes seven*). I knew better than to trust him. (*Nine dead and Liwan, ten*) I should have fought from the start, should have tried to reach Cadence, at least, even if my words never made it to Maryam's ears.

But the press of the gorging Mara crowds me away from the carnage. I have no choice but to swallow the rage, the betrayal, choking on bitterness. Gagging on my own helplessness.

I have to tell Ash what happened, *(dead, so many dead and gone and—)* to warn him that Ravel has betrayed us, could send enforcers after us at any time. He will need to—he is burning through prisoners at an alarming rate. The Mara only grow hungrier. Today's orgy of death sets a new baseline for tomorrow.

But exhaustion drags at whatever is left of me, slowing my progress, dulling my thoughts. Helping Ange heal earlier was draining. Everything since has just been burning through energy I didn't have to begin with.

Maybe Ash could feel it, from all the way in his hidden far corner of Under, because before I can make my way to him, he reaches out and pulls me to the other side.

⁕

"THERE'S NO TIME. My words slur with fatigue, even under the crisp starlight and sudden snap of night air.

"Shh. Everyone is safe for now. Just rest." He dials the light down to a cool dimness, muting the edges of the landscape until everything is as soft and blurry as I feel.

"Liar."

"Sleep," he says, though he knows I can't, or at least I shouldn't.

Everyone is not safe. Everyone is dead, or about to die, and I've wasted so much time trying every possible way to save them without getting my own hands dirty . . .

But exhaustion takes over, and fear and regret subside into muttering darkness.

⁕

TIME WITHOUT SPACE.

Pathways, branching, splitting, curling in on themselves . . .

Not paths—threads, tangling. I need to do something, to go somewhere.

I don't exist. Only the threads exist.

Ash is Ash. Cole is Cole. Ange is Ange . . .

Flames, rising like a tide, crashing over everything, scorching—

Not scorching. Pleasantly warm. The light is bright without burning. Soft, dry ground beneath me with ticking strands of tall grasses and the fluttering edges of exotically scented wildflowers kissing my skin. I sit up, shaking off the nightmarish vision.

Ash walks toward me, bringing with him the sharp tang of sea air and a rocky cliff overlooking the waves to replace the meadow. "Sleep well?"

"Ravel betrayed us." My voice is flat, my eyes dry. I am stone, and I will remain stone until the crushing weight of everything I cannot afford to feel, every mistake I could not afford to make, is gone.

"Did he?"

"He was on Maryam's side all along. You have to warn everyone before—"

"We changed locations as soon as he left, Cole. We're being careful, staying hidden. I won't say it's safe—nowhere is safe, not now—but we're not taking stupid risks, either."

I pace out over the open air, ignoring the drop from rugged heights to the sea below, and back, in no mood to bother with make-believe physics. "I should have known. I should have—"

Should have what? Taken Ash along, only to be captured and fed to the monsters instead? Gone alone, leaving the traitor with Lily and Amy and all the other helpless fools who followed him back into this deathtrap of a city?

What about the fools who followed me to their deaths? Does that make me as much a traitor as Ravel? Or is it mere incompetence that twists every single one of my plans off course?

"Why did you come back?" I ask Ash, still pacing. "You survive a shipwreck, and the first thing you do is throw yourself back into danger?"

"What do you want to hear?"

I freeze, one foot on the cliff, one off.

"If I told you I did it for love, what face would you make?" he says in that same strangled tone. "If I told you I couldn't bear to stay away, that if the world's ending, I might as well spend what's left of it with you, what would you say? No, don't look like that. Don't—"

He steps off the edge of the cliff after me, chasing me through the sky, and then, when I drop, beneath the waves. "Would you just stop running? Why is this so hard for you to accept?"

I cover my ears, eyes streaming, chest burning even though I know—I *know*—it's not the lack of oxygen, or the salt in the illusory water. I don't have any answers for him. I don't know how to even begin to describe the endless gulf between what I want and fear, between what he offers and what I can accept. "I'm not her," I finally choke out.

"You think I don't know that? I never asked you to be. Either you're trying to insult me or you're running out of excuses. Which is it, Cole?"

I shake my head. I can't let him distract me.

"She was more fun."

I stop.

"Is that what you wanted to hear? That Cadence was stronger, brighter, prettier, more full of life and power and all that's good in the world? Fine. She was a paragon of virtue, the perfect being. She's also a child, Cole. She's a memory of days spent under an endless sun and the watchful eye of parents, of naptimes and sweets and harmless mischief and dreams of a boundless future. She is not you."

My hands lower, my body swaying with the current. "But she—I'm not—"

"Stop telling me what you aren't! You think I can't see you? Can't think for myself? Just because I haven't known you forever doesn't mean I don't know you."

I shudder. He sounds so certain. He still doesn't understand. "You're wrong. You haven't seen—"

"Haven't seen what? That you're a mess? That you won't stop punishing yourself? That you've done things you're ashamed of, and you're not sure you can stop? That you're broken and powerless and lying to yourself that there's any chance left to be anything but a failure? Is that what I haven't seen?"

I can't swallow past the lump in my throat, my breath shallow and ragged, barely stirring the stately dance of particles in the water that surrounds us. An instant later, the rubbery fronds of a kelp forest spring up from the ocean floor.

"Stop hiding!" Ash roars. His breath is a little ragged too.

Some small part of my mind, the part that isn't drowning in irrational panic, worries about him, about what I've put him through.

His voice softens. "I don't need to see you to know you, Cole. You've made mistakes. Done things you're not proud of, and honestly, I'm not that happy about all of it either. You're stubborn to the point of insanity when it comes to the things that matter to you. You try way too hard. You give everything and do whatever it takes to save the people you care about, and that scares the shit out of me . . .

"But it's also one of the things I love about you. You see exactly how bad things could get, but you don't stop trying to make them better. You're not just angry—you're motivated. You've suffered more than most, but you keep getting back up. And maybe you've been trying so hard to be and do what you think you're supposed to that you don't know how to just *be*. But I see you, Cole. I've always seen you—just you. You're more that you realize. And I'm not going anywhere."

I shrink into the kelp bed, drawing the fronds close for cover. "Why? Why won't you just leave me alone?"

"You don't want to be alone," he says. "You just don't want to be scared anymore. But we can learn how to let go of the lies we've been taught. Even if the whole world is crashing down around us, we can choose a better way for as long as we have left."

That 'we' cries out with the parts of his story I'd forgotten. The loss of his parents—he'd hoped to find them still living, before his ship went down. The oppressive expectations of the overbearing grandfather who raised him, who sent his mom and dad to their exile, or death. Dead like Liwan and all the other kids I failed . . .

Trying hard isn't enough, no matter what Ash says. I unclench my grip on the kelp fronds, letting them flutter off on the current, along with all the possibilities for a future I don't dare hold onto. "Enough. You're right—the whole world is crashing down. I need you to stay focused."

There's a beat of tension, an extra weight to the water. Then it's gone. "I—I know. Sorry. I wasn't trying to pressure you. I just—here." He shoots in front of me, twisting one wrist, palm up, fingers curled to hold—nothing. He follows my stare, blinks, and shakes his head. "Hold on—"

The waters drain away, the seabed turning to rolling dunes, dry as far as the eye can see, except for a glistening orb slowly spinning on Ash's upturned palm.

"What is that?" I step closer, fascinated by the flickering way light shifts and glistens off particles suspended in the water. I turn my palm up and summon water to it, but the effect is lacklustre, little more than a wet, transparent ball. "How are you doing that?"

Fluffy winds its way up my arm and pokes a tendril through the bubble of liquid in my hand. It bursts, splashing into the sand. Ash holds his out to Fluffy instead.

"It's for you."

"You're giving the treespawn its own fishbowl?"

"Not for the forest, for you, C. The waters sent it. Sent me with it."

"The waters." Maybe he needs to get some sleep, too? But there's something about the shimmering thing he extends toward me, something almost alive. I reach for it despite myself—and he draws back. "I thought you said it was for me?"

"It is. Or I think it is. Just . . . be careful. The forest, I know. It's slow, steady. The waters aren't. I didn't think I'd make it back to you. I don't know why they sent this or what'll happen if you—"

I grab it from him, letting Fluffy hang on or drop as it likes. The treespawn anchors my dreamscape to the forest outside Nine Peaks—maybe to all the forests. If the ocean's gift works the same way, who knows what I'll be able to do now?

But nothing happens. That cool, smooth surface is inert. I squeeze, prod, bring it up to my face to peer into its depths. No response.

I glare at Ash.

He shrugs. "Okay, so maybe it's harmless. Pretty, though, right?"

I don't need pretty. I need power. "How's a floating puddle supposed to help me stop Maryam?"

"Uh, not sure that's what it's meant for."

I chuck the orb into the distance. "Then I don't need it."

He jogs after it. I don't bother staying to watch him hunt among the dunes. I'm done watching other people do the work. That way leads only to disaster—death, or betrayal, or both.

I need to find a way to fight back for real. If whatever power or magic I once held was Cadence's all along, fine. If the trees and the waters can't or won't help me, so be it. I just need to find something of my own. And I think I know where to look.

Only, Ange isn't sleeping anymore.

"Figures," I grumble. "*Now* you're up and about?"

Her fingers dig into the sheets. "Cole?"

"You can hear me?"

She frowns. "Where are you?"

"No time for that. Go to sleep. I need to test a theory."

She shakes her head but obediently rearranges the bedding and folds herself down under it.

"Can't you hurry up? This is taking too long."

She cracks an eyelid. "You try falling asleep on command. Especially after sleeping for like three days straight. Why do I have to do this, anyway?"

Maybe I can bore her to sleep? "You were sick. I helped you get better. Me. Alone. Well, mostly alone. Ash was there, but he didn't heal you, I did. I found the threads again, fixed them. But I don't exist on this side of reality, not really. I can't see or feel the threads unless I'm in the dreamscape. Deep in. I think. I don't really know. I need to try again."

Ange sits up slowly. "I'd rather not have you rummaging around inside my unconscious brain if you don't mind."

I consider this very reasonable perspective. "Fair. Counterpoint: playing test subject might help me stop the Mara from devouring the world. Also, not to nitpick, but you would be dead right now if it weren't for me, so you kind of owe me."

Am I being pushy and inconsiderate? Yes. Am I going to apologize for my rudeness? Who has the time? I am stone, and stones don't get embarrassed.

"What are you trying to do?" Ash says, stretching and stifling a yawn as he returns to his body.

"Can you take me back there? To her threads? I'm going either way."

Ange waves. "Still awake over here, by the way."

Ash points. "She says she's still awake, so you're not going anywhere for the moment. Why don't you try explaining what it is you're hoping to do?"

"Why? So I can get more people involved, get betrayed or get them killed? Nah. I'm good."

He blinks. "Cole, right?"

"Who else would it be?"

"What happened to you?"

"Try to keep up, sparkles. Failure. Betrayal. Hard deadline rushing up to smack us in the face. Ring any bells?" I've never been this mean in my life. Or un-life. It's kind of freeing, not needing anyone on your side.

Do I feel bad about alienating my friends for their own good? Maybe a little. But if there's one thing I know how to do, it's burying squishy, useless feelings to get the job done. I am stone. I will not crack.

Fluffy nudges me worriedly. I nudge back, hard. "Mind yourself, treespawn."

"Treespawn?" Ange says. "Also, who broke the kid?"

"You know you don't have to do this alone, right, C?" Ash says. When I don't answer, he scratches his head, making his tangled hair stand up in clumps. "Look, at least take this."

He turns his palm up. The orb is there, suddenly, glistening and casting ripples of light across the room. Ange sucks in a breath. I don't blame her. It was mesmerizing in the dreamscape. It's miraculous here.

I reach for it, without hands, and suddenly Ash's are empty. The light is gone, the sea's gift vanishing in an instant, at least from their point of view. From mine, it rocks up against Fluffy and burbles contentedly, coming to life and following me around with the same mysterious ease the forest's gift exhibits.

Disappointingly, I don't feel a sudden surge of power, and threads don't materialize out of thin air. Not that I was expecting any such thing. It's not like the ocean was going to magically give me my, well, magic back. But it would've been nice.

In the waking world, Ash starts bringing Ange up to speed on what she's missed, so there goes any chance of her falling asleep in the immediate future. Guess I'll just have to find someone else to practice on.

Up in Refuge, drones are busy carting away the bodies from the monsters' feast. The remains will probably be fed to the same insect masses that will eventually be processed into ingredients for Noosh. Thankfully, in my current form, I have no stomach to turn.

The Mara are quiet for now. Digesting, maybe. Ravel and Cadence are yawning through Maryam's slate of official audiences for the day, all the excitement of mass slaughter apparently over and done with. What would happen if I could get inside their heads and tangle some threads on purpose? Or Maryam's, for that matter? There's a thought—

But that takes me right back to where I was, trying to manipulate others into doing everything for me. It just doesn't work out. It's too easy to miss something, to send them in the wrong direction. I can't afford to wallow in circles repeating past mistakes. I need to focus on what I can do.

And apparently, what I can do is heal. Which means I need to find someone broken.

Yesterday, there were dozens of options. But with the prisoners' ranks so dramatically thinned, today there are only two who fit the bill. Both are women, neither young nor exceptionally old. One has the greyish undertone of a former Refuge drone, Noosh leaching the warmth from her flesh, but her flaking paint and torn costume point toward recent time spent in Freedom. The other looks older, skin etched by the harsh fog of the streets. Both must have fought capture; they're bruised and broken and feverish.

I choose the dancer first, diving headfirst into the chaos of her fading mind. Ash isn't here this time to help me build an island of serenity inside the madness. Good. I don't want to waste time finding my balance when what I really need is to immerse myself in the overwhelming otherness and fight my way through to that hidden inner place.

But Ange was Ange, and this woman? I don't know her, can't locate the core of who she is in the midst of her illness, can't even being to know where to look, or how . . .

Fluffy pokes me, grumbling. The other one—Squishy, let's say—gives me a little slap, too. I look down to see them huddled together, forming a small, perfect bubble of clarity. They jostle and nudge until I lean into it, letting it grow around me until the island of stillness pushes the otherness back completely.

Maybe this isn't a waste of time, but the first step in a sequence. What did Ash do? First the island, and then a bunch of teasing nonsense that I definitely don't want to repeat. But I can't stop it from unspooling inside my head. The memory clicks forward without my permission. *Ash is Ash, Cole is Cole, Ange is Ange . . .*

No, that is not quite right, is it? What he really said was, "I'm me, you're you," not our names. Me. You. Them.

I repeat the lines, word for word, or as near as I can remember. But it doesn't work. He's not here with me. And this woman isn't Ange.

I don't have any idea what her name is. So really, it should go, "I'm me. You're you," and end there. Or, "I'm me. Fluffy is Fluffy. Squishy is Squishy. You're you," if I want to get really specific. But mouthing the lines does nothing but make me feel silly and useless.

It wasn't a magic spell. It was a lesson. Me. You. Separate. This is 'me'—the part that is contained, the part I hold together, that holds me together.

That is 'you'—the part that is other, that is not me, that stands apart or, in the case of the dreamer, that surrounds that which is me.

I hold my hand up to the curve of the bubble and let my island of stillness, of *me*-ness, dissolve. I let the other surround me, immerse myself in the feverish remains of the woman I am trying to save, reach for the core—

—and step onto an obsidian sea reflecting a ravelling tapestry of living threads.

I don't recognize these fragments of memory the way I did some of Ange's, don't resonate with these dreams and longings and fears the way I did hers. This woman is familiar only in her humanity, in our shared experiences of Refuge, of Freedom.

It's easier, in some ways. I don't feel the same guilt at exposing her deepest self, don't cringe from the intimacy of holding the fabric of a stranger in my hands. But the difference comes in the re-weaving. I hesitate, less sure of which threads to twine, clumsily grabbing at whatever's nearest, artlessly stuffing loose cords wherever they might fit, knotting them together recklessly.

I will heal this woman because that is what I set out to do. Not out of a need to restore her individually, but out of a general sense that healing is, on the balance, better than not healing, and more importantly, is something I can do.

The result is messy, but it'll hold. When I crash back through that mirrored surface into the stranger's dreamscape, she's huddled in the corner of a dark room, arms clasped around her knees, shoulders hunched to protect her head.

I hesitate. "What's your name?"

She peers out at me, wary. "What did you do to me? Who are you?" Then her shoulders draw back, her grip relaxing. "You're her, aren't you? Victoire of Freedom. Did you kill the monsters again?"

I stumble back out of her dreams. I had forgotten what this felt like. It's been so long since I lost that power, but for a brief moment, I'd been a hero. The dancers' gazes had followed me in amazement and gratitude. Underfolk had sought me out, finding excuses to visit, in awe of my power, my ability to protect them. Not Cadence, a talented child with more power than she knew what to do with. Not Victoire, as the woman had named me, not Ravel's preening puppet, a creature of sensation without thought. Not Ravel himself, or Ange, or Ash, or Maryam, even. *Me.* I was the one they looked to.

And now I am again.

This is what I'm meant to be doing. This is why I wanted that magic in the first place. I can help people, save them. Beat back the monsters. Make a place for myself.

Or not even that, really. It is a chance that I could just . . . just have a reason to be. To keep being more than just another broken-down ghost haunting the halls of someone else's nightmare . . .

The thrill of discovery ebbs in another wave of exhaustion, but I don't want to rest, can't afford to. High above, Cadence is arguing with Ravel about what needs to happen with the barrier. Far below, Haynfyv fires question after question at Ange while Ash tries to keep Lily from escorting a parade of new friends in to meet her hero.

Far, far away, Nine Peaks will be readying an attack that could ignite the end of the world if I don't find a way to turn it back.

Luckily, I think I might just be able to do something about that.

26

UNRAVELLING

I MAKE IT through two more healings before collapsing into my own dreamscape to recover. Ash finds me there.

I refuse to tell him what I've been up to. He refuses to be upset about it—or to leave.

He could. He could even take one person across with him. What he can't do is come back, not in a hurry, not when the barrier does so much damage to dreamwalkers.

But even for Lily's sake, he won't be persuaded to go. So I leave him behind and hunt down more broken people to set to rights, doing my best to ignore how the ones I've just healed are being lined up for sacrifice at this very moment.

I don't watch it happen—the press of the Mara makes that nearly impossible, even if I wanted to, which I very much don't. But people keep getting carted away from the prison dorms and sickrooms, and the crowd of ghosts at the edge of realities thickens, an ever-growing number of familiar faces grimacing and shrieking and snapping at me as I struggle to pass, already worn down from pushing through yet one more healing than I really should have.

"I think it's time to talk about Cadence," Ash says. "You haven't tried to—you know—yet, have you?"

I look away from Cass's staring eyes and Suzie's withered ones, drawing back from the edge, putting off pressing through the ranks of the dead and returning to the waking world with regret and relief both. "It's her body, Ash. Let her die in it."

He hesitates, scanning my face. Her face, because I don't have anything better to imagine myself as than the girl I used to be. "How can you be so sure, C? When you woke up the first time in Refuge, Cady was the ghost. And neither of you are dead—"

"Yet," I interrupt.

He frowns. "Fine. Neither of you are dead *yet*—"

"That you know of."

"Cole. You're not dead. Cady's not dead. Let's try to agree on that much, at least. That doesn't necessarily mean you're alive, either. What if it's not even a 'life' thing, it's something else entirely?"

I press at a growing ache in my forehead. "I don't have time for word games. Spit it out."

"What if Cadence isn't Cadence? Or you're not you? What if you're Cadence? Or—or the reverse—"

"Not helping."

He sighs and scrubs a hand through his hair, rolling his eyes up at me in an expression that is probably meant to be exactly as distracting as it is. "No one has heard of anything like you two before. We're dreamwalkers—ghosts aren't exactly a foreign concept. But a person can't be living and ghost at the same time. So what if one of you is something . . . else?"

That gets my attention. "Like what? You think I'm a monster masquerading as a ghost now?"

"Or Cadence is—or at least, she could be. I don't know; that's the point. And neither do you. Maybe she's an embodied memory, some kind of fragment of who you used to be. Maybe she's a new type of monster, or the Mara have gotten a whole lot more creative."

"You keep saying "Cadence, Cadence," like it couldn't just as well be me that's the freak. At least she remembers life before Refuge. What if I'm a—a clone, or something? Artificially produced, like Ravel."

"If you were a clone, wouldn't there be two bodies instead of just one between the two of you? And you want to know why I'm talking to you right now instead of Cady? Easy: which one of you is trying to unleash the monsters, C? Which one of you is wearing yourself into oblivion trying to heal people?"

"But that's—she's—"

"Cole, come on, don't—"

I shoulder through my dead and lunge for the other side of reality. I can't deal with this right now. He just—he doesn't understand. Cadence is a pest, but she's *my* pest. Working on the side of evil doesn't change that. Maybe it would if she really meant it, but she's just . . . stuck in the past.

Like a ghost. Or a fragment. Or—or a monster playing at being a ghost.

But she's *Cadence.* It's not just the memories of the past; it's the way she is. And the way I am. I'm nothing like that child everyone remembers, fierce, and strong, and full of mischief and schemes . . .

Ash is trying to turn me against her. He probably believes it's the right thing to do, making it easier for me to end her. He trying to sacrifice his childhood friend for the sake of the world and use me as the weapon to do it. His whole big confession under the sea was probably calculated to begin with . . .

Except I'm not playing along. I can't take back a body that was never mine to begin with, especially not if doing so could destroy Cadence. I won't. She's just a kid. She doesn't understand what she's doing. She doesn't really mean to hurt us. And she's *mine.* I don't want her back in my head, no way, but I can't imagine a world where she's not there, somewhere.

My skill at healing people from the inside out is growing. Maybe, just maybe, there's a chance I can make a future for the both of us and everyone else too.

The hours drain away like spilled Noosh, sticky-slow and queasy-making. Though every viscous second that passes weighs on me, whispering that I'm too slow, too weak, too new at all this, I am getting faster at slipping through the inner dreamscapes to that deeper reality at the heart of people, at mending the tears in the fabric of their bodies and minds. I can heal minor injuries all the way now, prisoners waking up to marvel at skin that's suddenly smooth, broken bones strong and pain-free. I can pull the dying back from the brink, far enough for them to heal if Maryam doesn't end them first.

My endurance is growing, too. I run out of prisoners in Refuge to heal and start ranging further afield for people to practice on. Ravel's betrayal has come with one unexpected advantage—he really has gotten Maryam to take a break from chipping away at that barrier. But Nine Peaks' attack will hit in two days. We need that wall stronger than ever.

I think I can do something about that.

But first, I need to try to heal a ghost.

Ravel calls out to me before I can choose a victim—or practice subject, if we're being optimistic.

"Testing. Testing. Hello? Can you hear me?" he says from over twenty floors away. "Quick as you can, flame. Not to rush you but we're a little short on time . . ."

It doesn't take long to shoot up from Under to Maryam's opulent suite. Ravel has wedged himself into a corner between his bed and the wall. He whispers his summons into a pillow again; looking so ridiculous I could almost forget this is the scum who betrayed me—all of humanity, actually, come to that—just to grab the last couple days' worth of power for himself.

Finally getting into Maryam's good graces doesn't seem to have done him much good, though. Under his richly woven and excessively ornamented uniform, his skin is pallid and dull, bruise-dark shadows underscore his golden eyes.

He raises an eyebrow and sniffs. "Rude. And after all I've done."

I should know better than to let him bait me into an argument by now. I really should. But— "After all you've done, you deserve more than a bit of exhaustion. What's wrong—mommy overworking her little man?"

His lips thin, but all he says is: "Still so untrusting, darling? You wound me."

"Not enough, apparently."

"Don't." He twists, wedging himself more comfortably in the corner. "It was the only way. You know we're almost out of time. Your plan never would have worked. Maryam has had lifetimes of manipulating those around her into dancing to her tune—and outlived generations of those who would have manipulated her if they could. She'd have seen through your story in a heartbeat, even if your little doppelganger hadn't been there to bust the scheme wide open. But me? 'Mother dearest' was all too ready to believe I'd do anything to get in her good graces, especially if it meant more power for myself. Consistency, you see, and human nature. It all fit."

"Uh huh."

"See? See? You bought the story. I impress even myself." His grin fades. "But give me a little credit, flame. I'd hardly trade less than a week's worth of power over this decaying tower for a lifetime of opportunity outside it. I don't need the mayor to hand over the key to her city when I've already started building a base outside these walls. If you won't believe that I'd be on your side because I want to, because that's always where I'll be, believe this much: playing Maryam gets me further ahead than pleasing her."

Smooth talker, as usual, I'll give him that much. But his false earnestness is less convincing than he thinks. "So you've been on the side of the good guys all along? I guess you have managed to get Maryam to back off the barrier . . ."

He nods eagerly.

"On the other hand, you completely failed to stop Liwan's execution. You and Cadence handed over those kids to the Mara in cold blood."

His eyes darken. "Cole, you have to understand—"

"Is wasting my time just another part of your plan? 'Keep the enemy occupied until she runs out of time?' Or is this just recreation for you, some quick mind games before bed to cap off another successful day?"

"You want to hate me? Fine. I had to make a tough choice, flame. It's part of being a leader. You should try it sometime."

"Oh, is the game over so soon? Don't give up now—surely there's something you can say to convince the stupid, clueless girl that—"

"You really haven't been paying attention? Why would I have bothered to come back here for—I mean, come on, Cole. You know me better than this. You know I'd—For you, I'd—"

"You're right. I do know you. I know you're a shameless, desperate loser who will never amount to anything more than a pathetic shadow of the dictator he so desperately wants to be. Maryam's right. You're not her son. You're not anything."

His soft inhale almost stops my heart. I brace against the coming onslaught.

But all he says is, "I forgive you, flame. When this is all over, I hope you'll remember that."

"Don't you dare—"

"Go see Ash, Cole. If you can spare the time from whatever it is you're up to. He needs to talk to you too before the end."

"What—"

"I have to get back to work now. There really is no time. Go see Ash." He levers himself up with a sigh and marches, head down, through all my protests and insults. Cadence isn't waiting for him, but Maryam is, smiling a small, secret smile as if she has been listening in on our bickering. Or maybe she's just pleased at the increasingly panicked reports being mumbled in the general direction of her shoes.

If Ravel's mission was to distract me and waste my time, mission accomplished. But as much as I would like to check in with Ash and see how Ange is doing, there's only a day left before Nine Peaks' attack, at most, and I still haven't tested my theory. Obviously, the barrier needs to be as strong as possible if it's going to protect us. Cadence hasn't chipped away at it in a few days, which is good. But damage has already been done. It's weakened. Not enough to let the Mara out, not yet, but even at full strength, it might not have been able to turn back the level of assault Ash claims is on its way.

In Maryam's efforts to destroy the barrier, she's made a mistake. Through Cadence, she has exposed more than she knew about the source of its power. She probably has no idea that part of Cadence's heritage, the part I seem to be able to tap into now, is not just the power to strike down monsters, but the power to heal. If I go deep enough, I can see—and manipulate—the threads of people's inner selves. It's just a guess, but if I can do that with living humans, what if I could do something about the other kind?

It's a huge stretch, but if my ghosts are ghosts indeed and not just nightmares, can I dig inside of them to restore them to wholeness—whatever that means to a ghost? And, even more of a stretch, but what about *fragments* of people? That tortured, undead mass of threads that makes up the barrier itself?

If Cadence can reach into that and rip the threads of its "life" free, can I find a way to re-weave it and restore what has been damaged? Even strengthen it beyond what it was? Maybe it's because of what I am, because of the weirdness of my existence, that I even have a chance to try this.

It's a lot of 'ifs,' but they all add up to a future I hardly dare dream of—one where maybe, and only just maybe, not only could I stop the world getting destroyed, but this city and those I care about within it will get to keep going just a little longer.

And for that tenuous promise, I'm willing to throw myself into the heart of a ghost and challenge whatever awaits me there.

They've been waiting for me all along, surrounding me, clamouring for my attention. Nightmares, perhaps, at least to me, but ghosts nonetheless.

I just have to pick one.

27

UNDEAD

IWAN HAS JOINED the crowd in the seam between realities. Black ichor drools from the edges of a twisted grin; eyes a pinprick of red in a sea of shadow. Suzie is there too; a childish form cobwebbed with wrinkles, old and young at once. But it is Cass who I reach out to in the end because I can't bring myself to touch the children, even one that only masquerades as a child, and also because if it's Cass, I will not allow myself to fail.

He died because of me. I can't let whatever is left of him be destroyed too.

The monster he has become feels solid. His flesh scorches, his grip bone-crushing, broad fingers tipped in claws. That warm grin of his has become a fanged snarl, his wide brown eyes, so soft and adoring when he gazed at Ange, have become hollow pits flickering with flame, threatening to pull me under when once they extended that steady lifeline I so needed in those early days in Freedom.

Instead of tearing away from the horror he has become, I lean into that painful embrace. I let myself be burned, torn, drowned, devoured whole, clinging to that tiny "if" of hope through the pain and the horror. If I can do this; if I'm not wrong; if there is another side to reach, a deeper reality to dive into, a true Cass to find and make whole once more . . .

The ghosts are gone. This is not the seam between worlds. This is nowhere. The tension between one gasp and the next; a flicker between thoughts. Void and greyness shot through with the barest of sparks. A slow, muddy churning.

Out of habit, or instinct, I reach for that island of stillness that I first found with my fingers buried in the rich earth of Susan's garden in Nine Peaks. The same bubble that Ash formed around us in Ange's dreamscape.

It resists my call at first, but it comes. I strain to hold the island in place, strain to balance between peace and surrender in the midst of what remains of Cass's dreamscape. That this place exists at all, that I can even be here, is a miracle of such magnitude I can hardly take it in. But I can't stop and marvel at the implications.

There is a pattern to healing. First find stillness in self. Then embrace the chaos of otherness. Finally, a sudden bursting through to that deepest level, that innermost layer. The one that may no longer exist in him. The one that I am terrified to reach because this is *Cass*, who Ange loved, and who, in hindsight, I adored, and who almost certainly blames me for setting fire to his deepest and most precious dream of a future with her.

But because this is Cass, I let my bubble of safety dissolve. I find him in the muted chaos of death almost instantly. All I have to do is look for the brilliant cord that leads back to Ange.

The obsidian ocean that underlines his deepest self is shattered, splintering cracks marring its surface. The endless expanse above is more dark than not; a bare handful of fraying threads drifting apart instead of the myriad glowing strands of the living. What is left of him can hardly even be called fabric. There's no frame to fill in; more holes than weave left to patch. And the light of what threads remain is mottled and tarnished.

I reach for the brightest cord, offering up a silent apology for whatever this meddling might bring. I imagine Cass's flesh has long since been devoured, reprocessed into nutrient slurry.

There is no healing his physical form. And strengthening whatever else is left of him could simply make the monstrous thing he has become more dangerous. But I don't hesitate in wrapping my hand around the pure light of his lingering love for Ange and reaching for the next piece of his soul.

If healing the living was draining, taking me to the very limits of my endurance, reweaving the dead is like being sucked inside out and liquefied alive. And, because it is Cass, every shred of memory and hope and longing and desire I catch hold of is a fresh stab of guilt.

But it's also a gift.

I knew him for such a short time. Back then, I was so caught up by my own fear and confusion and anger that he and Ange had barely registered. In Freedom, everything was strange and new and overwhelming at first.

Now, glimpses into his past and dreams for the future round out those faded impressions, adding depth and dimension. I had made him into a saint in my imagination, a martyr to the ongoing saga of 'Cole's Quest for Power and Revenge.' He wasn't, quite. He had frustrations and resentments and regrets and failures. But his fears were more for others than for himself, and he gave his life more gladly than not.

I keep those fears and failures, using them to brace up the love and the devotion, turning the fraying ends of thread back into a fine, tight woven patch of fabric drifting in the dark night. The effort to gather and bind the fragments of what's left proves beyond me.

I lose myself for a time, opening eyes I don't remember closing to see the fabric fraying once more; picking myself up off the cruel edges of the cracked sea to gather his loosened threads back into a rough mat and begin again, finding yet one more unexpected thread in my hands each time I think I've finished. But, finally, beyond pain, beyond exhaustion, I run bloodied fingers along a patch of knotted and spliced-together fabric and nothing more comes loose in my hands.

I drop, then, the black glass shattering beneath me, the once bland void of Cass's dreamscape now sparking with unexpected light. But I can't stay, can't linger too long or I may never leave . . .

And he holds out a hand, draws me into a crowd of ghosts, and gives me a little push through to the other side. Cass smiles, teeth even, eyes clear; whole and human. He waves and steps back into the crowded band of the lost that linger in the void between sleep and waking.

I did it.

I—well, I probably didn't save him, exactly, but I restored his ghost to some semblance of what he once was. And if I did it once, I can do it again. And again. Not just for the haunted horde surrounding the dreamscape, but for the band of death that circles us all in the waking world as well.

I might just have a shot at saving the world after all—if I can only find the energy.

Satisfied, helpless, I rest.

⁕

"WHAT DID YOU do?"

Ash shakes me. I yawn in his face.

"You don't look so good, C."

It takes both arms and some rocking, but in the end, I manage to stagger to my feet without his help. "'M fine."

"You're practically transparent."

I take a closer look at my hands, at the way the scenery bleeds through at the edges, and shrug. Crystal is still a type of stone. There are worse things to be. "Neat?"

"It's not a good thing. Whatever you're doing, stop it."

I busy myself brushing bits of gravel and grit off. I must've unconsciously summoned an echo of Refuge's rooftop again.

Ash flicks a breeze around me to speed things up. "Ravel said he talked to you."

"Since when are you and Ravel chatty?"

"Since he started smuggling people to safety? He tried to tell you he was on our side."

Unlikely. "That liar is on no one's side but his own."

"Look, if you'd just take a moment to come see—"

"And waste what little time we have left?"

He runs a hand through his hair, making it stick up in clumps. "Or you could just trust me when I say *he's helping us.*"

"It doesn't really matter, not if I can't do something about that barrier. Which is what I should be doing. Right now. So listen to me or don't. Trust slimy Ravel or don't." I hold up a hand in the face of his objections. "On the balance, I really don't want any of you to die, but stopping you from committing suicide by idiocy is not my first priority right now."

I make for the ghosts. If Cass is there, I can show him to Ash in passing. One glance will be more convincing that any amount of argument.

On second thought, better not. Don't want news getting back to his new best buddy Ravel.

But Cass isn't waiting among the ghosts between worlds—and Ash yanks me back before I can call out to him anyway.

"Just listen for a minute," he says, tightening his grip. "Ravel is only posing as a traitor so he can smuggle people past the enforcers. I know it looked like he betrayed you, and yeah, people died. I'm sorry about that, Cole, I really am. He is too. But we're working like crazy to make it all worthwhile.

"Ange has been rounding up people across Under. Haynfyv is working with Amy to get messages to the ones in Refuge who are ready to go. Lily's even helping Sam scout for stragglers on the streets and guide them to temporary shelters. Ravel has been spending every night ferrying people across until he can barely stand.

"We're talking about dozens of people safe and free because of him, C. Hundreds, with your help. We can't afford to slow Ravel down with the sick and wounded, but if you can heal them enough so they can walk and he doesn't have to carry them—"

I am stone. I will not be swayed. "And then what? You want me to spend all that energy getting everyone all nice and healthy so the Mara have more fun hunting them down after they break free? I'm done getting other people tangled up in this, Ash. Do what you want. Just stay out of my way. I have to go."

I leave him standing there, stammering a protest. I know I sounded harsh, but it was for his own good. I hope he gets through this in one piece; I really do. I hope Ravel is actually getting people to safety, however tenuous and temporary it might be. I hope he can continue even after I heal the barrier. If I can stop Nine Peaks' attack and Ravel can clear the city, we have a real chance at saving almost everyone.

But Liwan's ghost wrenches at me in passing, glaring a venomous reminder that, no matter how many lives Ravel does or doesn't manage to save, it can never make up for throwing him and his friends to the Mara.

I almost stop to heal him then and there. Maybe I should practice once more with a ghost, just to be sure the power works properly . . .

But that is mostly the guilt talking. Even if I spend every last moment and every spark of energy I have left strengthening the barrier for whatever time is left, it might not be enough. And if it goes down, we all do.

Besides, the temptation to stay and do something about Liwan is at least partly out of fear of the barrier itself. It *hurt*. If the forest hadn't pulled me out, I'm not sure I would have survived.

I hesitate, hovering the barest breath away from one of the cracked, solid patches where Cadence has torn lives from the cursed dome. I might get trapped. I might get burned alive. And the most terrible of all horrors—I might join the lost ones, become yet one more tortured soul eternally decaying in its toxic embrace.

I reach out, a quick tap against the hard surface. It stings on contact.

Fluffy strokes my hand, concerned. Squishy rolls over to press its coolness against the slight burn. I curl around them, just for a moment, before disentangling Fluffy's tendrils and slipping away from Squishy's clinging wavelets.

"Not for you. Stay here."

The moment I think I've pulled free, they grab hold once more. I should leave them behind, safe. On the other hand, the treespawn and—seaspawn, I guess?—have passed seemingly unscathed through every other landscape I've bumbled through, so maybe they can take care of themselves . . .

And maybe I'm procrastinating because I really, really don't want to touch—

Pain.

More than pain: Anguish. Suffering. Torment.

But not just mine.

28

SHREDS

THEY'RE NOT EVEN people anymore, not really. They're shreds of what was: a broken shriek, the gnawing of a bottomless hunger, the reflexive grasping of tendons long since severed.

If I hadn't run the undead gauntlet of the Mara's prey before, this would be so much worse. But the edges of my own worlds have been bordered with the dead for so long now. At least these fragments are barely identifiable as human. They're not waiting here to torture me; they're simply lashing out in self-protection. The ground gold mixed into their undoing keeps them here, cementing them into place as they tear one another into continually lesser bits of wounded flesh and spirit.

It doesn't burn them, though, not like it would my kind. Not like it does me. This strange half-existence, or maybe my drone's upbringing in Refuge, was supposed to have granted me some resistance to the gold, but I appear to be dreamwalker enough for this much of the powdered element to eat into me like acid.

So I'm going to go out on a limb and guess there may be a time limit attached to this little experiment. Besides, you know, that whole great big, red, flashing countdown to the end of the world.

I laugh, and wince, and dig my hands into the mass of shredded scraps of humanity, searching for a way into whatever remains of these, uh, remains' inner life.

It turns out there's a threshold of pain and horror where you just kind of have to shrug and get on with it, ignoring the panic giggles, or lay down and die.

And I'm not the only one who isn't quite ready to die.

The barrier's muddy, sluggish current seems to be fuelled by the human scraps jostling for escape. And if there's enough will left in them to fight after all these years, maybe there's enough to grab hold of and—

I reach for the dreamscape and nearly split apart. Hundreds of fragmented worlds open up before, and around, and through me. Too many.

Squishy flows up, stretching to create a weightless bubble of protection around us. Fluffy unspools tendrils in every direction, pushing one reality aside while dragging us into the other.

The resulting space is featureless: dim, and sluggish, and somehow thin, like a soap bubble about to pop. Squishy flows back into a compact ball. I focus. Spin my island of peace in place of the creature's protection, taking a moment to review the essentials.

At the moment, that means remembering I'm me, and Squishy is Squishy but also the sea, and Fluffy is Fluffy but also the forest, and whatever we're in right now is . . .

Uh. Well, it definitely *is*.

It is only a scrap of once-life generating this reality, no longer even identifiable as human. But it's still *here*. It's still holding onto something important enough to give shape to this space. Which means it has a tenuous hold on at least one soul-deep longing or fear or—*ah.*

There it is.

Her spite pulls me into the shattered cavern of her deepest self. That's really about all that's left—darkness, and broken glass, and an amorphous sense of *she* and *loathing* and soul-deep desire for retribution.

The few tatters of memory and hope for an unreachable future are wispy and colourless, but I capture and lace one after another through my fingers, ignoring the way they slice my skin, and then turn them back on themselves, working the scraps into the tiniest of webs, finding fine, translucent threads to add each time I'm sure I've finished.

By the end, she's still hardly more than a sliver of being.

I don't know her name. I don't know what she looked like, who she loved or hated, what she feared or longed for. But I know that she *was*, that she lived and died and has remained trapped here for years upon years.

There's not enough left of her to bring her back to the fullness of the person she once was. There is no healing what she has become. But there's a softening of her desperation and anger, a rounding-off of the grasping, grating edges of her.

And when I pull back from her innermost self to her dreamscape—and then back further, into the shocking anguish of the barrier itself—I catch the grateful brush of her before she's sucked into the churning mass. The other shards of once-life can't hurt her now, and she won't hurt them.

Which . . . is exactly the opposite of what I'm here to accomplish. To strengthen the barrier, to help it stand against whatever Nine Peaks or Maryam can throw at it, Cadence included, I should be sharpening its components, stoking their desperation, not soothing it.

The barrier's dead zone—that is what I need to "heal." Those scraps Cadence tore apart need to be stirred up again or replaced, and I'm not about to feed it new sacrifices— though I wouldn't say no to Cadence bleeding on it again if she happened along.

Squishy gives me a nudge to let me know it's ready for another round. Fluffy rumbles agreement. I set my teeth and dive in once more. The dreamscape—any dreamscape—is harder to reach this time. The sea envelops me, protection against being pulled apart by the immeasurable force of too many worlds opening up at once. The forest reaches out to guide me into just one. But even cocooned in my island of safety, the pressure is crushing.

It's as if time itself moves differently. Each breath is an eternity, each blink a struggle against immense forces, even before I let my bubble collapse and immerse myself in the overwhelming inertia.

I search for echoes of hate, resentment, jealousy, even, and come up short. But this place exists—which means the someone it's tied to still exists in some form, beyond their own death, and the further destruction of whatever remained of them in the barrier.

I don't expect the thread that finally snags at my fingertips to speak of love, but it is unmistakeable. This scrap of humanity once loved so fiercely and so deeply it still echoes throughout the final vestiges of their soul.

I follow that tarnished cord into the deepest recesses of his being. At first, there is nothing else. Even this one, solitary strand is indistinct and fraying. But when I twist it back on itself and go to tie off the end in a knot, another strand brushes against me, and another. Enough to braid together once and then again, remembering, as the light of his renewed fabric grows, to leave a few ends straggling. It won't do to revive him but make her inert. Not yet.

I leave him with a promise to come back and finish the job one day if I can.

I barely have the energy left to claw my way from the barrier. The patch of cracked stillness on its churning surface—did it shrink? Does the sick lambency of the thing seem more vivid, the churning less sluggish?

Fluffy squirms encouragingly, which is as close as I'm going to get to an answer before I drag myself into the safety of my own dreamscape and pass out.

THE NOTES ARE low and winding. Thrumming, almost. A lilting tune voiced but wordless, or else of some flowing language I don't recognize. Soothing, yet desolate.

"I thought you couldn't come here." I sit up, her hand falling from my head.

The crooning stops.

"I found a way." Susan runs a work-roughened thumb across my cheek where the imprint of her skirt is slow to fade. "The forest has little respect for walls."

Fluffy chuckles and rolls around us, darting in to nudge her knee affectionately before resuming its joyous loops.

"So? What is it this time?" I sweep the ground up into hard, straight-edged chairs, the kind you can't stand to sit in for long. Squishy bobs to keep its balance on my knee and burbles a scolding.

Susan searches my face, her own heavy with a sadness that hardens, after a moment, to flint. "Your childish insistence on getting your own way isn't just hurting you, granddaughter. Don't you go snapping at me when you're the one who ran away from home."

Not my home. Not your grandchild. But we've been over that before. "If you think I'm going to apologize for being the only one who cared enough to try to help these people—"

"Is that what you've been doing, granddaughter? Helping people? Because from what I hear, you're about do more harm than we've seen in generations."

Ah. So she has been talking to Ash. Or maybe she's back on speaking terms with the council in Nine Peaks. "I'm taking responsibility for my actions. Tell me, were you on the council already when they sent your child and grandchild off to die? At what point did you decide *you* were done 'wasting' people on trying to save innocents?"

She draws a sharp breath. But instead of striking back, she reaches for Fluffy, running her fingers over its whorls absently. "I'm not here to discuss the past. I'm here for you. You don't know what you're doing. But you need to stop, before it's too late."

"The only one who needs to stop is your council. Here I am trying to save the literal *world*, and you all decide the best thing to do isn't to send backup but to blow us up?"

"I'm not here to undermine the council's rulings. Right or wrong, they've chosen their path. I am here to help you."

"Great—so you'll stop the elders' attack tomorrow?"

"No."

"Perhaps you have a way to stop Cadence directly?"

"No."

"I don't suppose you've found a way for me to fight the Mara and end the threat that way, then?"

"There is no fighting back, granddaughter. I'm here to help you survive what will come."

"Then stop wasting my time and stay out of my way." I turn on my heel and head for the horizon.

"Stay." Her voice takes on a strange sort of echo. When I peer back over my shoulder, she's not alone. A taller, younger woman stands beside her. I've seen her face before. Or rather, Ravel has. Cadence has. And I through them.

Susan takes my mother's hand and reaches out her other to the equally unfamiliar man who steps out of thin air to take it as easily as—oh. "They're not real. You're just dreaming them, like Ash dreams dancing flowers and fuzzy marching bands in and out of existence."

"They're as real as you want them to be. I can give them back to you—if you stay."

My nails cut into my palm, the fist so tight my knuckles ache. "Who do you think I am? I don't know these people. I don't care."

She looks back coolly and nods. Ash flickers into existence, and Ange, and Lily, and—and then Cass. My hands fall slack at my sides. She continues bringing memories to life, one after another, familiar faces from Refuge and Nine Peaks alike. The last is Liwan, who gives me a smirk and a wave.

"You'll have everything you need. Everyone you want, as long as you or I remember them. Forever." Sweat beads her forehead, but she stands tall at the side of her phantoms.

This time, it's a struggle to say, "I can't stay. I have to go back. I'm running out of time."

"Time isn't all you're running out of." Susan snags my wrist and pulls, twisting my elbow to turn my palm up. "Look."

The light shines through. Must be a side effect of exhaustion. If I focus on dreaming myself solid again—

"You're giving too much away," Susan says without relaxing her grip. "You're not trained. You shouldn't even be able to heal. But you've been pushing yourself without safeguards or limits. You're reaching well beyond the edges of your patients, drawing on your own reserves. It has to stop. You are not enough. You can't save the world on your own, and if you keep trying, you'll only destroy yourself before it ends. But *it is ending*—so rest now and find peace and safety here. There is no need to keep fighting."

I make a fist again, hiding the weakening of my existence from both of us, and yank free. I've faced temptation before. This time it isn't even all that compelling. Run away and live in a fantasy while the world burns? Is that what she thinks I really want? "Did Ash put you up to this? I already said no."

I dive for the waking world before she can get a word out. But perhaps Susan isn't so willing to let me go without a fight after all because the seam between realities is full of all too many of the faces I've just turned back from. The father, flesh peeling from bone, the mother, needle teeth gnashing, Liwan, eyes oozing darkness, and even Cass, reverted to the broken shell he'd been before I healed him.

I push through, forcing my way through the illusion she has created to get to the real ghosts in the void between worlds but pop through into the waking world. No more an illusion than usual, then. All that effort I spent healing Cass, wasted. Did I screw up, somehow, or is that the way it is with ghosts?

And if fully intact ghosts can't be healed, at least not for long, not without reverting, what does that mean for the shredded souls of the barrier?

29

CAPTURED

ASH IS CALLING for me.

I need to check on the barrier, but he sounds desperate. When I reach him, he's one of the last left standing. Refuge Force have him backed into a corner in the remains of Freedom's blue hall. He won't pull blades on humans, but his hand-to-hand skills have clearly benefitted from better training than the enforcers'. It takes a half dozen of them rushing him all at once, and even then, they don't bring him down unscathed.

"Oh, do shut up, lover," Cadence says from behind a wall of enforcers in the center of the room.

"Do you even know what that means, dead girl?" Ravel's bloody nose and swollen lip mangle the words, but he manages a supercilious look despite the gleeful enforcers ensuring he doesn't get up off his knees.

Cadence darts a quick glance at Maryam for approval, gets the nod, and kicks him in the stomach. "Shut it, *loser.*"

She giggles as if this is clever. How far she has fallen. At least when she was the ghost, she was actually funny. Sometimes. Actually, in hindsight, she was always pretty childish. But I'm letting her antics distract me from what I should be paying attention to, as usual.

"Don't react. I'm here," I whisper.

Ash coughs from under his own pile of enforcers, which is a reaction, but they don't seem to be worried now that he's safely pinned. Ravel chuckles, apparently assuming I'm talking to him, and then moans, spitting red.

I roll my eyes. "I won't ask what happened. Just, if you can, tell me what you need."

"—late," Ash gasps.

"Yeah. I know."

"He means it's too late, flame," Ravel mutters. "All my fault, I'm afraid. Not that I won't be happy to share the blame for the next couple hours or so. Plenty to go around."

"I take it you've been elsewhere, darling," Maryam croons, overhearing. "Do I have you to thank for this one's rebelliousness? And here I was thinking his painstaking upbringing was finally paying off. I do so hate being disappointed."

She leans down and tips Ravel's chin up with one long nail. He smiles blearily—and spits in her face. His keepers gasp, stumbling over themselves to babble apologies while wrestling him back from her. Maryam merely smiles, wiping off blood-laced saliva with deliberate care.

"Perhaps his training was deficient. Such a waste. We'll have to start over." She turns to Cadence. "You play messenger instead, dear."

Cadence looks longingly at Ravel, clearly wishing for the opportunity to get another kick in, but he's already being dragged away. Apparently, their working relationship in Refuge hasn't endeared him to her.

"He's a creep, Cole. What do you expect?" she says. "I told you that from the start, but you never listen. Not that it matters anymore."

"I understand this was all your work, darling?" Maryam interrupts, addressing me directly. "I can't imagine these good children could have found cause for complaint on their own. Not that going through a rebellious phase is unnatural, of course, but I hardly see a reason to let nature take its course when there are much superior alternatives.

Wouldn't you agree? You really were such a good little girl until just recently. Such a shame."

But I'm too busy chasing enforcers down the hallway to listen to her taunting. I have no idea what's going on, and clueless is not the right position to be in when dealing with Maryam. "What happened?"

"Things got a little out of hand," Ravel whispers back. "We were trying to get people stirred up, you know? Jostle them out of complacency; convince them to run. Amy's sob story worked a little too well—a lot of drones have brushed up against the unfairness of regulation a time or two. Not to mention, the desire to cut loose on occasion is pretty much universal. That kid you were trying to save, Liwan?"

"The one you fed to the Mara to get into mommy's good books?"

He huffs. "Turns out he was kind of popular, too. You start talking about attacks from unknown enemies and the end of the world, maybe a few people get curious, but most cover their ears. But you start telling tales of kids getting killed and corruption from inside? Especially when there've been whispers of rebellion for a while now? Things start happening."

"Skip to the part where you and Ash get taken down by enforcers. Maryam's going to get tired of listening to herself speak any minute now, and apparently I'm expected to do something about this mess."

"Too late," Ash groans, barely conscious in another set of enforcers' arms. "Too late to stop her . . ."

"It will be if you two don't quit wasting my time." I need to get back to the barrier. We've got less than a day until Nine Peaks' attack hits, and I've barely gotten started fixing it.

"Sorry flame," Ravel whispers. "Thought we had a chance. Refuge only has so many enforcers, you know? I guess after all those years agitating for a revolution, I couldn't let myself get caught on the wrong side when a real one finally broke out."

"Wait, so you really . . . ?"

"Oh, flame—" He coughs. The enforcers give him a shake. He rolls his eyes, rasping, "You never trust me. Here I was risking everything to play secret agent for you, and for what?"

Yeah, unlikely. "Saving the world, remember? Again, no time. Hurry it up. What do I need to know to bargain with Maryam?"

"You don't get it. There's nothing to bargain for. She's captured everyone. She thinks we were lying all along and now she's done waiting—she's bringing down that barrier tonight. And sacrificing everyone she captured to keep the Mara busy until she's finished. She's won."

I look to Ash for confirmation. He's limp in the arms of his captors. Not unconscious, just defeated.

"No. I won't let her." What am I doing? It's not like my protests matter to these two anymore.

I'm not interested in trying to unravel whose side Ravel is on. I can't do anything for Ash, and he's in no shape to be useful at the moment. So I leave them behind to focus wholly on Maryam. She wouldn't bother taunting me if there was nothing for her in it, right? Maybe?

I mean, if she's anything like Ravel, she could just be doing it for entertainment . . .

"We're waiting, Cole," says Cadence, inspecting a torn nail. Her nails aren't the only ragged parts. Her cheeks are hollow, her skin and hair dull, worn down by her attacks on the barrier. "Or rather, she is. Not me. I don't care what you do."

But there's a glint to her shadowed eyes that says she's paying closer attention than she wants to admit. I scan back over the past few minutes, trying to pull the correct memory from my split focus. Ravel, self-flagellating. Or flipping from double agent to triple—or is it back to double, again? I've lost track. Ash, defeated. Maryam . . . What was it Maryam wanted from me?

Doesn't matter. This is a waste of time. If Maryam is determined to bring down the barrier, I just have to build it back faster and stronger.

"She wants to bargain for Ash's life," Cadence chews the peeling edge of a nail as if she can hardly be bothered to mumble the words in Maryam's general direction. "*Just* him. She says she'll get in my way if you don't agree. Weaken my powers. We're still connected, you know, and she has been working on ways to get control back. But if you spare Ash, she'll stand back."

I—what? I said no such thing.

Maryam yawns. "That boy just now? Finc, I don't see why not."

"Cadence, what are you—"

"Uh huh," says Cadence, as if in response to some invisible, inaudible conversation partner. "Yup. Oh, really? Okay, it's a deal then. She says it's a bargain."

I stare. "Did—did you just fake talking to me?"

She angles her head, says briskly to Maryam: "Now that is out of the way, we should get moving. Busy night and all."

Maryam lifts one elegant eyebrow, clearly too intelligent to buy Cadence's clumsy ruse. But the mayor merely flicks some dust off her diaphanous skirts and sweeps off to destroy the world.

"I won't let you ruin this for me," Cadence mutters under her breath, trailing Maryam at some distance for privacy. "But since you're apparently too useless to remember to protect Ash, I had to do *something*. Don't worry. I'll keep him safe. I'll even let you talk to him on special occasions. If he still wants to chat with the imposter after I save the city, of course."

As if. "For the last time: if you destroy that barrier, it won't stop the Mara. It'll only unleash them on the world. You'll die. Ash will die. *Everyone will die*, Cadence."

She sways, paling, fragile as a bubble blown to its very limit. Then her wide, tragic gaze hardens. "Don't be silly. Monsters don't kill dreamwalkers. Only defective weaklings like you."

I almost do it. I reach for her with every intention of ripping control of that body from her stupid, selfish fingers. It's probably even the right thing to do.

But it's *Cadence*. If I take power from her, will she have anything left? As impossible as she's being, she's just a child inside, trapped in her own memories, desperate to turn back time. And even lost in the past, she remembered to save Ash.

She's not evil. At least, not all-the-way-through evil.

So I leave her behind. I leave all of them behind, grateful I won't need to pass through the prison floors again and face down more victims to get where I need to be.

The barrier is still healed. Actually, it's *more* healed. The wide, hardened area seems to have shrunk to the size of a closed fist.

Only, as it turns out, I haven't been the only one working to fix it.

Haynfyv is stretched against one wall, apparently capable of sleeping anywhere, arms awkwardly twisted beneath him in a sort of pillow. He mutters even in his sleep. I can't make sense of any of it. But if he's found an easier way to fix the barrier, I need to know what it is.

30

LIFEBLOOD

"**Y**OU'VE RETURNED. HAYNFYV doesn't get up from his chair, scribbling notes even in his sleep.

But where the last time I visited his dreamscape, there was nothing but a tangle of pinned notes tethered by string, now, it's cluttered with beakers, small, sharp, silvery instruments, and numbered diagrams.

"You've been busy." My finger squeaks against the cool, smooth curve of a beaker.

He tips his head in faint acknowledgment. "You have been absent. Challenging, you know, to make progress when one repeatedly loses hours' worth of work at a time. But I think I've got it sorted on both sides now. More clarity here, of course, than there. It is a complex formula: blood, and life, and ground gold, and a few other elements besides. Over there, I've only worked out the blood part, which, I'm afraid I must admit, isn't going terribly well for myself or the others presently on their way."

"Others?"

He blinks. "Your associates in the tunnels, mainly. They were off to see about gathering donors more widely before coming down to bleed."

"Bleed?"

He frowns. "A touch slow tonight, aren't we? Blood powers the barrier, in essence. Ha—'essence.' That is very good. Don't you think?"

"Hilarious. You've been *bleeding* on the barrier? And it came back to life?"

"It's not strictly alive, you know. But then, I suppose from a certain perspective one might—"

"And it works no matter whose blood is added? Even just a little?"

"Well, the minimum effective dose is quiet small, yes, but—"

"And no one has actually died?" It was one thing for Cadence's blood to revive the damaged fragments, but if mere human blood could be donated to strengthen the barrier without harm to the donor, that could change everything.

"Well, not as of yet. But, as I've mentioned, the formula does seem to include life as well as blood. Regrettably, I failed to ascertain that input prior to involving, ahem, myself in the experiment. I don't suppose you could warn off the volunteer donors on the other side for me?"

"You don't mean—"

He holds up a hand to the light, tilting it thoughtfully. His deep grey-brown skin glows as if lit from within, but that is nothing more than a pleasant illusion masking the horrifying truth: he's fading, just as I've been, the light shining through. At least according to Susan, I've been damaging myself by weaving myself into my healings. In his case, there's no such—

"I can feel it pulling on me," he murmurs with unnerving fondness. "Hungry little thing."

I back away, my elbow sweeping a beaker off the edge of a table. It shatters. "It can't—it shouldn't work like that. Just—just stop feeding it!"

He flexes his hand. "It won't help. I told you. 'Life' is part of the formula."

"No. No, it's okay. I'll—" I'll what? Save him? Stop him from feeding himself to the barrier to make it stronger when that is exactly what I was about to do? He's a grown man.

It's a shame he'll die—but if this works, he will die a hero. Like his brother.

And if it fails, he'll die anyway.

So I leave him to his dreams and take a moment to bow in thanks to the still body slowly bleeding out onto the tunnel floor, instead of staying to upset him with my useless horror. The last thing he needs to spend his final moments on is appeasing my worthless, self-indulgent *feelings*. He has already given too much. He may not wake at all before it's over. Because one way or another, this will all be over soon.

The barrier wails.

The stony dead patch on its surface swells from the size of a fist to the size of my head, doubling in size again, and then again as the lives trapped within wail and sputter into darkness. The cracked surface spans both walls now, completely reversing the effects of Haynfyv's sacrifice.

But Cadence is nowhere in sight.

"So look harder, stupid," she says from the other side of the city. "And stop pretending you have eyes."

And because she's right and I don't, I find myself unable not to see her brush a finger against the barrier. It wails, and another patch goes silent.

When did she become this powerful?

She shrugs. "Maybe it's because of that lovely rest you and the traitorous scum so thoughtfully provided?"

Her brows furrow, her scarred palm flat now against the hard surface of the barrier, sucking the life from an underwater section half the length of the city border. Her knees buckle, but she just leans in, bracing her forehead and both hands against the desiccated shell. Flakes stick to her clammy skin, paper-like dandruff of the undead.

Half a city away, water starts to bead through to the inner surface. Fluffy trembles against me. Squishy sloshes apologetically.

She smiles. "What's wrong? You're not going to whine and nag like usual? I know you can see it crumbling. Not much more to go, and the ocean will finish the job for me."

But she's wheezing, her lips cracked like the barrier. It's the only thing holding her up, as if every ounce of life she tears from it is being sucked back from her.

"It's killing you." Is it because she bled on it? Like Haynfyv said, is it taking both blood and life? Or is the incredible power she's drawing on making her waste away before my eyes?

"You really don't *see*," she whispers. "Look further."

At first, I think she means beyond the barrier, but as I strain to expand my focus wider, higher, further, it all opens up before me.

Haynfyv's 'donors,' trying to shake him awake. Shrugging at his lack of responsiveness. Opening their veins to splash blood against the stone. Cadence winces at the renewal pressing back against her, slowing the seeping waters, rallying against the weight of the wild, careless sea on the other side.

A dozen levels above, my awareness skitters across the sick and injured and recently captured prisoners cowering at the sight of the enforcers streaming through the door, come to take them away. Ash is there. And in a separate room, Ange. And in yet another place, Sam with his arms protectively around Lily. Yet another child I've failed.

I look away, pushing to see higher still, glossing past the unconscious forms of dreamless children who I can only hope will never wake again. More likely, when the rest of us are gone and the equipment fails, they will wake to a dead city, living only long enough to register its horror before their untouched minds call down the monsters. There is nothing I can do for them now.

Further up: Ravel, huddled in the corner of a locked room at the top of a tower he has never truly escaped. Shivering in absolute darkness. Rocking, covering his ears against the gleeful, taunting whispers of the Mara. Shaking his head, knocking it against the wall. Gasping in pain and fear and misery.

Good—he's the one who brought them back to die. Brought my friends, brought a *child*, even, back to this deathtrap of a city. No excuses. Their suffering is on his head. And if there's some shred of comfort in having someone to share all the guilt with, I won't have to be ashamed of it for much longer. The bloodbath has begun.

Because even higher yet, Maryam presides over a grand sacrifice like this city has never seen. One shuddering, wailing prisoner after another is dragged to her feet, chained in place, and subjected to her spidery touch as she offers them up to the Mara. No quelling drugs, no bleary tumble into darkness for these. They go shrieking, cursing, fighting to the last.

Until Amy.

Shoulders back, bruised head high, Ange's mousy, timid sister stalks across the killing floor to stand over Maryam with blazing eyes. Gracefully, she kneels, glaring all the while. Her slim hands are knotted in front of her, knuckles in sharp relief, as if her dying wish is to wrap them around the elegant neck of the woman in front of her.

Maryam appears amused. "Any last words, my child?"

"Don't you use that word. You don't have children," Amy says, high and clear and unhurried. "You have pawns. Drones. *My* child is proud of me. Would yours be?"

I gasp. I never would have thought she had it in her. Maryam's smile flattens. Her hand shoots out, the words of the ritual savaging the air like shards of broken glass.

I rise against her, throwing everything I can muster into a force barely strong enough to stir Amy's long dark hair as she falls.

I choke on bitter regret and helpless fury. There is absolutely nothing I can do about her death—besides make sure her sacrifice isn't in vain.

"Well?" Cadence gasps in the distance. "See anything good?

Her hands shake, sweat rolling down her skin. She's stretched out on the floor of a tunnel deep under Refuge, nose to the barrier, hands pinned against it with the weight of her body. I can practically hear her heart stuttering. If I had known she was going to kill herself trying to fulfill her dead parents' final mission, I would have taken back her body sooner.

At least, that's what I should be thinking. But after the way Amy went to her death clear-eyed and unbending, seeing my own almost-sister like this just makes me sad.

Such a waste, all of it.

Then I plunge into the shrieking morass of the undead and start undoing her work.

CADENCE HAS ALWAYS been stronger than me.

I've seen the memories—both hers and Ash's. She was a gifted child; clever, athletic, and powerful in the ways of her people on top of it all. When I came onto the scene, even as a disembodied ghost she retained that natural dominance; that belief that she always knew best and I should just fall in line.

So I don't know why I'm surprised that she can shred the barrier faster than I can build it back up. Even worn ragged, she is faster, more powerful. And she has the natural advantage in this, too: it takes far less effort to destroy than to heal.

She reaches in and tears apart the scraps of life trapped in the barrier by the handful. I have to go one by one, fishing with painstaking care for those fragile, corroded, gossamer-thin strands of individuality and purpose. I strain to puzzle out and piece together something with a semblance of life, taking care to leave it ragged enough to wound, as is the nature of the barrier. And every time I wrap up another stunning effort in healing beyond the grave, beyond humanity, even, she has gone and crushed a whole swathe of once-lives into so much dust.

Fluffy braces me, keeping me from being swept away in the morass. Squishy soothes and protects where it can. But even with both of them lending me their strength, there is only so much I can do—and Cadence unexpectedly has the sea on her side.

She tears and I rebuild, and all the while the vast power of the ocean presses, presses, presses against a surface growing incrementally more brittle and porous every second. First the barrier seeps, water working its way through tiny flaws to bead on the other side. Then it fractures, surface cracks deepening, slicing through to spurt thin streams in airy fans.

Then it buckles, all at once. Dozens of gushing spigots turn into one gigantic grinning mouth, gaping to let the waters rush through. The speed—the crushing *weight* of it—does more than fill the tunnels and chambers and halls. The raging torrent punches through walls and bursts through ceilings, sweeping away the lesser obstructions in an instant, pounding relentlessly against the more sturdy until they give way beneath the assault.

If the tunnels hadn't been scoured over and over again to fill Refuge's prisons, Ange's Underfolk would have been the first to die, every escape route cut off at once as their deep hideaways gather the rushing waves. Instead, the first casualty is Haynfyv. He drowns without ever waking—and there is no time for guilt or regret, because Cadence is next.

"Get up," I snap, hardening my tones to hide the fear. "It's coming—you know it is. You have to run."

She sighs, stretched across the floor. "I did it, didn't I? I broke the barrier."

She's too spent to lift an eyelash. She threw everything she had into fighting me. And even if she hadn't, even if she were in the best condition of her life, if she were at her most powerful, she couldn't outrun this. Not now, not unless the current slows and the tide reverses in the next instant, and even then . . .

It's such a waste. I—I should have ripped that body from her stupid fingers ages ago. If she was going to die like this all along, it would have been worth the risk. I could have saved her. Might've killed her too, but at least—at least—

No. No time for regret, not right now. The water is rising, roaring through the tunnels, nearly at the door now, and there is time for only one thing.

One last word with the last person I ever expected to have to say goodbye. But that's not what she needs to hear from me.

And, whatever she has been or done to me, here at the end all I want is to give her this: "Well done, dreamwalker," I say, as the water crashes around the corner. "You did it. You completed your mission."

She smiles and closes her eyes—and I can't just *let* this happen. I focus on the waves, unchaining my rage and fear and desperation. The air stirs, curling the leading edge of spray back into the waves. There's a beat of tension, a moment where the water almost bubbles out around my own wave of force, and I'm really doing it—I'm holding back the whole ocean for her—

My control slips. My energy gutters like a flame in the breeze. I used too much fighting her. Even at my best, I could barely stir the air in the waking world. The forest isn't here to help, and Squishy can't or won't provide the same kind of link to the waters.

The sea races in, battering our body against the remaining concrete. It froths its way to the ceiling and past, curling back from the walls and ricocheting off on its quest to continue up and out.

I remain.

The roaring grows distant. Bubbles cluster against the ceiling.

Finally, all is still but for the drifting of short, dark hair in the current.

This is wrong.

It should feel different. More . . . I don't know. More *something.* Freeing, or empty, or shattering, or—or anything but numb. If I were truly stone, this emptiness wouldn't feel so wrong. But there is nothing left here for me but failure and a lifeless shell, so I chase the mounting sea up, break through its surface, and keep climbing.

The prisoners are gone from their dorms. All of them.

I continue, past Ravel, still rocking in his lightless cell. The Mara who tormented him have moved on. They're occupied elsewhere, with the final dregs of their feast.

I arrive as Lily hits the floor, an empty-eyed doll draped over the prone forms of her adoptive father and her aunt—and the very world seems to shake at her fall. Her mother's corpse has been heaped with the others in one of the side rooms. The enforcers have been kept too busy to cart the dead off properly.

"I failed," I admit redundantly, still absolutely numb, as if the icy depths have seeped through to my very soul.

"I know," Ash says, staring at the fragile line of Lily's arm where it reaches for Ange's limp hand.

"Oh, is the other one here too?" Maryam flexes her hand, working out a cramp. "I wasn't sure if you would last beyond our dear Cadence's passing, darling. I'm so glad you're still with us."

"You promised not to hurt him." But of course she can't hear me.

"Apparently, she sent for me as soon as Cadence, uh . . ." He swallows hard, choking on the loss. "Sorry, C."

Maryam twirls her fingers in a hurry-up gesture. Two enforcers muscle Ash over and through the field of dead.

"I was lying," I blurt, desperate to get the words out the end. "Or hiding. You were right all along. I was scared. Not of you, but of what it would do to me to be seen. But I was wrong, Ash. I was wrong to hide. I can do it, I know I can. I can choose you back. I would have, if we had more time. I will—I mean, I do. Choose you. Even if it's only for a moment, I choose—"

"I know." His voice thick, blood running down his face, his eyes fixed on Lily's corpse. "It's okay. You did your best. I didn't want anything from you but the truth. Go now. Don't stay for this part."

"Can't you fight her or something? Don't just . . ." I trail off, weary beyond words. Why should he fight? Why should any of us cling so desperately to this pointless, hopeless life?

The barrier is crumbling. The Mara are gone—or, no, actually, they seem to mostly be here, still. Maryam's feast has drawn their full attention. I'm not sure they've even realized they can escape.

"They will," Ash murmurs. "The sea must be filling the gaps right now. It's not their element; they can't pass through. But when the tide turns, they'll go. There won't be enough food to keep them."

"And good riddance," Maryam says, her eyes shining. "It's about time those monsters left my poor city in peace."

She reaches for Ash's head. She doesn't make it. Her fingers are the first to go, shrivelling and curling, claw-like, skin turning papery, nails thick and yellow under flaking polish.

"Ah," she sighs, her honeyed voice turning hoarse and dry. "Finally."

She raps Ash on the head with thick knuckles. "Don't forget to let my boy out before you go. He knows what to do, how to start over, where the supply caches are. Look for more on the other side of the inlet, if needed."

Her spine curls, flesh sagging from her bones, hair falling in clumps. She nods, her withered lips curling. "My boy," she sighs, wilting back onto her throne, a withered shell with oddly bright eyes peering in fanatical satisfaction to the last.

From the distant, numb place where I now exist, I watch dispassionately until the beautiful, powerful, terrifying architect of our suffering is no more than dust and scraps of fabric stretched over misshapen fragments of bone.

"Cole—" Ash starts.

By the time I look over, he's gone too, folding to the corpse-strewn floor with a sigh, wide, dark eyes filmed over with the telltale pearlescent sheen of the Mara-taken.

And then he gets up.

31

TAKEN

THE GHOSTS HAVE all gone from the edges of my map. Tired of the borderlands, they've left for the real world once more.

My nightmares are real. I knew this, of course, but I'm not sure I really *understood* it. Not even when I travelled into Cass's inner self to heal his broken ghost.

But that's the thing. They were *all* broken. Every one of them trapped inside the barrier with the Mara. Not just the Mara-taken, but the others, too. I think everyone who's died inside this city ever since the walls went up has been trapped, the Mara feeding on the fading vestiges of their dreams even beyond death.

But the walls are crumbling and the monsters are still here.

Only, apparently, what they've really wanted all along wasn't just dreams, but flesh as well. They're wearing my friends like badly fitting suits, slipping beneath the skin and deep into muscle and bone, in some cases before the corpses have a chance to get cold. Ash still moves with some measure of grace, as does Ange, and Lily. Amy, not so much.

They even march Cadence and Haynfyv out from under the surface, water streaming off—and out of—their cold, sodden forms.

I'm grateful now to the uncanny but persistent numbness. It lets me gaze dispassionately on the macabre spectacle without succumbing to screaming madness. It's more than loud enough around here without my adding to the pandemonium.

Maryam's grand scheme has failed. The barrier has not crumbled into nothingness. It has only grown smaller. The combination of Cadence's campaign of destruction and the sea's relentless force carved a layer clear through its base, but the remaining dome simply dropped a few stories, settling into the gap.

The Mara romp through the tower, sucking the souls from the remaining workers and inhabiting their newly-emptied corpses, either unaware or uncaring that their hunting ground has shrunk and their prey been pushed to the brink of extinction. Beneath the waves, a fresh batch of sea monsters cavort with the long-trapped ones of my city, seemingly content to hunt the bounty of fish and other sea life newly swept in on the waves.

This is the new normal, but it won't last. Nine Peaks still hasn't struck. Though the barrier is nominally in place, fissures and flaking dead patches mottle its remaining surface. I don't know exactly what form the dreamwalkers' coming attack will take, but my chances of propping up the damaged dome against a force of nature equal to or greater than the sea are vanishingly scarce.

Not to mention, I'm not all that motivated. It's hard to see anything past the tortured, decaying souls of my friends. No longer clustered around the seam between worlds, ghosts roam everywhere. The air is thick with what's left of them. Death was only the beginning of their torment. Now that the Mara fully have their hooks in them, their suffering is seemingly unending, fuelling the monsters' power and feeding them long after the flesh has been stolen.

I almost welcome whatever Nine Peaks has in store for us. If only they could burn us all up, monsters and ghosts alike scorched into oblivion. But if they destroy the barrier without annihilating everything within, the horror my city has become will only be the beginning.

"Are they close?" Ravel whispers.

He's taken to talking to me. At first, I ignored his muttering. He was halfway insane, anyway. I can't release him. Can't free him. No point in giving him false hope.

Then, when he wouldn't shut up, I told him exactly what was going on behind the locked door of his isolation cell. He didn't take it well, but after a brief period of shunning, he seems to have caved to the need to talk to someone once more.

"Flame? Are they close yet?"

"They will be if you don't shut up."

He considers this. "At least I'll make a pretty monster."

"Am I supposed to laugh?"

"You could always try to console me." He smirks. Then shivers. "I think the monsters forgot to turn on the heat this morning."

"Or they ate the last of the building engineers."

"Or that. Cole, for real, though: are they close?"

I ignore him and his forlorn tone, and the way he's rocking in the dark, alone and afraid, and desperately hoping for someone to come and throw open the doors to let the light in.

It's hard to see him when Ash's shade is in my way, half his face shredded, the rest contorted in a rictus of pain. He's got hold of Lily's ghost, somehow, and is dragging her by the neck, her head tilted at an awful angle, her teeth clamped in an empty grin as ichor boils from the pits of her eyes.

I turn away from their pawing hands, curling myself smaller. As if that will help. Everywhere I turn it only gets worse. Cadence—and her parents. Ange, and Liwan. Amy and Sam. The dead crowd around me as if . . .

As if they're as desperate for my attention as Ravel is.

"I know you're there, flame," he says. "Talk to me. Please."

The floor shivers beneath him. Perhaps the foundations are so damaged by the ocean's release that it will fall and end the walking nightmares entirely. I consider sharing this promising hypothesis with him. But he's not the only living being that would be wiped out if Refuge crumbled.

Maryam's stolen children, the untouched youngest ones, are still held in their chemically frozen sleep not far away. They'll be invisible to the Mara until they wake, or at least uninteresting. Some few other living humans run from the monster-ridden undead or cower in odd corners of these halls too. Death by crushing or by soul-sucking nightmare is hardly likely to be an appealing choice.

I start to explain. Stop before I get a word out. He's a monster in his own right. He used me, hurt me, drew me into the same darkness he has been trapped in so long.

He also saved me, freed me, helped me in the only ways he knew how. "I don't have anything to say that can help. Yes, they're close. Yes, they're coming. Yes, they're probably going to suck out your soul. But don't worry; I'm sure you'll be just as much of a pest as a ghost. If not more so."

"Thanks darling, you always know what to say to make me feel better," he whispers, eyes closed, still rocking. "So I guess it's my turn. If I had the chance to do it all over again, I would still come back for you. I can feel you rolling your eyes, flame. 'Oh, that Ravel. Such a tease. Tee hee.' You know you're thinking it."

"I have never thought, said, or so much as imagined the phrase 'tee hee' in my life."

He snorts. "As always, glad to expand your frame of reference. For real, though. Sorry. I wouldn't change a minute I got to spend with you. Not even the ones you spent glaring daggers. Those were some of my favourites if you want the truth."

"You're sick."

He shrugs. "Aren't we all? But let me finish. I'd do it all again, for *me*. I'm selfish like that. But if I weren't, if I were more like—like him. Sparkie—you are sure he's dead, flame?"

Ash's grimacing shade waggles Lily's squirming form under my nose. "Oh yeah, he's dead."

"Good. But if I *were* more like him, maybe I would have been able to protect you. To give you the world without hurting you. To let you be free of this place.

So, uh, sorry I wasn't your hero, I guess." He sniffles, rubbing his nose. "It really is freezing in here."

But darkness doesn't mean the same thing to me. I can see the heat rising under his skin, tinting his face red from collar to the tips of his ears.

"And here I thought you were supposed to have a way with words."

"You know me, flame. Always another angle up my sleeve."

The Mara in their skin suits really are getting closer. When they're wearing humans they don't seem to be as powerful, but they are reasonably clever. They'll find a key or improvise a battering ram once they get hungry enough.

"What's the angle, Ravel? What's this pathetic act going to accomplish? Might as well reveal the trick before it's too late."

He swallows. "Don't suppose you'd agree to be my girl, seeing as how I'm about to die and all?"

"Nope."

"Or you could forgive me for, you know, stuff."

"I could, but then what would we have to argue about?"

"Whether my eyes are my best feature or my devastating smile?"

I shudder at his hollow laugh—and the prospect of those light-filled golden eyes clouding over. "If it's any consolation, I don't think you'll care about your looks after they take you." The others certainly don't seem self-aware about their new fangs and leaking voids and shredded flesh . . .

"Oh, I'm sure I'll be a very vain ghost. Pity the monster who messes with this hot bod."

Fluffy gives me a jab. My bubble of detachment wobbles. "Say that again."

"What? 'Hot bod?'"

"Definitely not that."

"'Poor monsters?'"

Squishy bobs agreement. The world speeds up around me, the screeching of the dead raking my ears, the horror of their visible torment drilling into my soul. "Pity the monster . . ."

"Uh, flame? What is up with the echo?"

Pity the monsters. It's so ridiculous it might just be worth a shot. Even Ravel, without his minions, stripped of his web of connections, is nothing more than a powerless boy huddled in a dark room.

What would the Mara be if I could take away the source of their power? They grow stronger by siphoning off our dreams, tearing us apart thread by thread, even after death.

But I'm a weaver.

"Goodbye, Ravel. And thank you. If this doesn't work, I'm sure you'll make a lovely monster."

"Wait, flame—"

But there's no time to waste. I can't afford to hesitate.

I reach for the one who scares me the most. My mother.

⁂

THERE ARE THINGS here I don't want to see. I sort through the threads quickly, careful not to waste more than a glance at each set of memories, fears, longings, desires . . .

This woman deserves some shred of privacy—or that's what I intend. But her threads have a weight to them, a kind of friction against my skin that pulls me in despite my fear.

Susan: her face unlined, her long braids dark and thick. She's scolding the obstinate little girl this woman once was. Another time: teaching, her calloused hands guiding the small, soft ones of a child. Another time: scolding, then laughing, then fighting.

Another face appears. My father. Then an infant—a toddler—a child with twigs in her hair, and scraped knees, and a mutinous expression. Cadence.

Even later still, a journey like so many before. But this time, there's a growing sense of uncertainty that gives way to fear. Near the end now, a desperate race through a crumbling landscape. Loss. Pain.

The scraps of her life are still here, ragged and snarled from the Mara's relentless hunger, tarnished and faded, but somehow still clinging to the framework of her deepest self. She's not a fragment, not like those poor souls fed into the barrier. She's still a person. And I am not stone after all, but water and wood and fire, my heart burning as the tears run down my face.

It doesn't even take that much to heal her.

I tie off the last knot and stand back to admire the shimmering fabric of the woman who brought Cadence and I, whatever our current forms, into this world. There's more love in that weave than despair, more laughter than anger, and not one single loose thread left for the Mara to draw on.

I almost hate to leave it behind. But there are more ghosts to restore. To heal. I step away from my work, sinking through the smooth, perfect surface that surrounds her deepest self into her dreamscape, only to find myself swept up into a hug.

She holds me out, studying my features. I open my mouth to apologize, to explain that I'm not her daughter, not really—but a tugging sensation stops me.

Somehow, I missed one. A stray thread, clinging to me like an anchor. A final, lingering vulnerability that will call out to the Mara like a beacon. I need to go back, to reweave it into the fabric of her life, or else cut it free before they use it to unravel her once more.

But she touches my face, drawing my attention back to her form in the dreamscape. She smiles wordlessly. She still hasn't spoken. I—I'm not sure she can. Maybe she's been dead so long she's forgotten how. But, though I don't look anything like the child she left behind, she seems to know me. Or Cadence, rather.

Cadence, who owes her something only I'm left to give.

"I'm sorry." I lay my free hand over hers, folding myself into the form of the child who made a mistake that would cost her parents' lives and the world's besides. "I only wanted to help. I didn't mean for you and dad to get killed. I'm so, so sorry."

Tears well in our mother's eyes. She shakes her head, pulls me close. When she died, Cadence was just a child, so I find myself small enough that I have to stretch, lifting onto my toes and reaching to press the loose thread to her heart, even as she bends to press a kiss to my forehead.

The light is blinding.

The darkness in its wake crushes me. Exhaustion and emptiness drag me down even as the renewed wailing of the dead batters at my raw edges.

But deep inside, there's a spark of this incredible, aching exhilaration. *That* was a healing unlike anything I could have imagined.

Now I just have to do it again. And again. For a city's worth of trapped souls. Before the dreamwalkers' impending strike sends them scattering across the world.

32

DEADLINE

LL GHOSTS WANT one thing. Or rather, they all want *at least* one thing. Some of them want so many things it's like a web, clinging and binding tighter and tighter no matter how I struggle to work myself free.

But, in the end, it comes down to a single thread. And, after I heal the first few dozen, I don't even really have to guess what they need from me. A love fulfilled, a loss restored, a regret released. The patterns become familiar, if no less exhausting.

My friends prove the hardest to release, not because their longings and attachment to this broken world are stronger—though in some cases, they are—but because of the inescapable intimacy of piecing together their deepest selves and then the wrenching pain of letting them go.

Mostly, I get good at running away before the end. Identify that final tie, figure out what I need to say or do or become so they can accept it, and turn tail before that awful, glorious light overwhelms everything and leaves me stunned and exposed in the waking world.

The youngest are the easiest to release. Not emotionally, but practically. They take back their dreams with both hands at the slightest opportunity, as if welcoming old friends. The very old are sometimes like that, too.

Ange fights peace even harder than I expect. So does Ravel, newly dead and, as it happens, not at all attached to his now-Mara-inhabited physical form, despite his quips.

I manage to draw away before the light comes to take them. Ash's freeing, too, I can't stand to watch. Nor Grace's.

Her death is the first sign I've been moving too slow. It's not the last. I've been so preoccupied with Refuge that I missed the moment when the Mara realized the fissures in the barrier were deep enough to sneak out through.

They're growing desperate. I've been stealing their food, snatching their power back from them. The embodied ones are trapped now by the rising floodwaters like their prey so many generations ago, unable to flee the tower. The remainder of the formless Mara squeezed out and pounced on the nearest source of energy they could find—Ash's Spectre squad, Steph's Nightwitches, and a few others from Nine Peaks as well. I'm shocked to find Susan in her most recent memories. Our grandmother hadn't abandoned us after all. The dreamwalkers, elder and trainees alike, must have been waiting to help the refugees as Ravel spirited them across. He really was on our side all along.

The young dreamwalkers are fighting as hard as they can, but the Mara are reckless in their hunger, willing to risk the flashing silver blades to steal the energy of the living.

Grace's memories tell me all this and more as I race to release her and catch up to the monstrous nightmares. With each ghost I can steal back from them, their threat diminishes. Soon, even trainee dreamwalkers should be able to contain them.

But the fight is wearing me down, too. In each new spirit's dreamscape, I grow more and more transparent. I look more like a ghost now than they do.

I can't afford to rest, to retreat. But I know if I stopped to inspect the fabric of my own soul, I would find it threadbare and ravelling, too many strands stolen to bolster another's healing.

It's okay, though. It is.

It doesn't matter that I don't have the energy left to turn back Nine Peaks' attack. There's no one left in the city but monsters wearing human skins. And they're hardly even monsters now.

I've released all the ghosts but one, and without the trapped spirits to feed on, the Mara have become simply *creatures*. They leave their skins behind and drift, lonely and formless and, if not entirely benign, at least neutral. Like the forest's strange, shifting tree-like form that I first encountered in the forest outside Nine Peaks, or the sea creatures who saved Ash when his ship was sinking, the Mara had been simply responding to the pain they felt humans were inflicting on them.

No humans, no pain; no pain, no counterattack. Or so they convey, wordlessly, apologetically, even, before pressing on me a swirling little ball of fog, not the diseased yellow of my city's toxic fumes, but nearer the pure silver light of a dreamwalker's power.

If I weren't refusing to acknowledge its existence, I might name it—

"Puffy, right?" the last ghost says. "You have the worst naming sense ever. It should totally be something cool, like Zephyr or Atmos or something. All your ideas are so lame."

"How are you talking right now?"

"How are you talking right now?" she mimics in a squeaky, high-pitched tone. "Please. Don't lump me in with all those other pathetic ghosts. It's not like I've never been bodyjacked before."

I'm too tired for this. But I can't rest until she's free. It's time I finally let her go.

"Don't you come near me," she warns, skipping back.

"It won't hurt, Cadence. I promise."

She squeals, darting away almost playfully. But there's a real edge of fear to her screech when I draw close.

"Stop it! I don't like this!"

"It's okay. It's not scary at all. You should have seen mom—she was so beautiful. And then when dad went—" I keep up a steady stream of babbling as I reach for her, soothing her with stories and memories and promises of a world better than this one, the way she once distracted me. I don't think she even notices the moment we slip into her dreamscape.

It's solid, fully formed and bright as if she's still a living human. But it's also small, full of brilliant primary colours splashed across a landscape no larger than Susan's great room. And then there are the cracks in the paint, the gaps that look out onto nothingness.

Cadence glares. "You're really planning to send me away, aren't you?"

She's wearing her child form, still clinging to the past. She even has the same streak of mud on her cheek that she had that awful day her world fell apart.

"I'm sending you to the same place mom and dad went." I kneel in front of her. I'm about the same size as our mother was when she died. Maybe that's why Cady sighs and leans into me instead of fighting.

"I didn't mean it," she whispers, clutching her small, unmarred fists on the cloth of my shirt. "I just wanted to help."

"I know. They forgive you."

Her inner fabric is remarkably even, bright and tightly woven, but so small. If I'd still had any doubts, seeing her deepest self would have resolved them.

I am not Cadence and she is not me. I don't know any more than that, not how it's possible that we are separate, not how it came to be that I became, and grew, and changed, and wore myself threadbare trying to heal everyone else, nor how she came to be frozen on the edge of childhood.

But the fabric doesn't lie.

There's surprisingly little to do. A few snagged threads to nudge back into place. A raw edge to smooth. A few tarnished spots to wipe clean again. The stains crumble like dried blood and blow away on a breath.

I don't mean to weave myself into the healing this time any more than I did the last dozen—or hundred. I've lost track.

But when I drop back into her dreamscape, that one loose thread that always remains has itself wound deep into my very soul. Just the slightest tweak on it has me keeling over.

Cadence peers down at me. "Is this what's supposed to happen?"

I shake my head, gasping.

"Oh. Well, maybe you should take a break? And come take a look at this—"

She points. I crane my neck—and her small hand at my back shoves me into the void.

I WAKE UP stiff and smelling of seawater.

"Took you long enough," Ravel says.

"She was busy," Ash shoots back, leaning over to push me back down when I start to rise. "Better take a minute, C. Most of us didn't get a full-system saltwater cleanse while we were out."

I flinch, frantically replaying his final moments in his head as my skin heats. What had I said? What had I *promised*? I wasn't expecting to have to face him again.

"So, was I a pretty monster?" Ravel croons, shouldering his rival aside. He bats deep brown eyes at me—the inhuman gold apparently stripped from his body along with the possessing monsters—and lifts one eyebrow, as if in reassurance that, yes, it's definitely all him in there.

Ange grabs him by the back of his shirt and yanks. "Leave the poor girl alone for five minutes."

A groan comes from somewhere behind me. Everyone looks. I take the opportunity to spit up some more water and then cradle my aching head.

"Ah, here comes your drowning buddy," Ange says dryly. "Right on schedule."

I set my teeth in the briny-tasting flesh of my inner arm and bite.

"Whoa, okay," Ravel says. "So, yeah, you're alive. Not a dream. Try not to hurt yourself."

Ash wipes blood off my lip and slips an arm behind me so I can look around. It's an unremarkable Refuge workroom, chairs overturned here and there, consoles in pieces on the floor, and a half dozen or so familiar faces staring back at me.

"How—?"

Ange shrugs. "I was pretty sure I was done for. Then I woke up here."

"Same." Ravel waves languidly. "One minute the monsters were knocking down the door, the next—boom."

Ash sighs. "Don't let them bait you. I've already explained everything they need to know."

"'Monsters go bye-bye' isn't quite doing it for me." My attempt at snark is interrupted by a coughing fit. The water burns on its way out. "You're *alive.*"

If Ash weren't propping me up right now, I would be flat on the floor—and not just because I have never been more exhausted in my life.

"Mmhmm. So are you," Ange says. "Life all around. Ash tells us you beat the Mara into submission, so they spit us back into our bodies."

"Uh, that's not exactly what I—" He starts, looks down at me, and shakes his head. "Doesn't matter. We can hash out the details later. Right now, let's just be happy everyone's safe and leave it at that."

"Everyone?" I crane my neck, counting.

Liwan takes that moment to stroll through the door. My jaw drops.

"Everyone, um, intact," Ravel confirms. "Practically speaking, that means most Mara-taken over the last few days or so should have made it back in one piece. Plus, uh, drowning victims, apparently."

I close my eyes. None of this is possible—which apparently, in my overtired brain, means anything is possible. But Cass isn't walking through that door anytime soon. Neither are my parents.

"Our parents," Cadence says. "Also, hi: you're in my body."

"That's enough, Cady. Leave her in peace for five minutes, won't you?" Ash turns to me. "Don't worry. She can't do anything more. It's really over now."

"As if," she sniffs. "You guys forgot about the fogeys, didn't you?"

"The what?" Ange goes on alert. She's not the only one who scans the room for danger.

"Nine Peaks," I rasp, each syllable a stone around my neck. "How long?"

"At least one of you has been paying attention," Cadence snarks. "Yup, the good old homeland is about to wipe us out in a storm of earth-shattering fire. So maybe everyone should take this opportunity to thank you again for getting stuffed back in those nice, flammable skins?"

Ash stands, pulling me with him. I had forgotten how crushingly heavy a body could be. He tightens his grip as my knees sag. "We should have a little time still. A couple hours. Maybe more. If we hurry, we can—"

"Run away from a volcano? As if. Even if you leave the slowpokes behind, you'll be lucky to clear the city. And it's not like molten fire attacks come with pinpoint accuracy."

"What about the barrier?" Just the thought of the energy I'd need to marshal to even begin to strengthen it again makes my vision go wobbly and dark around the edges, but if it's the only way—

"Long gone," Ange says matter-of-factly. "And good riddance."

This is it, then. I don't have anything left to give. No one I can use, no power I can draw on, nothing to fight back with. So the world will survive without us. Great. Everyone I care about is in the path of destruction, and all I can do is . . .

"I got nothing." I laugh a little at the thickness in my own voice. "Sorry. Guess we're doomed."

33

LINKED

FIRST ONE SOMBER face cracks in a smile, then another. Ravel sputters. Ange snorts. Sure, some of the giggling is a little frantic, but I think hysterics are called for, given the circumstances.

"So, what should we do in the meantime?" I say when the laughter has died down into scattered chuckles and muffled sobs. "Anyone know any good games? Ravel?"

But for once, he doesn't seem to be in the mood to play. He stares back wordlessly, blinking so slowly I start to get worried.

"Earth to Stupid?" Cadence prompts. "Calling Stupid. Is anyone home?"

He pinches the bridge of his nose. "I'm thinking."

"It's that hard?"

"Shh. Wait."

His face clears.

"Oop, did it just have a wittle thoughty-woughty?" Cadence singsongs.

If we all weren't about to die, I would really need to have a word with her about her attitude. *Someone's* got to parent the brat. Luckily, I'll be off the hook within the day.

"Nine Peaks is sending us a volcano, yeah?" Ravel finally says.

Ash wobbles his hand. "Not exactly. More like redirecting the potential force of an eruption through subterranean channels."

"And that's the elders' work?"

"Not necessarily. But most likely."

"And the elders of Nine Peaks are like you two? Mystical string-pulling powers, right?" He wiggles his fingers in illustration.

"Is that what you think we do?"

"Just answer him," Ange interrupts, moving closer.

"Cole's 'string-pulling powers' as you put it, are unique. A bonus skill, if you like. But we're all dreamwalkers, yes."

"And dreamwalkers can manipulate fire?" Ravel persists. "Send it to attack other cities through—what was it? Underground tunnels?"

"No, that's—that's not—"

"But your elders are sending the volcano, right? Your *dreamwalker* elders? The ones that are the same kind of whatsits as you?"

"It's not that simple. I can't—"

"Yeah, we all know you're useless, glitter boy. But what about her?" Ravel nods toward me, dark eyes gleaming. "She comes with all the upgrades, right? So she can send it back."

"Whoa, no way." I hold up my hands. "I don't have anything left, remember? Even if I did, I'm not even totally sure what a volcano is. I can't stop it or—or send it anywhere."

"Maybe you could try, though?" Ravel spreads his arms as if this is some brilliant revelation sent to him from on high. When I stare him down, he shrugs. "Or not. But it's not just you two now is it? I know you've got a whole pack of your kind babysitting the refugees just outside the city. What about them?"

This time it's Ash's turn to shake his head.

Ravel hisses in frustration. "How about you just *ask* them to try, huh? It's not like we have a lot to lose here."

"They said no, Ravel. Learn to listen." Ange brushes past him to take my hand. "You fought hard. Thank you."

Her touch sends sunlight fizzing through my veins. I clamp down on it like a lifeline. She jerks back, pulling me away from Ash.

The moment I'm free of his support, my knees buckle, the rush of energy snapped off like a switch has been flipped.

He catches me before I hit the floor. "What—"

"Shh." I stare at my hand, still clamped around Ange's. The current is back. "Something just happened. Ravel, come here for a sec."

He trots over, both arms out as if I'll throw myself into them.

"Don't let go," I say to Ash, tightening my grip on Ange at the same time.

With my free hand, I reach out to Ravel. "Take it. It's not like it'll kill you."

He laughs—but this time, when the jolt hits, his eyes fly wide and he tries to yank away. He makes it less than a hand-span before I catch an invisible thread and hold him in place.

"What are you doing to me?" he whispers, staring at his own hand frozen in midair—at least from his perspective.

"Playing." I pry my fingers from Ange's, lifting away just enough to catch sight of the shining strand linking our palms. "Aren't you having fun?"

Ravel bares his teeth, a little frantic. "Always, with you, flame."

"Cole? What's happening?" Ash is steady at my back, but his voice cracks.

"Just a little experiment. I need you to try something for me, okay? I want you to take Ange's other hand. It's okay. Just go slowly. Good. Now let go. No, of me, not her."

He reaches gingerly, poised to catch me when I inevitably sag to the floor. But the chain of energy keeps humming even when we're not touching, passing from him to Ange, Ange to me, and on the other side, flowing in from Ravel.

"You—your hands—" Ash inches further away, evidently growing more confident I'm not about to crash to my knees. "Your powers came back?"

I study the glowing threads. "*Something* came back, anyway."

"Can I put my arm down now?" Ravel says.

"Not a chance. Here—take her hand."

He huffs but extends a hand to a woman standing a few feet away. She blushes, looking around as if this might be a good time to run away from the crazy people. But then she reaches back, her energy fizzing through him to me.

He might not know her, but I do. I know each and every one of them, the survivors. It's more than I can keep in my head, all the minutia of their lives and deaths and the dreams that transcend both, but traces remain.

I smile, trying to be reassuring. She looks away, but she doesn't let go. And the threads I lent her buzz with every ounce of the energy I spent weaving her hopes and fears and longings back into the fabric of her soul.

There is more power in just these four than I could have ever imagined. And there are dozens more like them. Hundreds.

But is it enough power to turn back a volcano?

"We need to get out of the city. Now." Reluctantly, I release all the threads but Ash's, sagging at the sudden drain. Some of the energy must have, I don't know, recharged me or something, though, because at least now I'm standing on my own.

I flap both hands at a room full of blank stares. "*Now* would be good. That's right. Everyone. All together. Right now. Off we go."

Once they get moving, it's not so bad. We pick up steam and more bodies as we go. Children. Workers. Underfolk. We even snatch armfuls of supplies when they're along our route. There are some who refuse to follow; division heads who try to order us back to prison, dull-eyed workers clinging to their consoles, unwilling or unable to understand that their devotion to regulation no longer serves any purpose, angry enforcers who have to be disarmed. I don't like leaving anyone behind, not when I know what's coming. But we can't slow down to persuade everyone. It's all we can do to try to help those who'll let us.

By the time we're wading from the newly barrier-free tunnel through a soggy stretch of low tide, the crowd is mostly even on the same page about what comes next.

Which is good because I don't have time to explain it from the start to the waiting refugees, not to mention the squads from Nine Peaks *and* a city's worth of drones, rebels, and everything in between.

We only have one shot at this. I'm not even sure what *this* is. Only that something's happening, something exponential—and tapping into our power together is our only hope of surviving what comes next.

It starts with a tremor. Pebbles rattle on the beach—but when hundreds of feet are shifting and scuffing along, that's hardly a surprise. The waves are more telling. The sea creatures stop watching curiously from the sidelines and start swimming—away. Even I can tell the water shouldn't be moving like that.

"Earthquake," Ash murmurs.

"I thought we were expecting a volcano?"

He shrugs. "It's a more complex process than you would think."

"Better get started, then."

But we both hesitate. I've lost him once already today. If this doesn't work, he won't be coming back from a second death. None of us will.

"You've got this," he says, brushing calloused fingers against my cheek. "But, just in case. Whatever happens. Wherever we end up. I'll find you again."

I nod, catching my breath at the heat in his touch. Then he goes. I won't stand shoulder to shoulder with him, or Ravel, or Ange, or any of my other friends, surrounding myself instead with those I've only ever met on the other side. Many of these people have no idea I saved their lives not two hours ago. They have no reason to recognize or trust me.

But they recognize the mercurial founder of Freedom and heir to Refuge and move to obey his orders out of fear, if not awe. Ange has pull with this crowd, too, well known and trusted throughout Under as well as, to a lesser extent, with some of those from Freedom and the streets.

Liwan gathers the young rebels from both the tower and the tunnels, and Ash's words are enough to bring the Nine Peaks contingent into the circle. They're each needed elsewhere. And I need to focus.

I don't know how much power this will take, or if we even have a chance. But whether we live out this day or die, it'll be together.

Besides, if we weren't holding each other up, the shuddering earth would have us flat on our faces by now.

Haynfyv works his way through the crowd, murmuring apologies for those unfortunate enough to be in the path of his elbows. "Do they need to hold hands?"

"Huh?"

He peers down at me. "Judging by your agents' movements and the present environmental disturbance we are in imminent peril. And the strategy that suggests the greatest chance of success involves gathering in close proximity. I'm offering to lend my aid in whichever way you deem best suited to the occasion. Now: do you need people to join hands, or is proximity sufficient?"

I grab his hand—for balance. The earth seems to be trying to yank itself out from under me. "You don't actually remember *anything*, do you?"

"I'll take that as confirmation. You: hand," he barks at the man standing beside him, and then the next one down the line.

"It's coming," Ash shouts from somewhere in the crowd.

The water is roiling in front of us, thick clouds of steam hissing into the air. If this doesn't work, it's anyone's guess whether we'll boil or suffocate first. I reach for the threads. First to those nearest me, and then through their neighbours, the call reverberates out.

The very air seems to come alive with the response. Energy crackles through each strand as it finds my fingers. The sudden force almost breaks my grip. Each and every sliver of myself I've given away seems to be finding its way back now with twice—no, dozens of times the energy I spent healing the victims of the Mara. I feel *amazing*.

A thin sheen of silver ripples from my hands to my neighbours, and to their neighbours. Instead of using this power to cross over to the safety of that other reality, where the crowd cannot follow, I yank the shielding silver manifestation of a dreamwalkers' power into the waking world.

When Ash realizes what I'm doing, he pushes back through the crowd to reposition the gifted from Nine Peaks, spacing them evenly around the perimeter. They tap into the dreamscape one after another, distinctive frissons of energy forming a series of anchors to weave my impromptu barrier around. A living barrier this time, not made of pulverized elements and shattered souls, but woven of life shared and returned. A feedback loop powered by hundreds of separate sources.

It's more than I dared hope for. But is it enough?

The earth shivers beneath us. The air is thick with choking fumes. The water boils, followed by the land. Deep crimson and flaming gold spark from the heart of the city and fling chunks of it into the air. They batter the surface of our misty shell. I strain, pushing it out another inch, two, a hands-breadth, an arms-length. But the drain of every flaming missile is tangible. Each scorching coal seems as if it rakes across my skin, even as each terrified cry from those on the outer edges echoes in my head.

Together, we're more than I ever could have imagined. But if I crumble under this assault, the few dreamwalkers scattered among the crowd may manage to survive, but they won't be able to shield the powerless.

Now the city is burning. The sea itself is boiling. And friends and strangers alike are about to lose not just their homes but their lives.

"On the plus side, you've spared us all an eternity of undead torment, so there is that," Cadence says.

There is that.

Sweat trickles into my eyes. My knees tremble. There's a resistance, now, when I draw on the power running through the threads, a sort of tension that warns I won't be able to keep on at this rate much longer.

It's like all my efforts to heal had been sequestering energy, but now I'm drawing those reserves down to the dregs—and soon, I'll hit bottom.

"Dark much?" Cadence laughs.

"What do you want? Sunshine and rainbows? Just look at it! Everything's getting destroyed! Where are all these people supposed to live, huh? No homes. Nothing left alive. Even the sea is ruined."

Squishy wobbles against me.

"Oh. Um. Sorry. I'm sure it's not the whole sea. Just, you know. This bit."

I try not to think of the creatures getting boiled alive under the waves. At least there wasn't much growing around us on the shore to get ruined.

That's when it splits open beneath us.

34

ERUPTION

Y FINGERS SLIP. The ground drops out.

"Are you stupid?" Cadence yells.

I'm scrambling too fast to argue, snatching at loose threads no one else can see, shifting the energy of the mist to cover a crowd crumbling apart as we speak.

Ash and the others do their best to organize the chaos, hauling people out of fissures and herding them back together so no one slips out of my reach. Children to the center, dreamwalkers and healthy adults to the outer edges.

But another tremor like that, or the worsening heat, or a renewed storm of scorching hail . . . We can't survive this without help, and I'm out of tricks.

Fluffy nudges me, looping a soft, fibrous tendril around my wrist.

"Not now." I block out the choking smoke and focus on keeping my grip on hundreds of threads at once.

The treespawn nudges harder.

"What are you—"

The little creature drops, its thin tendril unspooling to maintain contact with my wrist as it tumbles into a crack in the earth. The scorching, gnashing, lava-fissured earth.

Trees are made of wood. They burn.

"Fluffy!" I drop to my knees, lunging after the little wood-grained knot, but it's already gone. Everything but that one thin strand. And no matter how I yank on it, it doesn't budge.

The earth trembles again. I brace myself for the tremor, pushing power we can't afford to waste into extending our shell of protection beneath our feet to keep anyone from falling this time. But the sudden, violent jolt doesn't arrive. New cracks aren't splitting the earth. There's just a slow, steady creaking as the existing fissures narrow. And seal.

Leaving Fluffy locked in the earth.

I dig my fingers into the dirt where its lonely remaining tendril vanishes. Something pushes back. A lot of somethings.

Soft green sprouts spring up underfoot. One shoots up taller, a young plant, then not so young. A sapling, thickening as I stare. A tiny yet grizzled form steps out from its smooth bark and cocks its head, looking up at me. It spreads both forelimbs. Fluffy is almost too big for it to hold.

"Did you do all this?" I reach for the wooden knot. It extends a sleepy loop and clings to my arm. The forest creature steps back into its sapling, leaving the treespawn behind. "You're holding the earth together for us? Isn't it hot?"

Fluffy grumbles and squirms in a pleased sort of way, but its smooth brown whorls and satiny curves are looking a little charred around the edges.

And the few extra moments' safety the forest has bought us, though appreciated, doesn't change anything. The city is still burning, melted slag mixing with lava and hissing into the boiling sea. The young dreamwalkers seeded around our perimeter are flickering and going dark one by one as they burn through their reserves and run dry.

The ordinary humans are worn out too, leaning against one another or sprawled on the renewed ground, despite its growing heat. Fluffy's miraculous ground cover is already withering.

Squishy steams gently, and even my sweat is starting to evaporate. I can't draw enough power to push back the heat, not if I want the dreamscape's protective mist to last more than another few minutes.

The seaspawn flicks a wavelet at Fluffy as if in farewell. It melts, losing its shape and patters down on the wilting sprouts at my feet.

A fine rain spatters across my face. The roiling sea surges, a fresh current sweeping in high from the far side of the inlet. The waves calm, steam hissing up from the points where molten rock still invades the newly cooled water.

Squishy coalesces on my shoulder, giving me a damp nudge before sloshing down to cuddle with Fluffy. The newest member of their uncanny little trio hovers uncertainly near my face.

I blink at it, considering. The other two seem tired but unharmed by their efforts to protect us. "Well? What do you do?"

Puffy gives a little roll in midair. Then it, well, puffs apart. A breeze filters through the crowd, cool and heavy with the lingering remnants of Squishy's rain. It sweeps the remaining smoke from the air, leaving it sweet and clear.

The fog-creature spins itself back into a visible mass and bobs at me hopefully.

"Very nice. Now if you can just keep that up for . . ." How long do we still have to hold out? The rumbling underfoot has calmed, but outside our little oasis of protection the volcano still churns, throwing chunks of earth into the sky, spitting fingers of flame, coughing fresh smoke in our direction. It's nowhere near done yet.

The energy I can draw from the crowd is guttering. I lock my knees to keep from falling as the manifesting dreamscape sucks at the last of our reserves. It is not going to be enough to just shelter from the storm. If I can't find a way to stop the volcano itself, none of us will survive.

"I don't suppose one of you could do something about that?" I eye my unexpected allies doubtfully.

The forest's gift doesn't bother answering, clearly weak against the fire. The sea's wobbles uncertainly, but judging by the state of the inlet, its waters can only do so much. The sky's is tracing lazy figure eights in midair—I'm not entirely sure it's even listening.

But I already knew the answer before I asked. There's no last-minute rescue waiting in the wings. I'll fight until the end, of course. It's just . . . It won't be long now—

"So, uh, the self-sacrifice shtick is cute and all, but I have a better idea," Cadence says. "Why don't you give me your anchor?"

"My what?"

"Fluffy. Ugh, I cannot believe you named it that. Whatever. Just gimme the tree thingy, and the other two, and I'll see what I can do."

"About what?"

"Are you stupid? I'm gonna stop that volcano."

"Cadence, stop distracting her," Ash says.

I twist to acknowledge the backup with a nod—and the world goes glittery around the edges.

There's a slow, grey moment. My stomach dips, turning sour. I'm somehow freezing and feverish at the same time.

Then I'm sitting in the middle of a ring of worried faces with silver mist leaking from my fingers.

"I think this is it, C." Ash tries for a smile. It doesn't go well.

"Yuck. I mean, sure, go ahead," Cadence complains. "Have your tearful goodbye scene if you must. *Or* you could give me your toys and let me save the world for a change."

I go to rub my head, remember halfway that I was supposed to be doing something, and reach for the web of threads woven through the crowd. The pulse of energy in return is sluggish, the resulting layer of mist stretched thin, but I can cover everyone still, if only just.

"It's okay," Ash says bravely. "You tried. You can let it go now."

"Or, again, you could stop ignoring me," Cadence insists.

"Yeah, it's not like power totally goes to your head or anything," Ravel says, popping out from the crowd with Ange in tow. "Might as well party on at the end of the world, right?"

But his smirk is forced, and Ange's expression tense.

"We've made sure the kids are in the middle," she says. "They'll have the best chance of surviving. One of your young ones"—she nods at Ash—"will guide them north later if—if they can . . ."

She swallows hard, looking away.

"Again. Hi. Right here. Offering to save the world." Cadence says. "What's the worst that can happen? You all gonna die twice or what?"

I blink. She's not wrong, but—"What's in it for you? You let half these people die once already. What's different this time?"

"Do we have time to rehash the sins of Cady? No? Cool, let's move on. Gimme the sprites. I'll say "please" if it helps."

"Will you really?" Ravel snarks back, apparently unable to help himself.

"Well, not to you. Cole, I know how you just love the limelight and all, but how about instead of martyrdom you just let me have this?"

I pant, shaking my head against the stars dancing at the edge of my vision. I can't catch my breath. The world keeps greying out around me, except that's not right, is it? It's not the world but me that's fading.

Cadence won't stop pestering me to the last. It's nice to know some things never change, I guess. But— "Why are you still here? I know you don't have to be. You can run away to the other side anytime you want."

"Would you let me?" Her voice is hushed, as if she doesn't want the others to overhear. "Will you let me go now, Cole? I saw you free them, you know. Mom and dad. If you'd be okay with me hiding out in the dreamscape, you should be able to let me go for real. Please. You don't need me anymore."

I stammer, breathless and dizzy, straining for the words to express how shocked, how absurd her—

"*Don't.* I stayed for you. Set me free now, Cole."

Maybe it's because I'm tapped into the dreamscape. Maybe it's some trick of the mist and the dregs of the crowd's power boost, but I can almost see her: a child with wild hair and a lace-like birthmark a few shades darker than the rest of her skin framing deep brown eyes. She holds out a hand. There's apology in her face, and regret, but that hand is imperious.

"No. You can't—" I wheeze, head spinning with the strain of holding the hopes and dreams and lives of hundreds of people in my hands and now *this* on top of it all.

"I'm sorry. For all of it. Let me go now, Cole."

Still that small hand, outstretched. Demanding something I can't give.

Except—what right do I have to leave her behind? To force her to remain alone. Forever the villain of the story. Eternally the lonely child who sacrificed everything to bring back what she herself had destroyed.

But the past is gone. It's time for both of us to let it die. And that means letting it all go—both the past and my need to control the situation—and trusting her one last time. So I don't stop her when she reaches to take these strange creatures that have come into my life away again.

"Thank you. It wasn't all bad, was it?" She curls her small arms around Fluffy and Squishy, snuggling them close. Puffy nestles in her hair.

It's unexpectedly cute. Little brat. "I'll miss you."

"Well duh," she calls back over her shoulder, darting weightlessly out of my reach—and into the heart of the volcano, flames spurting up in her wake.

There's no time to mourn.

I throw everything I have left into holding the eruption at bay. Flaming chunks of the city batter our misty shelter, each one pressing in further than the last before being deflected.

The heat is unbearable, the smoke choking without the sea or the sky to brush it away. The earth shudders and rips open beneath us without the forest's roots binding it together. Ash's quick thinking is the only thing that keeps me from sliding into the fires deep below. Not everyone is so lucky.

I spend the remaining power to its dregs and beyond, drawing more than magic down my web of threads. My hands grow cold and clumsy, but there are only a few strands left to cling to, the crowd long since released lest I reach beyond what I had given them and drain down their lives too.

The fiery reds and smoky blacks of the volcano-rocked landscape fade to featureless grey. The blistering heat slips away, leaving only this icy numbness.

If I can't protect us, at least I won't be the last to die this time. Maybe I'll catch up with Cadence, and ask mom and dad if they're really hers, or mine, or—

No more questions.

No more thought.

Just . . .

Stillness.

HERE ONCE WAS a girl.

And then there were two.

One to wander in the labyrinth of memories and mistakes of the past. One to stumble through the pathless mists of the future. And one dancing through the endless present, forever waiting for the moments her sisters might call.

So really, there were three.

"YOU'RE NOT REAL."

Victoire shrugs and pirouettes in place, colourful flowing layers fluttering in her wake. Four orbs dance with her, bobbing and pouncing joyfully.

"What are they doing here?"

She catches the flickering one, peeking over its flames of blue and red and yellow mischievously. The ball of fog nuzzles her face while the little wood knot spins excited loops around her feet.

Squishy sloshes over to me sedately, apparently done playing.

"You weren't supposed to die, too," I inform the ocean at my feet. "Or are you just visiting?"

"No one's dead," Cadence says.

She's sitting cross-legged on the ceiling, hair hanging down in a ragged mane. It's not a particularly remarkable ceiling. The paint's a bit blobby, truth be told.

"You're babbling. Stop it." She rolls her eyes. "Fine. I'll come down if you think of somewhere more exciting to hang out than . . . wherever this is supposed to be."

Victoire swirls into midair and extends a hand.

Cadence crosses her arms. "Not until she stops imagining us into a cell. It's depressing."

Victoire flips upside down and mimics Cadence's posture, slumping her shoulders and putting on an outrageous pout.

Cadence snorts. Then she giggles. Victoire nudges her, and the giggles turn into full-blown, mouth open, eyes scrunched, red-faced laughter.

"Fine, I'll come down." She pushes off the ceiling, flips twice, and lands neatly in front of me. "Don't tell me you thought she was a figment of your imagination? Not likely, when the best you can come up with for scenery is a bland set of four walls and a blobby paint job."

Okay then. That's about enough regret-fuelled nostalgia for me. "Go pester someone else. I don't remember inviting you to my afterlife."

"Again. *Not dead.* You're free to wake up anytime, princess."

Victoire nods, shaking her finger with mock solemnity. The fiery orb bobs along with it like an oversized ring. My frustration ebbs. She winks. Has she been working me this whole time?

"If you name it 'Burny' I'm never speaking to you again," Cadence says, pulling my attention back to the newest member of our little flock of weirdoes.

"Where did Flicker come from?"

She blinks. "Flicker? Actually, that's not bad. For you, I mean. The volcano gave her to me. Turns out she wasn't too happy at Nine Peaks sending her so far from home like that. Messing with the natural order is totally the opposite of what they're supposed to be doing, after all."

"She?"

"Well, it's better than calling them 'it' don't you think? Besides, she's really more of a she." Cadence holds out a finger and Flicker flutters over to perch on it. "Also, she says she's staying with me. You can go now."

"They talk to you?"

"It's a gift."

Victoire twirls by, gathering Flicker and the other three back into her orbit with a reproving glance. Cadence deflates a bit.

"You're sure you're not just imagining things?"

"Are you?" she snaps. "Only one way to find out, right?"

She marches over and shoves me into the wall. And then through it.

"SHE'S GOING TO wake up soon, right?" Ravel says.

A cool hand brushes my forehead. "There's nothing wrong with her," Ange says. "Just overtired."

"It's been days. No one's that tired."

"What do you want me to say? She has a pulse. She's breathing. The kid is alive. Beyond that, it's not like I'm an expert on the repercussions of being a human shield."

"Did you ask *them*?"

"No. It never once occurred to me to check with the other people with strange powers to see if they knew any way to help this person with strange powers. I've always been incompetent like that."

"You could have just said yes."

A rustle. Footsteps. A breath of air on my cheek.

I can feel the world, raw and grating against my awareness. I can hear it. I just can't see it. I should open my eyes, right? That's the obvious next thing to do.

I just . . . can't quite muster the energy . . .

"Anything yet?" Ash says from further away.

Ash, and Ange, *and* Ravel? Either this section of the afterlife is better than the last, or maybe, somehow . . .

"Shouldn't you be able to do something?" Ravel complains. "It can't be good for them to just be lying here like this."

Them?

"Oh, that's right. I forgot to wiggle my fingers and chant the magic words. I'll get right on that."

"Why is everyone so sarcastic today?"

"Out," Ange orders.

"Good idea," Ash says. "They're probably just waiting for you to leave."

"I know I am," a fourth person says. Her voice is a little slurred. It's rougher and higher pitched than I'm used to. But the bolt of pure electricity it sends shooting through me not only snaps my eyelids open but has me nearly to my feet before the vertigo catches up.

I grab for the edge of her cot to keep from crashing to the floor. She frowns blearily. "Clumsy. Hope I don't grow up like that too."

"How—You—You can't be—"

But that trademark eye roll is unmistakeable.

The girl in the cot beside mine is shorter, with a rounder face and longer hair. Otherwise, we're identical.

"Told ya no one was dead," Cadence says smugly. She coughs. "Also: ouch."

In the background, Ange swats Ravel. "Go help if you're going to stay."

He fumbles for water, gingerly sliding an arm behind Cadence to lever her up enough to take a sip without choking. She glares and pointedly dribbles on him.

Ash appears at my elbow. "You should probably lay down again. You were out for a while."

I let him steer me back to the makeshift cot—more a heap of flattish rubble padded with a couple dusty blankets, really—without taking my eyes off Cadence. "How is this possible? You're—you're—" Real. Visible. Also, weirdly, either a lot older or a few years younger than she should be?

Ash clears his throat. "Same question."

"You two are hopeless. You really had no idea what you had all along? C'mon out guys." Cadence snaps her fingers, and then groans at the sudden weight of the orbs on her chest. "Cutesy nicknames aside, you made some very convenient friends. When I met Flicker, she insisted on a gift to thank us for helping the fires return home. So they all teamed up to build us this."

She examines her nails and sighs. "I did suggest a little more creativity in the design. And before you ask, yes, it's real. It'll grow, and get hungry, and do all the usual sorts of obnoxious human things. Oh, and Victoire says hi. She decided to stick with me. We prefer to be addressed as Cady, boss, or My Queen and will accept the use of singular pronouns, though the plural is obviously more accurate."

"Oh," says Ash faintly, sitting down beside me all at once. "Wow." I pat his shoulder tentatively.

"Yeah, wow." Ravel echoes sarcastically. "Great reward. You couldn't have them build us a new city instead?"

Ange smacks him again.

"What? We've got hundreds of people to house in burnt-out rubble and feed with scraps of broiled seaweed."

We do? "Wait, where are we?"

I haven't had much of a chance to look around, given the circumstances. But the 'walls' seem to be some kind of textured fabric, billowing with the briny sea breeze, open to a murky sky. The 'floor' is grainy sand and rubble.

"Home. Where else would we be?" Ravel says with a smirk, gesturing at the makeshift room. "Our own lovely ruins."

"But—"

"You've been unconscious for a few days," Ash says more gently. "We did talk about trying to move everyone to Nine Peaks, but it's a long way on foot, and the elders aren't likely to respond well to a crowd of refugees appearing on their doorstep at the best of times."

"Not to mention they're the murdering assholes who tried to, you know, *murder us all*," Ravel adds helpfully.

My mouth goes dry. What do we do? Why had we never talked about what came after? I mean, besides the obvious: we didn't really expect there to be an after. But now there is, and someone is going to have to figure out how to keep a city's worth of people safe and, like, alive.

"We can talk about this later," Ange says, looking at me with a worried expression. "You really should get some more rest—"

"Who's in charge?" I interrupt. "Somebody has to be giving orders out there."

They exchange guilty looks. Ange is the first to confess. "We kind of told them you were, actually. It was easier than trying to get past what they thought of each of us before. People saw you protecting them. They seemed to figure if you could keep fire from raining down on their heads, your orders might be worth following."

"I haven't given any orders."

"They didn't need to know that," Ravel says. "And they still don't. Like Ange said, you can get some rest. We'll pretend to consult you and then tell people whatever they need to hear."

"But you just said they're starving, and—"

"Nah, they're just sick of seaweed. And we're not totally out of supplies. Yet. We managed to grab more than we expected on our way out." A strange expression softens his features, and he slips one hand into a pocket, accompanied by the faint crinkle of paper. He shakes his head. "It's fine for now. Seriously, flame. You don't have to figure out everything right this minute."

"Yeah, *flame*," Cadence says sarcastically—which is more than usually upsetting coming from a face that looks so much like mine. "You can always screw everything up tomorrow."

Then she closes her eyes and shakes her head. "Oops. Sorry. Habit. We'll behave."

I groan and flop back against the blankets. This is too weird. Too much. I was counting on a nice peaceful afterlife, not getting appointed head of a city's worth of refugees.

On the other hand, it's not like I don't have ideas about what needs to happen. Maybe it's exhaustion talking, but this . . . is not the worst thing to happen to me lately. I'm alive. My friends are alive. The city is destroyed, but a bunch of people got saved after all.

So maybe Cadence got the starring role in the end—but the battle's not over yet. There's still more to be done. And somehow, as usual, I've got myself all tangled up in it.

When it comes right down to it, I don't even mind. If anything, I'm kind of excited to get started.

"I'm going to sleep," I announce. "And when I wake up, I expect a full report of our situation. I want headcounts—make a list of useful skills, too. I want supply inventories. I want the squads patrolling in case any nearby creatures get curious. I want people sorting rubble for anything salvageable. And somebody get me Haynfyv."

"You don't actually have to be in charge, flame," Ravel says. "We just said you were to get everyone on board."

"Don't worry," I say, yawning. "I'll make good use of your talents too."

36
BEGINNINGS

ESPITE CADY'S PREFERRED title, neither she nor I end up being crowned queen of the refugees. I think it's going to be healthier for me not be in the spotlight, at least not on my own. As partial punishment for nearly causing the end of the world, she doesn't get to be.

Instead, she's going back to school—Grace and Susan have set up an ad-hoc child-minding-meets-education program in the midst of the rubble. We've managed to reunite a few of the stolen children with parents or older siblings, but most were orphaned by Refuge. Maybe we can get to the place where they can be adopted by other survivors, but for now, we're all operating as one big, not-so-happy family anyway.

The basics—food, shelter, clean water—were secured while I was still unconscious, along with a rough leadership structure mirroring what existed before the fall of the city. Ange represents Underfolk, Ravel has mostly been recognized as the successor to Refuge by its inhabitants, and Sam stands in as the voice of the unaffiliated survivors from the streets. Ash speaks for the dreamwalkers, with Susan and the squad captains for backup. Turns out the Nine Peaks elders' hostility didn't sit too well with a number of their people, and my grandmother was all too pleased to bring more supporters our way, even if there wasn't much they were able to do on arrival.

And, by virtue of technically saving the world and accidentally getting named leader of the whole mess while I was out of commission, I'm also on the council.

Actually, as far as the general population knows, I'm in charge of it. That doesn't necessarily mean anyone listens to what I have to say, though.

"Of course they'll let you in," Susan insists. "It's your home."

"But not ours," Ravel points out. "If you remember, they weren't exactly thrilled when I showed up the first time. Nine Peaks stuck the last batch of survivors in a quarantine camp outside the city walls when we first showed up. What do you think they're going to do when we arrive on their doorstep with ten times as many?"

"And that's assuming we can even move everyone," Ange adds. "There are some pretty young kids, not to mention the sick and wounded to think about. We don't have nearly the amount of transportation needed to carry the ones who can't make the trek on their own."

"We're better off moving to the island," Ash says. "At least they want us back."

"'Cause sailing worked out so well for you the last time," Ravel snipes. "No thanks, Sparky."

"Really?" Ash takes a step toward the shorter boy. "You really want to try me right now?"

"Enough." I shove them apart to take the center of the small ring we've cleared as an open-air council chamber. "Let Kurt finish his report."

The former Inspector Haynfyv clears his throat, looking as if he'd rather be anywhere but in the middle of our meeting. "As I was saying, upon consultation with experts from the communities formerly known as Refuge and Under, and with the specialist recommendations of our guests from Nine Peaks, the feasibility of restoring a sufficient number of dwellings and supplying occupants with the essentials of life within their previous territories is inadvisable."

"Which is why Nine Peaks—" Susan starts, at the same moment as Ash says, "So we'll take the ships, then—"

I motion them to silence, not taking my eyes off of Kurt Hayne. "And the other possibility?"

He shakes his head. "It is far from ideal, but engineers and fabricators from all three populations agree it could be viable. It would take time to construct a new city on this side of the inlet, of course, but there are sufficient resources in the vicinity to maintain the settlement."

"Here?" Susan sweeps an incredulous hand toward the long-overgrown rubble. "There's nothing here but sand and ruins. Hasn't been for a hundred years."

"Thanks for your input, Gran," I say dryly. "We can carry on from here. I'm sure your students are missing you."

She nods, conceding the floor with good grace, but steps into the center of the circle to give me a hug before heading out. Ash straightens at her departure, settling under the responsibility of speaking for the dreamwalkers alone.

"I'm for it," Ange says. I'd thought she might be. "We've built in worse circumstances before. Underfolk know how to survive, and take care of one another. It's your lot who're the liability."

Ravel snorts. "The sheep'll do whatever I tell them to." Then he slips a hand into his pocket, his eyes darkening. "Sorry. I meant I'd be happy to help no matter what we choose. And there are worse places to try to rebuild. But as much as there's no love lost between me and the fogeys, it might be easier in the long run to join Nine Peaks. Or check out glitter boy's mythical island paradise."

"You know my vote, C." Ash's face shines with hope at the thought of reuniting with his parents. "I can't guarantee Grandfather wouldn't make life difficult if we head north, but the islanders would welcome us with open arms. I'm sure their ship will be arriving any day now."

"There's not much here," Sam puts in doubtfully. "I'd like folk to have a better life, you know? Even if we're not much wanted by those up north, they live easy up there.

And they owe us for turning our homes into slag. Wouldn't hurt to play on their guilt a little. Besides, what about the ones we left behind?"

I nod. No matter what happens, we'll need to send word to the first wave of refugees we'd left in Nine Peaks and offer them the option of rejoining us. But there's one more council member to speak.

"Lily?" I say gently.

She's the voice of the people for today's meeting. We draw one at random each time we meet. My idea. I've seen what power can do, how it twists things and separates leaders from the people impacted by their decisions. Lily's our youngest citizen representative so far, but I'm glad it's her. She's struggled to survive in a crumbling city, been separated from her family, and made the trek to Nine Peaks and back again. I don't know about the others, but for me, her voice will carry the most weight in this decision.

"You want to build a city here?" she asks, digging a toe in the sand doubtfully.

Haynfyv kneels beside her, gingerly putting an arm around his niece and darting a look around our circle as if someone will tell him to stop. He gestures. "Not just here. We're a big crowd, right? Lots of people. So we spread out a bit. Some over there. Some further inland. Some back that way."

She furrows her brow. "Then where will the wall go?"

I blink. She's right. Nine Peaks has its wood and earth barrier ringing the entire city. Refuge existed within the four walls of its tower, and the dome was a sort of wall around the whole city. She's never seen people live without borders. Neither have I.

Maybe it's time for that to change. "What if we didn't have one?"

She tilts her head, her small face furrowed in concentration. "No walls?"

"Just for the buildings," I clarify. "To hold the roofs up, okay? But no big walls, not like a fence around everyone."

"Cole, I don't think—" Ravel's interrupted from a cough by Ash and a kick from Ange. He subsides.

"You really want to do this?" Ash says.

I catch Lily's eye. She grins. I turn, studying each council member. Ange will back me up. As much as she tries to look out for her people, I think it's as much so she can stay close to Cass's final resting place as anything. Ravel will want to stay wherever there are people to work; that much will never change. Though he has seemed to soften a little since the fall of the city. Sam's not sentimental, but he'll go where Lily goes. Ash . . .

Ash wants to rejoin his family. They weren't on the ship that went down with him on it, but people who claimed to know his parents were. He hasn't seen his mom and dad in over a decade. It makes sense that he misses them. And I hope that they get a chance to reunite. I'll do what I can to make that happen.

But I don't want to leave. I want to start over. I want us to do better, this time. There's more here to heal, and to rebuild. And I want to be a part of that. "Yeah. I really do."

"SO?" I SETTLE gingerly on the damp bit of concrete beside Ravel. "You going to tell me what's going on or am I supposed to guess?"

He shrugs. "Thought you had more important things to worry about."

"True. I should probably get back to all that big important stuff I'm in charge of now—" I hop off the concrete.

Ravel snags my sleeve and drags me back. "Wait." He grabs my other arm, turning my palms up, then down, to examine the backs of my hands. "The burns are still there."

Both hands are etched with the uneven whorls of the barrier. They used to be a near twin to his black tattoos, but those marks vanished along with his nightmare-gold eyes when the Mara gave back his body.

"We don't match anymore," I say softly.

He huffs a laugh. "You're not getting rid of me that easily, flame. Besides, ink can be replaced." But when he lets go, it's only one hand. He reaches into his pocket, draws out a folded sheaf of paper.

I eye the pile of pages. A confession? Song lyrics? Blackmail material? "Do I want to know?"

He shakes his head, taps the papers on his knee, and finally extends them toward me. "Found them in one of the supply caches. They're from her. My . . . From Maryam."

"From your mom."

He flinches. Nods. Shakes his head. "Just read them."

He sits in silence while I read, his knee bouncing a bit, his hands clasped to keep them still. I take my time, pausing to watch the birds wheeling over the waves, not just seagulls, but herons and geese. A robin hops across the rubble toward us, hoping for crumbs. Heads peek from the water and nudge up against the shore—seals, and otters, and once, the sudden spurting fountains of a pod of whales daring the inlet, seemingly unperturbed by the creatures that share the deeps with them. We leave them alone, and they don't bother us. We haven't lost anyone to the sea monsters yet.

How different could things have been for Ravel? For Maryam? The pages are a letter for her only living son—a secret history, a tragedy, and a plea for forgiveness. She hadn't been able to stop her people from destroying their world and stirring the wrath of the unseen creatures around them. I can only hope that we've learned to see and to share better. For my part, I'll do whatever I can to make sure of it.

"I won't forgive her," Ravel bursts out. "She can't just write a letter and make it all go away."

I nod. "She did terrible things. They can't be erased so easily."

He rips the letter from my hands, stalks to the edges of the waves, and raises it.

I dart after him, catching his wrist just as he makes to hurl the pages into the sea. He jerks away, whirling, arm upraised and eyes wild. I flinch.

Then I raise my chin. I won't be afraid of him. "How many lives did you sacrifice to the Mara?"

This time it's his turn to flinch. I don't give him a chance to respond. "I can't tell you how many lives I sacrificed. Nor Cadence. I can't even tell you we thought we were doing the right thing, or the only thing we could, at the time. Will you throw us away, too?"

He backs down, backs away, trips, landing with a squelch in the damp, pebbly sand. He tips his head back, inky lashes fluttering against damp cheeks. "So where does that leave me?"

"Alive. Broken. Healing. In debt to the other survivors. So pay up." I offer him a hand. "Your mom hurt a lot of people. I'm not saying that what she did wasn't awful. It scares me that she could do so much wrong and still believe it was the right thing to do. I'm not giving myself a pass, either. Or you. But we're still here. We're going to listen, and do our best to see, and try not to turn into crazy fanatics who think they're the only ones who carry the weight of the world. And, starting today, we're going to be okay just being us. Okay?"

He takes my hand, but I don't pull him up just yet. "She loved you, you know?"

He blinks fast, ducking his head. "She didn't know how to love."

I lean back and pull. Standing, he's barely taller than me, his eyes damp and his bare face startlingly vulnerable, though it's been some time since I've seen him painted and masked and costumed in the extravagant lies he used to cling to.

"I think she just forgot, for a little while. Or walled that part of herself off along with the rest of the world. You were the last thing she spoke of, at the end."

Ravel scrubs his forearm over his eyes, leaving it there to whisper, "I don't know who I am without her."

I think about Cadence, and the memories she took with her. I think about the family I still don't feel a part of, and the rule-bound life Ravel's mother's regime required of me, the one I never managed to live up to. I think about every life I failed to save, every choice I wish I'd made differently. But for all our failures, we're still here.

I duck down to peer under his raised arm. "I know. Me too. So let's find out."

37

ENDINGS

CADENCE FOUND ME the night I surrendered to the Mara. We've been together, one way or another, ever since.

And now, it's time for her to leave.

"Be careful," Ash says. "Don't forget to look where you're going. You can't just float through walls anymore."

She rolls her eyes.

"She'll be fine," Ravel says. "Or she won't. Either way, off you go kiddo."

He makes a shooing motion. She sticks her tongue out at him.

"We'll watch out for her," an older woman says, slinging an insistent arm around Cadence's prickly shoulders. "We did manage to raise three without too much damage, after all."

This time it's Steph who rolls her eyes, but she and Grace are having a hard time keeping the shy grins off their faces. The oldest sister, Banshee or whatever, is practically glowing, which is a weird look for her. But understandable. My cousins had believed their parents dead for years. Getting both of them back like this is more than they ever hoped for.

The ship appeared two weeks after Cadence and I woke up. I had given up on help from the island after Ash's ship went down, but apparently, they hadn't forgotten about us.

Would it have been nice if they showed up a couple weeks earlier? Sure.

Would it have changed anything? My newfound aunt and uncle don't think so, but then we don't agree on lots of things, not least of all what should happen with the refugees. They want to load us all up on their ships and sail back to their island—and I see the same longing in Ash's eyes. But I look at what we've built already, and I'm not so sure.

The dreamwalkers, whether those in Nine Peaks or those from the island, say their purpose is to 'heal' nature. They're supposedly trying to undo the harm humans caused generations ago through a slow and careful process of research and ecological restoration.

But then they go around doing stupid stuff like pretending kids' parents died to try to stimulate the development of stronger powers and insisting on intruding on damaged landscapes and then killing the creatures who react to the intrusion, and—oh, right—redirecting nearby volcanic activity to attack people thousands of miles away.

It's almost like hiding out in their painstakingly engineered and cultivated walled cities is keeping them from noticing just how crazy and unnatural some of the stuff they've been doing is.

At least, that's what the Regen City Council has been talking about for the past few days. We'd started organizing people, and shelter, and stuff out of necessity, each of us bringing whatever skills or network we had to the table and adding voices as leaders emerged from the crowd. Now we're working toward something more than just survival.

We want to try something different, right here on the blasted, broken shoreline. Instead of running away to untouched land high in the mountains or across the water, we're navigating life in the midst of monsters—and we haven't lost anyone yet.

Sure, we have to move a little slower than we might like when it comes to scouting for salvage, or picking a site to plant on, or wading into the water to harvest sea life, but we would rather take our time and get a little less done than take more than our share and start a fight. At least, that's the plan.

It's not easy getting everyone on the same page when you start with a bunch of homeless strangers that includes everything from unthinking rule-followers to anti-authority revolutionaries, but I think it helps that every single one of us lost our home and our ways of life at the same time. We all have to adjust to a new world.

And it doesn't hurt that we've got people with a little extra magic at their disposal—including the four orb-like creatures that bob around helping out here and there—but when it comes down to it, most of us have *something* to contribute. Ange's underground engineers, in particular, were thrilled to compare notes with the kids from Nine Peaks and the newcomers from the island. Grace's insight and Susan's experience have been particularly useful. They're already looking at ways to draw energy from the waves and the wind without disturbing the creatures around us. It turns out to be exciting—if, at times, exhausting—to look for new ways to build a better life for all of us.

Which is why I can't believe Cady is willing to sail away from it all.

"You know you're not getting rid of me that easily, right?" she says, tracking my thoughts a bit too closely as usual, even if I'm mostly sure she's not really in my head anymore. "As if. Think of it as a small vacation. You'll enjoy not having anyone around to call you out on your crap. Just don't get too comfortable."

Steph smirks. I eye her narrowly, not at all pleased that she and Cady will be spending some quality time together on this trip. I can already see a future where she and Cady are inseparable tag-teaming bullies.

"We really shouldn't be gone long," Grace chimes in. "We know you could use more supplies. And Mom said things are done differently on the island. We can bring back more teachings to help Regen City."

Cady snorts, as she does every time she hears the admittedly grandiose name for our makeshift smattering of structures along the rubble-strewn coastline. But she lost the vote to call it Trash Town nine to one, so there's nothing she can say.

She turns to leave, and hesitates. "Look, I'm just passing on a message, okay? They want me to tell you you're doing great. Keep it up, and it'll all turn out."

"They?"

She holds Fluffy and Squishy out impatiently. "They. This lot. The sprites, or whatever. They said they're glad they chose you. Even though they're with me now."

Puffy wafts over and nuzzles my cheek. I flinch back from Flicker's lick of flame on my other side. "The, uh, 'sprites' *talk* to you?"

Cady shrugs. "We share a wavelength. They said they liked your restraint. Like, sure, you want stuff, but you also know how to hold back and, y'know, share. Empathize. Maybe you'd know how to be less greedy than the ones who came before."

My jaw drops. Cady peeks over her shoulder and hastens to add, "Don't let it go to your head. I bet it was really just that you're the only dreamwalker who'd developed a resistance to gold. So, like, you'd just suffered enough to maybe survive a revolution 's all. But you're not special, okay? So don't go acting like it."

She stalks off, the sprites bobbing in her wake. I call a shell-shocked thanks after her, though I wouldn't put it past her to have made the whole thing up. Still, it was a nice conciliatory gesture either way.

Maybe it'll be good for her to get away for a bit and figure out who she is without me. I certainly could use some time to get used to who I am without her. And I cannot wait for her aunt and uncle to try parenting my little trouble child. I stifle a smirk and turn to face the next wave of goodbyes.

Grace hugs me and Steph gives me a bruising cuff on the shoulder. Her older sister—who definitely has a name, but since everyone calls her Banshee, I can never remember it—sniffs and casts a frustrated look at Ash. He's carefully examining his toes.

I'm too busy laughing at the look on his face to dodge my aunt's embrace. Thankfully, my uncle shows no inclination to give me a hug; so all that's left is to wave awkwardly in Cady's general direction as she lounges against the ship's rail. She rolls her eyes and turns her back.

"She'll miss you, you know," Ash says, casually slinging an arm around my shoulder. He refused to go with her, even though I know he's longing to see his parents. But I talked to Grace's mom and dad. They'll see that the next ship out is carrying a surprise for Ash. It's literally the absolute least I could do for him after all he's done for me.

Ravel glowers.

I shrug free. "She'll just have to find someone else to pester."

But my chest stays tight and my eyes prickle as Cady's ship shrinks into the distance, the long, straight line of her back oh-so-casually propped against the rails merging into the amorphous dark blob of the distant boat silhouetted against the late afternoon sun.

Then Ange jogs up to say the council needs to convene—something about a wastewater disagreement—and Ravel makes a very childish joke that sends Lily into fits of giggles. Amy, red-faced, tries to explain why her daughter should most definitely not repeat it to anyone, ever, and Haynfyv turns an interesting shade of purplish-grey, sputtering.

Ash tries to cozy up again under the guise of escorting me back to the cleared area we have our council meetings in, and I sidestep, rolling my eyes at Ravel's pleased expression. One of these days, I'll have to sit them both down and have a chat about boundaries and independence. Right now, I just need a little more of both than either of them seems to have realized. Maybe that will change over time. Other things certainly have.

Maryam told me it takes an iron will and a heart of stone to lead. To provide. To stop the monsters at the gate and make a safe, healthy home. I am not made of stone or iron. I'm not totally sure what I am made of, but I'm not sure that matters anymore, either.

The more important thing is what I want, and what I choose, and what I do. I won't be the perfect leader—I'm pretty sure I won't ever be the perfect anything—and I've made a lot of mistakes already, but I'm going to do my best to keep dreaming of better ways to live and be, and to work with friends and rivals and everyone in between to help us get there.

This isn't the world I grew up in. No masks. No walls. No hiding. No monsters.

It's bigger, and more complicated, and difficult, and beautiful than anything I ever could have imagined. And for the first time in forever, I can't wait to find out what comes next.

38

CODA

"ANY MORE FIRES to put out tonight?" Ash drops into the chair beside me and prods the small fire pit in front of us with a long branch. The flies aren't too bad this near the water.

I sigh, letting the tension of the day drain from my muscles. Our furniture has come a long way since those early days; the satin-grained curve of this chair back is perfect for lounging at the end of a long day. "Just this one. I'm not worried."

He looks over, silhouetted against the ruddy light. He's cropped his hair short again; I miss the way he wore it when he was younger. "You're not, are you?"

"Should I be? We survived Ravel's idea of founding day anniversary celebrations. Hardly any fights to break up and no major injuries. Great food. Your band rocked. His dance routine was a little weird, but at least no one got hurt." I smirk at the memory. He's grown up in a lot of ways—we all have. But some things never change.

I snuggle down deeper into my chair. "Last I checked, nothing and no one is after our necks, we're growing enough for the winter, the water and soil samples for our next expansion site have come back clean, and after we finish the new build next week, no one will be bunking up who doesn't want to be."

Ash snorts. "I don't think Grace is in any hurry to move out of Liwan's place, even with those brothers of his."

I shrug. "I'm sure we can find someone to take it if she doesn't want it. Lily keeps insisting she's old enough to live on her own now, even if Sam's not too keen on the idea."

Ash cocks an eyebrow. I smother a laugh. "Fine. Call it a guesthouse then. We could certainly use one. And, at the rate people are moving down from Nine Peaks or over from the island, it won't last long."

"We have room to build," Ash says easily, stretching. "And you know how much the construction team loves testing new designs. They'd be crushed if we didn't have something on the go for them to play with."

I shake my head. I have to admit their latest homes have some pretty great features, but the overall forms keep getting weirder. Still, considering they've been working mostly with found objects in a wildly different setting than any of them had worked prior to just a few years earlier, it's amazing what they've managed to accomplish. It's amazing what we've all managed to do, really. "Aside from that, your parents finally went home yesterday, and Gran's been too busy keeping Cady occupied with Ange's youngest to nag me in, oh, at least six hours, so I'd say I've got nothing to worry about until tomorrow morning at the earliest."

Ash pokes at the fire again, sparks rising against the deep purple of the night sky. "About that . . ."

I groan. "No. Come on. How often do we just get to sit and take it easy like this? Can't it wait? Put that thing down and relax."

He chuckles, and obeys, stretching out in the chair beside mine. We listen to the even hiss of the waves behind the sweet crackling pops of dried driftwood. The silence is warm, comfortable. My eyelids grow heavy.

I sigh, pushing myself higher in my chair. "Might as well spit it out now. You know I won't be able to sleep until you do."

He shifts, looking over with no sign of drowsiness. "You asked for time, and space. You needed it. I get that. You were so young—"

"We both were." I'm wide-awake now. I pull my legs in and twist, crossing them awkwardly on the angled seat of the chair to face him.

He nods. "But you'd lost so much time. In a way, it's like you had to start life all over again after Refuge took you."

I glance at the fire, then past, to the starlit inlet. It hadn't been all *that* long ago, but these past few years had felt like decades next to my time in Refuge. So many people, so many fights—and triumphs. If I'd known what a challenge it would be building and running a city like this . . .

I'd do it all over again. In a heartbeat. But Ash isn't here to chat about the ins and outs of municipal leadership or my troubled past. "So we're really doing this now?"

"Feels like time, don't you think?" He leans in, his face shadowed. "Cole, I—"

I hold up a hand, smiling at the sudden memory. Amazing how a few years could make even the worst times seem tinted with golden-hued nostalgia. "You had dreamed of me for years—"

Ash hesitates, probably trying to decide if that's humour in my tone, or warning. "Decades. Well, at least a decade." He tilts his head, probably counting. "Years, sure. Let's go with that."

"I imagined this conversation, you know. My line was going to be either, 'While I have only just begun to dream again.' Or, 'While my dreams have only just come back to life.'"

The fire pops. Ash reaches for my hand. "And now? What will you dream of next, C?"

I lace my fingers through his. Ignoring the demands of the city at my back, the fears that I've learned to hear in whispers instead of shouts, the lies of a childhood that taught me the only safe way to be was forever and always alone, I whisper against his lips, "*Us.*"

※

COLE'S ADVENTURES ARE finished
(at least for the moment),
but yours don't have to be.

Join the author's newsletter at
kawiggins.com
for free short reads including series prequels,
insider content, and news about upcoming releases!

ACKNOWLEDGEMENTS

TO THE READERS who keep following me into—and through—the dark (why?! & thanks!)

To my parents, who support my crazy dreams and the equally prickly pets along for the ride.

To siblings, family, friends, and total strangers who graciously read the messy drafts and keep asking for more.

To Lisa Poisso for guidance through the dark and twisty plotting woods, Catherine Milos for the diligent copyedits (as always, any and all errors are stubbornly my own) and Christian Bentulan for the base cover design.

To the one to whom I am always enough. I can't imagine life without you. I'm so grateful I've never had to.

And finally, to all the awkward, prickly kids out there who are afraid to try, who try too hard, who try and fail, who try and keep on trying. You're enough. You're not done yet. You never will be. But you're enough.

Keep fighting on.

K.A. WIGGINS IS a Vancouver-born Canadian speculative fiction writer, speaker, and creative writing coach known for the acclaimed "climate change + monsters" YA dystopian dark fantasy series *Threads of Dreams*.

Her debut, *Blind the Eyes*, was a 2020 Page Turner Awards Book Spotlight Prize winner and Barnes & Noble Press "20 Favorite Indie Books of 2018." Her short fiction has been published in Enchanted Conversation: A Fairytale Magazine, Frozen Wavelets by The Earthian Hivemind, Fiction-Atlas Press, and Virgibooks (in translation).

Find her at kawiggins.com or @kaiespace on social.

www.ingramcontent.com/pod-product-compliance
Lightning Source LLC
Chambersburg PA
CBHW021307190726

48288CB00003B/736